CHAPTER 1

Brussels, Belgium

The informant was late.

John "Reaper" Kane leaned in the alcove of a building just off Place des Armateurs, the rippling water of the Brussels-Scheldt Maritime Canal directly across the street. A speed boat waited there, its supercharged motor burbling, SEAL Chief Borden Hunt at the wheel, ready to go full-throttle once Kane jumped on with his informant.

But the informant was late.

Kane was in Brussels to collect John Casiano, a minor cartel errand boy who had a tip about cartel players scattered throughout Europe planning some sort of strike back against the US after the capture of Jorge Sanchez, leader of the Chologos drug cartel. The informant had taken up the DEA on its offer of a big payday should anyone have information on the remaining members of the cartel, the back of which had been broken thanks to continued pressure from the DEA and Kane's own Team Reaper.

The extraction plan was simple. Pick up Casiano, hop in the speed boat, and race up the canal to the ocean where a Navy submarine waited to collect them. The submarine might have been extreme, but Kane wanted to avoid the obvious traps waiting at an airport or train station. Boat to submarine was the fastest way out of the area, and out of danger.

It was a quarter past 0400, the street was quiet, and Kane felt like the last man in the world.

He needed the mission after the previous week's leave, where he'd spent a day at a facility in Maine where his sister Mel, still in a coma, remained confined to a bed. He held onto the hope that she would wake up and recover, but that hope was on shaky ground. While he'd spent that one day by her bedside, reading out loud anything he could get his hands on, and talking endlessly once he'd exhausted the material, she showed no sign of knowing he was there. He was unwilling to spend too much time there due to the nature of his job and the associated dangers. He really wanted to keep Mel separate from that part of his life, away from any threats.

But now, Kane was back at work, and putting his mind to things other than the tragedy of his sister's condition. He was back to doing what he did best.

He had been on so many missions such as this, waiting in alleys and doorways, that he should have been used to the monotony. His senses always remained on alert, his focus sharp. He liked these jobs because they kept his edge honed. The alcove protected his back; the canal protected his front; his danger scan regularly shifted left and right. So far, everything was clear, and that was the problem.

Casiano should have arrived at 0330. They should be in the boat and halfway up the canal by now.

BLOOD RUSH

A TEAM REAPER THRILLER

BRIAN DRAKE

BRENT TOWNS

WOLFPACK
PUBLISHING
— EST 2013 —

Copyright © 2019 Brian Drake
Based on Characters Created by Brent Towns
All rights reserved.

Published in the United States by Wolfpack Publishing, Las Vegas.

Wolfpack Publishing
6032 Wheat Penny Avenue
Las Vegas, NV 89122

wolfpackpublishing.com

Paperback ISBN 978-1-64119-909-4
Ebook ISBN 978-1-64119-908-7

Library of Congress Control Number: 2019938104

BLOOD RUSH

Kane shifted in the alcove, the weight of the SIG-Sauer M17 9mm autoloader under his left arm dragging on his side. His lower back hurt from standing for so long, the three sides of the cold concrete hiding spot unmercifully uncomfortable. His feet were okay thanks to excellent inserts in his shoes. He wanted out of there, fast, with Casiano, but it was beginning to look like maybe cartel assassins had reached him first.

Unfortunate, because Casiano still had plenty of information inside his head that the DEA wanted very badly.

Tires screeched. Kane's eyes snapped right. A car turned the corner, fishtailing, sideswiping a lamppost and almost bringing it crashing down. The car crossed both lanes of the road before settling in a straight line heading for Kane's position. It screeched to a halt a few feet away from the doorway. The driver's door swung open and Casiano tumbled onto the sidewalk, letting out a yell as his body hit the pavement. His clothes were a wrinkled mess, but nothing was torn; his face covered in sweat and bloody welts. He struggled to get to his knees.

Kane raced from the alcove and grabbed an arm to help him to his feet.

"They almost had me," Casiano said, gasping for air. Kane checked the man's body for other wounds but found none. Casiano was in fight-or-flight mode. As close as he had come to getting caught, it had pumped his body full of adrenaline.

"It's gonna be fine, let's go."

"It's the daughter," Casiano said, coughing. "Sanchez's daughter!"

Another car rushed at them from the opposite end of the street, bright halogen lights highlighting Kane and Casiano as they stood in the open. The tires screamed as the driver slammed the brakes. A man leaned out the passenger side window, cradling a short submachine gun, and flame spit from the muzzle, the salvo of gunfire sounding like a buzz-saw.

"Down!" Kane shouted, violently shoving Casiano to the pavement. The salvo stitched into the car's metal shell and shattered the front windshield. Shards of glass rained on Kane's back as he covered Casiano with his body. Kane rolled away, up onto the sidewalk, as Casiano scrambled for the rear of the car.

Kane came up on his back with the SIG-Sauer in his right hand. Steadying the pistol with a two-hand grip, he sighted on the enemy car. The glow of the Tritium night sights provided a perfect picture. The passenger piled out, jamming a new magazine into his weapon, joined by the driver who raised his own sub gun to shoulder level.

The SIG spit twice, the muzzle flipping up, Kane's practiced trigger finger feeling for the trigger reset, firing twice more, the shots so rapid the pistol might have been his own SMG.

Driver and passenger closed in, and then another weapon joined the fray, Chief Hunt opening fire from the bow of the speed boat with his Heckler & Koch 416 carbine. A stream of 5.56mm slugs jerked the driver off balance and tore into his hip. As he fell, he sprayed more rounds at Kane. Kane's body tightened as the slugs split the air overhead. He fired again. The 9mm stingers from the hot barrel of the M17 found their mark. Two spurts of blood from the center of the driver's chest ended his assault, and his body dropped onto the pavement, his sub gun skittering across the pavement.

Kane triggered more rounds, and so did Hunt, the

louder HK carbine drowning out the SIG pistol. The passenger spun as multiple rounds ripped through his upper body, falling midway between his car and Casiano's.

As the echo of the shots faded, Kane's eyes scanned for further danger. He saw nothing. But that didn't mean they were home free. There could be another team on the way. They had to move fast.

Kane jumped up and grabbed the back of Casiano's shirt, hauling the man to his feet.

"Come on!"

Casiano kept pace beside Kane as they ran across the street. He suddenly stopped mid-stride, gasping sharply, but momentum carried him forward. His face hit the pavement with a sharp smack, and then the whip-crack of the sniper shot that brought him down echoed up the street.

Kane dived and rolled as a second bullet whistled past him. The crack of the shot followed. Hunt, aboard the boat, yelled something, the HK 416 chattering covering fire. Kane jumped up and ran the rest of the way, his shoes landing hard on the road's surface as he sprinted. No other shots reached him, the sniper likely having vacated his nest after the second shot.

Kane's body burned hotly as he leaped, leaving the pavement, clearing the gap of water between the concrete and speedboat. He fell roughly onto the deck, dropping to his knees, lurching back as the speed boat surged forward, the water behind exploding upward as the motor's twin propellers spun.

Kane sat up and looked back. The death zone receded quickly, and Kane felt a pang of regret. He hated leaving a man behind. He'd lost informants before, and they were always personal losses. One had to try and remain detached, but in Kane's experience, that wasn't always possible. To remain totally detached, one risked losing their humanity. He'd seen other men make that choice, and it had ruined their lives. Kane had too much to live for to take that risk.

The speed boat jostled over the water. The city rushed by on either side, but the view did not hold his interest. He stood and moved up the narrow boat to the seat beside Hunt and fell heavily onto the wet cushion.

"Are you hit?" Chief Hunt asked. The SEAL operator eyed Kane with concern.

"No holes I wasn't already born with," Kane said.

"But we lost our package."

"That we did."

Hunt faced forward and held course. If he had any other comment, he didn't share.

Kane sank against the backrest as if there was a huge weight on his shoulders.

Sanchez's daughter? What did Casiano mean? Kane knew of the young woman, but she'd never been part of her father's organization. Instead, she'd used his money to make the world her playground, part of the new jet set. She'd made no secret of who she was, and that seemed to make her quite popular. But while she'd been on the radar of Team Reaper, the CIA, and the DEA, there'd been no reason to think she engaged in the same activities as her father.

But Casiano hadn't mentioned her for no reason. He hadn't been killed for no reason, either.

Kane had to get back to the rest of his team. And fast.

Their mission against what remained of the Chologos cartel wasn't over by a long shot.

Three months Team Reaper had worked to smash the

cartel's operations and drag Jorge Sanchez kicking and screaming into a federal court in New York City. Three intense months of blood, sweat, and bullets. And now, the one person who had never appeared to be a threat was apparently becoming exactly that.

But how?

There was only one way to find out, Kane decided, as cold water splashed at his cheeks. Hunt held the wheel steady, the experienced Navy man effortlessly guiding the speed boat along the wide canal.

Time for Team Reaper to get back in the fight and deliver justice where there was none.

Berlin, Germany

The rain had stopped hours ago, but not even Diego Moreno's long coat blocked the 0400 chill that remained. His teeth chattered a little, his body shivering ever so slightly. The streets were still wet with what looked like sweat.

The cartel terrorist stood just over five feet high. The long black coat stopped around his ankles and a knit cap rode atop his head. The cap wasn't much of a defense against the cold, either. His pale lips and lack of eyebrows were his most distinguishing features, and his eyes picked out almost every detail around him.

He leaned against the wall of an alcove at the corner of Poststrabe and Rathaustrabe in Berlin, among darkened cafe fronts, the ghost-like buildings eerily silent. Across from him was a construction zone, half-walls and silent cranes and other equipment waiting for daylight. He didn't bother to read the signs identifying what the project was. A few stray cars lined the curbs on either end of the street, but no others traveled the roadway at this hour. The Spree River whispered nearby.

Diego Moreno stood with his hands jammed deep into the pockets of his coat, the right pocket bulging a little more because of the Glock-19 9mm pistol he held in his hand, fifteen rounds in the mag and one in the chamber. All hollow-points designed to rip a man apart. He had arranged the meeting at this location, over the telephone, but he also knew the rendezvous might be a trap. If the Americans were coming to get him then he'd go down fighting. Such a day had to arrive eventually. The last three months had proved one thing. Death comes to all, eventually—sometimes a fate worse than death. He was fortunate in that he'd managed to escape the assault on the Chologos Cartel that ended in the capture of his friend and former boss, Jorge Sanchez. But how long would that fortune last?

A long black car turned the corner up ahead. Its bright headlights flashed across the construction site and caused a glare on the wet pavement. When the lights hit Moreno with the ferocity of a stage spotlight, he couldn't help but raise his left arm to block the light and pull his Glock-19 with the other. His gloved finger curled around the trigger, fitting easily into the extended trigger guard.

The big car stopped a few feet away. Mercedes-Benz S600 limousine. Black with silver trim. The headlamps burned brightly. Those same lights flashed twice, stayed off, turned on again and flashed twice more. Moreno put the Glock back in his pocket. As he approached the car, the rear door opened on hydraulic hinges. The figure that opened the door, briefly visible as the interior light spilled onto the sidewalk, slid back as Moreno ducked to enter.

"You are the last person I expected to see in this car," Moreno said as he sat. The woman across from him cracked a polished smile showing perfect teeth. Moreno knew for a fact that those teeth had cost Jorge Sanchez a ton of money.

But he'd never been able to tell his daughter no.

"Yet here I am," said Blanca Sanchez.

The soft bench seats faced each other. Blanca had a rotating flat screen connected to a laptop on her side.

Track lighting in the roof brightly lit the cabin. There was almost no sense of movement with the lighting and tinted windows. The soundproofing deadened the engine noise to a dull throb. The warmth of the cabin and its plush leather seats might have been a womb.

Moreno regarded Blanca curiously. He removed the cap on his head as the heat wrapped around him. Blanca looked better than the last time he had seen her. The daughter of cartel boss, Jorge Sanchez had always been a little tubby—a testament to her lifestyle of all-party-no-work, but now she was lean and trim with a sharp line to her jaw and obvious curves under the tight-fitting dress. Her shapely legs crossed at the knees, six-inch heels, stockings, the whole nine yards.

"What are you doing here?"

"We're going to free my father," Blanca said.

Moreno laughed. "Your father is on trial in New York City. He's surrounded by armed federal marshals. He's not going anywhere."

"I have a plan," she said.

"I don't believe you. Your father kept you away from the organization, and all we ever saw of you was a drunken leech who partied away his money."

"Not all of it." Blanca grinned. She had a mischievous gleam in her eye.

A hot flush crept up Moreno's neck. Blanca had been a thorn in the flesh for too long for him to take any of this conversation seriously. Her father loved her, yes, but he worried about her, too, and not just for her safety, or the variety of worries that descend upon a father when his daughter is alone out in the big wide world. He worried somebody might use her to get to him. He worried she might say something to somebody who would use the information against him. In general, he worried. And Moreno had not liked seeing his friend worry.

Moreno and Sanchez had been friends longer than Moreno cared to admit, first as childhood chums, then as adults. But in between, there had been a break as they pursued their own destinies. Sanchez reached the top of the cartel leadership. Moreno fell to the bottom of the barrel. But then Sanchez found him on the street, by chance, and helped him restore his former self when alcohol and drugs were turning him into a dead man.

And if Jorge's kid wanted to play games. . .

"If this is supposed to be some sort of. . .whatever you call it," Moreno said, "all you're doing is pissing me off."

Blanca held up a hand, her long red nails matching her lipstick. "You're right. I was everything you accuse me of. Since the U.S. arrested my father, I've been doing some soul-searching, and I've had a change of heart. Now the least I can do to pay my father back is to free him from captivity, and we'll start by executing an event that will make the Americans do whatever we ask."

"I'm still not convinced, but try and impress me."

"Here's what you're doing." Blanca turned the flat screen toward Moreno and started pressing buttons on the computer. "American tourists cruise into Cabo San Lucas every day. Sometimes, there are certain VIPs aboard the ships. These VIPs, when the authorities learn of their kidnapping, will force the Americans to negotiate or face public humiliation. I need a man to make that happen. I need *you* to make that happen, Diego."

An image of the Port of Cabo appeared on the screen. Ships didn't dock at the port specifically; the pier wasn't large enough to accommodate them, but they anchored slightly off-shore instead. Tourists off-boarded onto "shuttle boats" that brought them the rest of the way to the pier. A plan formed in Diego's mind. If he had one or two men on those shuttle boats, the VIPs would drop right into his lap.

Moreno nodded. "Budget?"

"No expense spared. My father cannot be convicted. He cannot be sent to prison."

"When should I start?"

"Right now. The boat I want docks in three days."

"Who is the VIP?"

"Two of them. You'll get that information when you arrive in Mexico."

Blanca lifted a handset from the door panel on her right and spoke to the driver. The car made a long turn and straightened out. After the turn, there was once again only a small sense of forward movement when the engine surged.

The Mercedes slowed and swung curbside. Blanca said, "Much success. You're the first salvo."

"Who's the second?"

She winked. "That's a surprise."

Moreno let a smile pull at the corners of his mouth. He didn't know how Blanca had turned herself around, but she had. She'd convinced him. It was like when Jorge found him in the street. He'd get Jorge back, get his life back, get his dignity back. No more hiding like a frightened mouse.

He exited back into the cold of the early Berlin morning. As his shoes tapped a rhythm on the concrete, and the Mercedes drove away, he felt warm all over.

If the car had been a womb, he was now reborn.

After the capture of Blanca's father, with the DEA hunting his known associates all over the globe, Moreno had picked Berlin as a place to disappear because it seemed to be the furthest he could get from Mexico and still enjoy society, albeit carefully. The hermit's life had lost its allure very quickly. But now that had changed.

He'd entered the limo a hermit and emerged a warrior.

Time to get even.

The door shut quietly, and Blanca Sanchez sat alone, dimming the interior lights. She felt peace in the darkness. As the driver continued on, picking up speed as he approached the autobahn, she sat back and felt herself relax for the first time in several days. She'd been busy, mostly in Mexico, then the flight across the ocean to Berlin and the possibility that Moreno would tell her to go to hell. Thankfully, he had not. She couldn't imagine carrying on her father's legacy without him.

Moreno was the last on her list. The other remaining members of her father's organization, except for one, scattered across the world, had agreed to come back to the fold. If the U.S. refused to hand over her father, she would make the people hurt the way they had hurt so many others, not just in Mexico, but around the world.

She hadn't always been so radical. Blanca had lived high on her father's generous monthly allowances and enjoyed the best of everything: cars, clothes, shoes, resorts, whatever she wanted. Whatever man she wanted. Less than a day after news of her father's arrest shook her small world, she'd found solace in one such man named Fasil Mahlik.

The Eaton-educated man from Saudi Arabia had opened her eyes, forging with Blanca more than just a physical relationship. Her first act, upon taking her father's place, was putting Mahlik and his own crew of jihadist warriors in a position of partnership in her endeavor. He'd provided instruction in areas she knew nothing about, how to use bombs and guns; Blanca was a fast learner.

As the car picked up speed on the autobahn, she thought over the plan so far. Moreno would handle the American VIPs, the two daughters of a Senator from Arizona known for being a Capitol Hill war hawk, and a big proponent of the "war on drugs". She'd made arrangements with a trio of freelance cartel killers for the second phase of her operation. She checked her watch. By now they would be on their way into the United States. She'd told them to ignore facial recognition and enter without a disguise. Their sighting alone would send the Americans on a wild goose chase. They were killers, sure, but the kind of killing they were known for was not why Blanca had hired them.

She had her own work to do and planned to remain in Berlin for a few more days to accomplish the task. There was an arms dealer she needed to see who, Mahlik said, had plenty of C4 plastic explosive for sale that would suit their plans nicely.

And then, of course, her demands, which she intended to communicate directly to the United States President, a man named Carter; a man with more blood on his hands than had ever stained her father's. The irony of an evil people calling somebody else evil; she'd laugh if it hadn't affected her so closely. The United States had more blood on its hands than ten cartels put together. How dare they classify her father as an evil man and hunt him like a wounded animal.

She looked out the tinted window at the other cars. The tint blocked any indication of the scenery beyond the freeway. Instead, Blanca saw her face, partially reflected. The woman in the reflection looked strong. Proud. Confident.

Let her vengeance begin.

CHAPTER 2

USS Louisiana
Somewhere in the North Atlantic

The constant throb of the submarine's engine and the rocking back and forth of the sub as it sliced through the rough water made John Kane's stomach queasy, but that was life aboard a naval ship. As a former Marine, he was begrudgingly used to ocean travel.

He and Hunt were aboard the *USS Louisiana*, an Ohio-class submarine, also known as a Trident, powered by a nuclear reactor that didn't make Kane nervous at all. He felt perfectly comfortable with a proverbial ton of radiation mere feet from him at any given time. He knew how dangerous radiation was. He'd seen *Star Trek II: The Wrath of Khan* many times and still teared up during Spock's radiation-induced death.

Kane had hated, however, to leave the speed boat adrift in the ocean. It had been a good piece of transportation. Fast, agile, very capable of getting him and Hunt out of harm's way. He knew the hunk of fiberglass had no personality of its own, but he hoped somebody stumbled upon the craft and used it for their own purposes.

Kane's six-foot-four height and broad shoulders also made it hard to navigate the narrow passageways; he had to hunch over through every doorway and turn sideways through the narrowest passages. He'd had the same problem on every naval vessel he'd ever set foot on. Ship designers simply did not have six-footers in mind when they built big boats.

Hunt, the Navy SEAL, with his average height and build, didn't see the conditions as a big deal. He breezed easily throughout the submarine as if he'd been aboard one his entire life. Kane caught him smirking at his discomfort several times. Little punk.

Kane and Hunt were heading for a secure communication booth somewhere aft. The sailor who pointed the way said they couldn't miss it.

The booth barely had enough room for him and Hunt with a small desk and flat screen monitor with a built-in camera. Kane's stomach lurched some more, and, this time, the narrow walls felt like they were closing in on him. He focused on the task and pushed all other thoughts out of his mind.

A face filled the monitor, the face of General Mary Thurston, overall leader of Team Reaper, for which Kane was "Reaper One", and Hunt a sometime associate, who also commanded his own SEAL team. Thurston's normally long dark hair was tied back tightly behind her head, but her brown eyes seemed to see everything on their side of the monitor.

While Kane groaned with the push and pull in his gut, Hunt snacked on a Power Bar.

"What happened?" the General asked.

"Totally went to hell," Hunt said, adding, "Ma'am."

"That's fine for the abridged version," she said, "but I need a little more detail. Kane?"

"I met the informant as planned, but he was already blown. A kill team was waiting for us, couple guys in a car, plus a sniper on the roof. We got the guys in the car. The sniper got Casiano."

"We have nothing?"

"Not *nothing*, per se, just not a lot," Kane said. "Whatever he was going to tell us died with him, but Casiano did say something about Jorge Sanchez's daughter before he was shot."

"Her name is Blanca, right?"

"Correct, General," Kane said. "We didn't pay too much attention to her when we took down her father's cartel because she wasn't part of it."

"Party girl?"

"Right. Huge allowance, that sort of thing. Ran with the jet set all over Europe."

"Is she taking over her father's operations?"

"Whatever she's doing," Kane said, "we need a rundown straight away. Everything we have on her. She might be planning to take over, and she might be planning to try and break her father out of custody. Regardless, we need all hands on deck."

"How long till you're back in the U.S.?" Thurston said.

"Three, four days."

"Too long. I'll send a chopper to meet you halfway, and we'll get you back here ASAP."

"The sooner the better," Kane said.

Thurston smiled, but only briefly. "While you're waiting, we'll work on that background info and alert New York."

Kane nodded. Part of Team Reaper had been attached to a team of U.S. Marshals to help transport Jorge Sanchez to and from his trial.

"Who's on the job there?" Kane said.

"Cara, Brick, and Arenas."

"Good."

Sanchez's trial was due to start within 48 hours; meanwhile, the former cartel kingpin was cooling it in a cell in a Manhattan Correctional Facility, the normal security beefed up by armed federal marshals who ran things so tightly a mouse couldn't get through their blockade.

"We'll be standing by for the chopper," Kane said.

Thurston said good-bye and the monitor blinked out.

Kane turned off the screen and looked at Hunt, who was chewing a piece of his Power Bar.

"How can you eat with this thing rolling around as it does?"

Hunt shrugged. "I feel fine."

Kane shook his head and stood up. Shoving open the door, he hunched down as he once again entered a narrow passage, but still banged his head on a low-hanging pipe.

"Goddammit."

"Watch your head," Hunt said from behind him.

Kane looked back long enough to scowl at Hunt, a hand clamped where the pipe had struck. Then he turned and moved forward. He thought he heard Hunt laugh but didn't say anything. There were some battles even "Reaper" Kane couldn't win.

Team Reaper HQ

El Paso, Texas.

General Mary Thurston passed Luis Ferrero's office on her way to the headquarters operations room, but he was on the phone and waved her off after she paused a moment in the doorway. She walked with purpose into the operations room, scanning the row of computer work stations and the operators in front of the screens. She zeroed on the red hair of Sam "Slick" Swift, whose busy fingers tapped away at his keyboard.

"What are you up to, Slick?"

"Usual."

"Pause it. I need a rundown on Blanca Sanchez."

Swift stopped typing and looked up at Thurston. In his mid-thirties, Swift combined red hair with a thin frame. Thurston hated to admit that he was skinnier than she was. In her early forties, Thurston had proved herself in the Army Rangers and maintained an athletic build, but age and Mother Nature was a bitch, and it was a constant battle to maintain fighting shape even though she hadn't seen a battlefield in more years than she could count.

Sam Swift was a valuable member of Team Bravo, the headquarters detachment of Reaper, the man with the golden fingers, with the ability to hack anything containing a microchip.

"Is your request related to a certain drug kingpin we put in jail, perhaps?" Swift said.

"Exactly. I need everything we have, from where she was born to where she is right now, or at least an approximation of where she might be found. I need associates, friends, where she hangs out. The whole package, priority one."

"On it." Swift pressed a button to clear his screen, and his fingers began typing some more.

"What's happening?"

Thurston turned. Luis Ferrero, Team Reaper's operations leader, approached. The DEA man may spend most of his time behind a desk now, but he was a capable operator in his own right and had fought beside John Kane on a covert mission in Colombia. His hair was touched with gray.

Thurston gave him a quick update on the situation overseas, and a rundown of her orders to Swift.

"We need somebody on the ground in Mexico as well," Ferrero said. His hair looked a little grayer today, Thurston thought, or maybe it was just her imagination. She had a feeling they'd all be a little rougher around the edges after this mission. The chase for Jorge Sanchez had been tough enough, but now they had to fight his kid? It was an example of the never-ending war against drugs, and there were too many similar examples for Thurston's comfort.

"I have an idea for that," she said. "Where's Traynor?"

Pete Traynor, aka Bravo Two, would be the perfect person to put on the ground in Mexico. A former undercover DEA man, he had valuable contacts in the nation south of the border. If Blanca's cyberspace footprint was too faint for Swift to discover, perhaps Traynor's Mexico contacts would have hard data that could help.

Swift said he hadn't seen him in a few days, and none of the other operators knew either.

Thurston pulled a cell phone from the left pocket of her pants, scrolled to Traynor's name, and pressed CALL.

Pete Traynor was actually glad when the punk came in with a gun. He hadn't beaten the garbage out of a bad guy in several weeks, and the pangs of withdrawal ached through his body. He'd been loafing around the city and headquarters the last few weeks, letting his usually unshaven face grow even more so. His orders, along with the rest of the team, had been to rest up after the three-month operation to nail Jorge Sanchez, but too much inactivity made Traynor restless, and there was only so much practice shooting he could do at HQ, only so much jogging, and, heaven knew, only so much reality television one could watch. He needed a mission, and soon, before his brain cells melted.

He stepped into Liquor King. It was warm enough outside that he hadn't needed a jacket, and the short sleeves of his Iron Maiden T-shirt exposed the tattoos up and down each arm. He waved at the counter-man, who had a small radio blasting nearby, a football game, from the sound of the announcer's description—a Texas A&M game, to be exact, which one of the local radio stations broadcasted throughout the season.

He made his way to the back corner of the crowded liquor store, with its narrow aisles and shelves overcrowded with items, and stopped in front of the beer section, the sliding doors behind which his elixir waited slightly spotted with frost. He set his eyes on a six-pack of Coors Banquet. It wasn't a fancy beer, but indeed a good one, and nobody else seemed to like it so there was always plenty for him.

He reached for the sliding door handle and—

The bell above the door dinged and several voices, very aggressive voices, made the hairs on the back of Traynor's neck stand up.

"Turn that shit off, old man!" somebody, a male, yelled, and the counter-man let out a yell of his own as a loud crash, followed by the silencing of the football game, echoed through the store.

Traynor dropped low and moved carefully along the back wall, easing around each display stand making up the four aisles. He stopped when the counter came into view, along with the counter-man, his hands up, sweat dotting his panicked face, and the four punks standing before him. One held a shiny revolver. The other three held knives.

"Open that register right now!" the gunman said.

The counter-man's hands shook. He tried to talk, but the gunman shouted at him again.

"Don't make me ask again or I'll blow you away and get the money myself! Move it!"

Traynor scooted back, his mind racing for a solution. He had no weapon on him. He didn't carry off-duty. Who goes on a beer run expecting a gunfight? But here he was. Unarmed. Against at least one gun and three knives. The knife guys didn't bother him. The shooter, however, bothered him very much.

Traynor's eyes darted back and forth. Just ahead, against the wall, a shelf contained a variety of canned goods. He snatched some pork-n-beans and started up the aisle toward the counter.

The counter-man finally opened the register and started taking out big handfuls of cash. The punks encouraged him to move faster, the gunman holding the pistol on the counter-man's chin.

Traynor stepped closer. His right shoe squeaked on the polished tile floor.

One of the three knifers spun around, raising his knife defensively.

"Hey!"

Traynor threw the pork-n-beans in such a way that an A&M scout would sign him to first-string quarterback. He didn't aim for the knife guys; his target was the punk with the gun. As the gunman turned to see what his partner was yelling about, the pork-n-beans smashed into his face with the force of a hammer. He didn't have a chance to cry out. His legs failed him and he dropped onto the floor.

The knifer who yelled the alarm lunged at Traynor, who easily sidestepped even in the narrow aisle space and twisted the punk's wrist, a delightful snap briefly sounding before being drowned out by the punk's scream. A knee to the punk's belly put him down.

Traynor pivoted to face the last two. One of them picked up the revolver and pointed it at Traynor, but then the counter-man jumped into the act, too. The shotgun he pulled from under the counter made a nice click-clack as he worked the action. The punk's eyes widened. He dropped the revolver like a proverbial hot potato.

"Freeze!" the counter-man said, with gusto.

"We make a good team," Traynor said. He dragged the unconscious knife man over to the rest of the crew, grabbing the revolver. "Call the police. I'll keep 'em covered."

The formerly-brave hoods were suddenly speechless. Traynor, however, felt quite alive. No reality show could top this kind of action.

Two squad cars arrived. The officers interviewed the counter-man and Traynor and examined the security footage of the fight. Once the officer drove away with the hoods in handcuffs, the counter-man gave the Coors Banquet to Traynor free of charge.

His day was getting better every minute.

While walking back to his nearby apartment, his cell phone rang. He pulled it from the inside pocket of his jacket and looked at the caller ID. Thurston.

"Traynor talking," he said.

"It's Thurston."

"Yes, ma'am."

"I need you at headquarters right away. Something's come up."

Traynor smiled. Hat trick. Who had it better than him at that moment?

Nobody, that's who.

"On my way, ma'am."

CHAPTER 3

Team Reaper HQ

"Who is your best source in Mexico?" Thurston asked.

Traynor sat in front of her desk, the plastic bag with his beer under the chair, while Ferrero stood beside the seated general. They'd given him the backstory on Kane's mission, and he suddenly wished they'd rounded up every last member of the Sanchez family to prevent such a problem from arising.

Blanca had been so far off the radar, they hadn't really given her much thought, other than what she might do when daddy's money vanished. Now he knew better. And they'd made a huge mistake. He figured Kane was thinking the same thing.

"Rico Ramirez," Traynor said. "Federal Drug Task Force. We worked with him a lot when we were down there."

"Call him," Ferrero said.

"Better yet," Thurston said, "go see him."

"How soon can a plane be ready?"

"One hour."

Traynor shrugged. "Plenty of time for a beer then. Either of you want one?" He reached for the bag. "They were free."

"What do you mean, free?" Ferrero said.

Traynor recounted his story, exaggerating just enough to make him look cool.

Thurston passed. Ferrero accepted the offer.

Manhattan, NY
Moynihan Federal Courthouse

"All we have to do," Cara Billings said, "is make a five-minute drive twice a day and pray that nobody tries to blow us up."

Cara Billings, aka Reaper Two, looked at the two men standing in front of her, both of whom appeared ready for a sarcastic comeback to her summary of their mission.

Carlos Arenas, Reaper Three, kept his square jaw closed as he looked at Billings. A former member of Mexico's special forces for ten years, he was now firmly part of Team Reaper, relocating from Mexico to the United States with his wife and two kids.

Richard "Brick" Peters earned his nickname for every one of his six-feet-three inches. An ex-Navy SEAL, he sported a shaved head and forearm tattoos.

Both were working with Billings on what they considered the most dangerous part of the Sanchez operation since they were more likely to be killed by boring routine than enemy fire.

Jorge Sanchez's trial was due to start in 48 hours. All the pre-trial shenanigans were over and done; witnesses were ready, prosecutors prepped, the defense team working overtime. The trio of Team Reaper operatives had to get Sanchez from the Manhattan Correctional Facility where Sanchez was currently cooling it in a cell and take him to the Daniel Patrick Moynihan Federal Courthouse. A five-minute drive. Only a few blocks. A few blocks where anything could happen, where cartel forces who wanted to spring Sanchez could find one of many kill zones for an ambush.

"Why do I think," Arenas said, "that I'm suddenly not carrying enough insurance?"

"What do the marshals have in mind?" Brick asked.

The saving grace of their mission was working with a team of elite U.S. Marshals who had done this sort of prisoner transport operation before. So many times, in fact, that they had a variety of ways to fool potential ambushers with decoy caravans and other methods of trickery.

Cara Billings glanced to her left where, across the mid-level outdoor patio filled with courthouse staff taking a smoke break or making an attempt at a spot of fresh air, the two federal marshals they were coordinating with stood having their own meeting. The two strapping fellows, Cara noted, wore no wedding rings—not that she was in the market, though with her tan, slim build, and short dark hair, she certainly had her pick of the litter. But until she figured out what she and John Kane were doing in their on-again-off-again-currently-off existence, she didn't want to open the door to potential suitors or encourage them in any way.

"Their idea," she said. "We'll transport Sanchez in an SUV, with a back-up team of marshals in a second vehicle, and two other SUVs will play decoy. I suggested disguising

Sanchez and using alternate transportation between here and there, but they seem to think the SUV trick will be all they need, since the jail is so close, and they've done this a thousand times before. They've also suggested running him through Columbus Park." She gestured northeast where most of the park was concealed by tall trees, but still visible in the distance. "But we can't get a vehicle through there, and I don't fancy the idea of running Sanchez through on foot. I don't care if we have an entire Marine battalion for backup."

Arenas said, "Have other prisoners had their kids gunning to get papa out of jail?"

Cara sighed. The three of them had listened to General Thurston's extensive briefing on the Blanca Sanchez matter and knew how Traynor and Kane had been assigned to handle their end of the case, but all the three of them could do was move Sanchez back and forth and hope nobody tried to kill them on the way. As somebody once said, hope wasn't a strategy.

It certainly wasn't enough of a strategy for Cara Billings. She wanted a more proactive role. No, she'd demanded a more proactive role. Put somebody else on the babysitting detail. Neither she, Brick, or Arenas, had risked their lives over the last three months simply to be sitting ducks at a traffic light now that the main event had concluded.

But the general refused the request. She wanted Reaper represented at the trial. Reaper *deserved* representation at the trial, she'd said. After all, they'd done all the work once corruption in the DEA had been exposed and made the agency virtually useless in the fight. Cara understood General Thurston's perspective but did not agree with it one bit. She didn't want to admit that to Brick and

Arenas, however. She had to maintain command discipline.

"We have our orders, so we need to make the best of it."

The two men nodded. They understood. This wasn't their first rodeo. If they played their cards right, it also wouldn't be their last.

"What you're really thinking," Brick said, "is written all over your face."

"And here I thought I was being so chameleon-like," she said. *Busted.*

She looked around. Whoever had designed the federal courthouse building liked gray. So did the designers of every other government and law enforcement-related buildings in the immediate area. It was as though the architects had been ordered not to include anything unique or attractive in their designs. The buildings were to be as efficient as the government wished it were, but for all the red tape and general unpleasantness of dealing with bureaucrats, a nice building to work in and look at might not have been too much to ask. The whole city looked gray to her, actually, and this mid-level break area provided no respite from the sounds of the city at all. Vehicle engines, especially those of big buses, rumbled from the street below. The exhaust fumes tickled Cara's nose. Horns honked. Pigeons flapped incessantly, trying to suck up any leftover lunch crumbs they could find, their cooing an odd punctuation to the city's soundtrack. At least it was cool. They weren't doing this in the stifling heat of the summer. She knew all about the oppressive heatwaves that gripped New York City and Manhattan like a vice in the summer. No thanks.

Cara let out a sigh. It wasn't the worst posting ever, but sure felt that way.

Thurston had made sure to take care of them, however.

All three were staying at a nearby Marriott Hotel, very good suites, and it allowed Cara to check in with her son Jimmy every night after she finished her shift. Jimmy was the only person linking her to her late husband. Being a widow was tough, and not something she had planned on when dreaming of her future when she was young. Luckily, she had the kind of job she could throw herself into and get her mind off the disappointments life had handed her. Jimmy certainly wasn't a disappointment though.

The marshals made their way to her and Brick and Arenas. The tall one, the one who had Cara's eye, was Wayne O'Neil. "We should run the route a couple of times," he said, "so you're familiar."

"Let's do it."

The SUVs would at least cut down some of the outside noise. She didn't understand how New Yorkers could stand the cacophony. Cara and Brick and Arenas followed the marshals.

Mexico City

"Target in sight."

Captain Rico Ramirez of the Mexican Federal Drug Task Force spoke into his wireless microphone. "In position. Standing by."

"Target exiting the building now."

It would be good to get out of the cramped van Ramirez and his two teammates occupied. The van wasn't meant to fit three men, especially if they wore bulky body armor and carried sidearms and submachine guns. They'd been parked in the same spot for several hours, the van plain white with no identification markings. They wanted the target to think it was somebody's personal vehicle.

Ramirez eased away from the wall of the van where he'd been sitting. He glanced at his teammates who responded with stony glances of their own. They'd been waiting hours for this opportunity; they were ready. Ramirez moved to the rear of the van and looked out the dirty window. They'd cleaned the glass in one particular spot, which was enough for Ramirez to peek through and observe the target's address.

"We see him," he said into the wireless.

Paco Jimenez was the worst of the drug thugs Ramirez tangled with. Ramirez hated Jimenez especially. He hated all drug thugs, but Paco Jimenez actually *manufactured* the poison that killed and made so many people miserable, not just in his homeland but across the world. Paco had been an elusive quarry the last few months; now, Ramirez and his team finally had a chance to capture the bastard and they had no intention of letting him slip away.

But they had to be prepared, hence the body armor and heavy weapons.

If they had to kill him, Ramirez would not complain.

Paco Jimenez was known to carry a machine pistol of his own, a 9mm Beretta 93-R so favored by cartel thugs, and he wasn't afraid to use the weapon. Several of Ramirez's colleagues were dead and gone because of that machine pistol.

The narrow street didn't offer a lot of room to maneuver, but there was cover. Cars lined one side of the street; alleys between buildings, hopefully none of them needed.

Paco Jimenez looked both ways before he stepped off the curb. The nondescript building he'd exited didn't have any allies in it, as far as the street intelligence knew, and

Ramirez hoped the information was solid. The last thing he needed was a bunch of gunners crowding his backside.

Ramirez had a mop of dark hair on his head and a wiry frame. He was all muscle and bone. He wrapped those bony fingers around the handle of the van's back door and shoved it open. His boots hit the pavement, followed by those of his teammates. With their weapons at shoulder level, shouted commands escaping from their lips, the trio converged on Paco Jimenez.

Paco wasn't going quietly. Ramirez realized that as the drug maker's face twisted in anger. He threw back his long coat and grabbed for the machine pistol slung beneath his left armpit. Ramirez's finger tightened on the trigger of his Heckler & Koch UMP .45 ACP submachine gun, but he wasn't fast enough. The fusillade of slugs from Jimenez's Beretta 93-R pierced the afternoon. Ramirez hit the ground hard, rolling out of the way, and then was up on his feet, swinging his weapon to where Jimenez had stood. Not there. He pivoted left. Shouting for his men to follow, he took off running, glancing back only once to see both team-mates still on their feet, and unharmed by the machine pistol's swarm.

Jimenez dodged between parked cars, turned, fired again. Ramirez felt the 9mm hollow-points slice the air—too close for comfort. He sighted on the drug maker's back and squeezed off a burst of his own, the HK bucking against his shoulder, Ramirez wincing from the recoil. He really had no padding where the stock met bone. Jimenez kept running, the SMG's salvo only smacking into the car he'd used for cover.

Voices in his ear advised him of where Jimenez was running. He had teams on the roofs above the street, but none of them could get to street level fast enough to supplement Ramirez and his teammates. They were on their own against a known killer.

Ramirez and his men pounded after Jimenez, shouting for pedestrians to get out of the way. The innocents indeed ran screaming from the action. They'd probably had a lot of practice doing so as cartel violence was so, unfortunately, common.

They raced by storefronts, dodging outdoor displays. Jimenez turned left up ahead. There was a park there, lots of open space, and Ramirez knew they might lose him there if he took off in any of five different exits the park offered.

Ramirez rounded the corner, too, his teammates moving up alongside him. They shouted for Jimenez to stop and surrender. He turned and raised his machine pistol once more, his eyes zeroed on Ramirez. The task force captain felt a strange sensation, as if he somehow knew he was perfectly aligned in Jimenez's sights. His own trigger finger reacted. The Heckler & Koch submachine gun bucked once more. This time, the salvo hit the target. Red sprouted across the front of Jimenez's shirt as the man-shredding .45 ACP slugs ripped his body open, knocking him back, arms flailing wide. The Beretta machine pistol fell from his softening grip, and by the time his body hit the ground, Ramirez didn't need a coroner to tell him the drug maker was on his way to hell via the HK Express.

Ramirez lowered his weapon and shouted into the wireless for backup and emergency personnel to respond to their location. Then he turned to his teammates for a celebratory high-five. It might have seemed cold-blooded to do so, but taking down Jimenez was a major victory. A lot of dead colleagues had just been avenged. There would be no courtroom tricks or paid off judges to return Paco Jimenez to the street.

It was a good day indeed.

Back at headquarters, Ramirez splashed water on his face. The sink in the men's room was so low Ramirez had to bent down to reach the faucet, which put a strain on his lower back. He wanted to ignore the fact that he was getting older and that his time in the field was now limited, but his body often forced a reminder. He wasn't ready to trade his gun for a desk just yet, but someday time and nature would make the choice for him.

He was still keyed up from the Jimenez confrontation, and had a lot of work to do to properly wrap up the day. There was a stack of paperwork to fill out, a report to file— he'd be in the office all night. Nights like this, he was glad he didn't have anybody waiting for him at home, not even a dog. Other nights, not so much.

He left the bathroom and followed the narrow hallway back to his office where the message light on his phone blinked. He stared at the light, wondering if the shooting was going to cause problems with the top floor. Jimenez' bribe money had spread far and wide. Those no longer receiving their regular stack of cash might have an issue with Jimenez or his crew.

He listened to the message and smiled. The voice of his American friend, Pete Traynor, came over the speaker. But his smile faded after the message ended. Based on what he heard, Rico Ramirez figured he wouldn't be going home for at least another week.

CHAPTER 4

Mexico City
   Mexico City International Airport

Pete Traynor cleared customs in Mexico with only his carry-on backpack. His lightly packed suitcase would be waiting at the baggage claim area. As he walked through the busy terminal with its shiny tiled floor, ignoring the smells of frying meat at a terminal restaurant, he was glad that he wasn't the only casually-dressed, unshaven and tattooed male in the building. He blended in nicely, except for his skin, but there were enough white foreigners in the terminal, obviously tourists acting as such, to not stand out like a bloody lip. He'd made arrangements for Rico Ramirez to pick him up and found the Mexican drug cop waiting near the carousel where passengers from several newly-arrived flights were collecting bags and trying to make their way through the crowd to the chaos of outside.

Rico Ramirez was slightly shorter than Traynor, less than a foot, bulky despite his slight build, dark hair and dark eyes. His most distinguishing feature was a scar on the right side of his neck, which was usually concealed by a shirt collar. The scar was a reminder of how close he'd come to losing his life in a cartel assassination attempt. Ramirez, in telling Traynor the story, took great pride in the fact that he'd shot the assassin instead, taking a major cartel killer off the chessboard in the process.

"Welcome back, amigo," Ramirez said, shaking Traynor's hand warmly. "I didn't expect a reunion so soon."

"It never stops, Rico," Traynor said. "You beat one bad guy, another takes his place."

"At least we'll never be out of a job."

"Sometimes I wish we were."

"We'll stop fighting when we reach Valhalla."

"Right on."

Traynor collected his suitcase and they left the airport in Ramirez's car, heading for the freeway. Ramirez didn't say much as he negotiated the traffic, and Traynor remained quiet as he took in the scenery. Mexico City could be anywhere in the world for all the cars on the road, and the imported American fast food restaurants. He didn't come all the way to Mexico to eat at a McDonalds, but as they passed one, he noticed the crowded dining room. The natives weren't so prejudiced. He often felt like he lived in a bubble, expecting only the United States to have the modern conveniences and annoyances the rest of the world lacked. Sort of his own "grass is greener" argument. He'd like to get away from all the noise someday, find a place to retire to that was quiet and free of the controlled chaos of a big city, the American big city in particular, because he considered it an extreme example of Americans' out-of-control appetites for sensory overload. But every place he visited, unless it was somewhere deep in a jungle, proved that society had advanced to the point where none of the hassles could be avoided. And who wanted to live in a jungle where you shared space with mosquitos, anyway? Mosquitos carried malaria.

Ramirez joined traffic on the freeway and finally said, "You're serious about the daughter?"

"Yup. We need to find her and her people before they launch a strike to get her old man back."

"You really expect a commando assault on a federal courthouse in New York City?"

"Manhattan, actually, not that it matters. And I don't know what to expect. I only know she's got a hair up her ass to break her old man free, and we need to stop her."

Ramirez remained quiet for a moment. Then: "We have a few options."

"I hope so."

"There are still some Sanchez loyalists scattered around that we can tap into, put under surveillance. Problem is, they're small fry. I don't know if they'll lead us anywhere."

"Blanca isn't in a position to argue with who was small-fry and who wasn't," Traynor said. "She'll need every warm body that she can find. If that means a sudden promotion for the guy who always got the coffee, that's what it means, and I'm sure dude will be happy with the bump in pay."

"Then when we get to my office, we can start organizing a proper operation. Get them all under a pair of eyes or two."

"As long as you can spare the men. This isn't exactly as formal an arrangement between our governments as we had last time."

"Not to worry," Ramirez said. "I've already updated my superiors and they're making this top priority. If Blanca Sanchez succeeds and frees her father, not only will she want to get even with the United States, but she'll come after us as well because we helped you."

"Bad juju all around," Traynor said.

"Juju?"

"Shit, Rico. We're up to our elbows in shit."

Ramirez understood that reference. He glanced at the clock on the dashboard.

"It's about lunch time," he said. "We can both use something to eat and probably a beer."

"Anywhere but McDonalds."

Ramirez laughed. "That's funny. I say almost the same thing when I'm in the U.S. No tacos."

"We're more alike than we realize, my friend."

Ramirez signaled for a lane change and left the freeway at the next exit.

Berlin, Germany

It was raining.

Not a heavy rain, just an annoying drizzle that couldn't decide if it wanted to be real rain or not. Gunter Bruner looked out his office window and wished the weather would make up its mind instead of going at the effort half-assed. He watched his reflection in the glass become distorted as the drizzle covered the window. He was eight floors above the street so he had a nice view of busy Berlin below. The buildings across the way were too tall for him to see any of the city's sights, but the Brandenberg Gate was behind them somewhere. They were constructing buildings in Berlin these days that were so tall that they blocked the views that made the city unique. It seemed to

Bruner they were trying to shield Berlin's history from itself.

Gunter Bruner maintained a respectable appearance, occupying the eighth floor of the office building under the guise of an engineering firm. He had a secretary whose duty it was to tell prospective callers that they weren't currently taking on clients. He had his nicely-appointed corner office, which was dutifully cleaned every night by the dedicated janitorial crew that Bruner made sure to enrich at every Christmas. A little cash in the pocket went a long way to encourage somebody to keep his or her mouth shut about all the empty cubicles.

Gunter Bruner's real business was that of selling arms and munitions to various groups, countries, and individuals the world over. Some of his arms dealing was perfectly legit-imate, with proper transactions, end-user agreements, and very clear and detailed records of who bought what, when, and how. That was the side of the business that kept the prying eyes of the CIA or BND, the German intelligence agency, away from his affairs. The rest of his arms dealing was not quite so up-and-up, hence his need to avoid loose chatter, and, especially, official government inquiries.

Bruner turned away from his reflection. There was only so much of his bald, narrow head, and pointed nose that he could stand to see. His office door opened. He didn't look up as he sat behind his desk. There were only two other people who had access to the office. His secretary, of course, who always knocked first, and his associate, another woman. Her name was Eliza Scheck.

Eliza Scheck entered the office wearing a tweed jacket over her tight blouse and skirt. Beige stockings covering her well-shaped legs. Her hair, slightly curled, flowed down her back, but it was her make-up that Bruner always noticed, because she caked it on her face as if putting on a mask. He always wondered what she was hiding under that false facade. Nothing physical, he knew, she was quite attractive without the make-up on the rare occasions on which he saw her without it, but it suggested to him that she was concealing something deeper, something unspoken. Something she wanted to hide.

"What is it?"

"I have Blanca Sanchez to see you."

"Who?"

"The woman you've had an appointment with for two days now, Gunter. Please try and keep up."

Bruner dismissed her remarks with a wave. Eliza's attitude was nothing new. If she hadn't been so efficient in handling his affairs, he'd have tossed her years ago. He let her deal with the appointments and client contacts. He never showed his face to a client until they had been properly vetted by Eliza. If she was bringing somebody to the office, it meant they weren't a threat—a direct threat, anyway. Some clients did try to get funny now and then. Some thought they could hijack his weapons and keep the cash they were supposed to pay him, One or two had tried to rip off one of his suppliers or make a deal behind his back with same. Bruner still being alive proved none had been successful. Thus far.

Even Gunter Bruner knew his luck wouldn't last forever.

"Bring her in. Will you be staying?"

"No," Eliza said sharply, turning on a heel. She exited the office quietly and returned with another woman who was taller and fuller-figured and didn't need a mask of make-up on her face. Bruner took in the sharp chin and high cheekbones of Blanca Sanchez, the long black hair, the simple dress that made her obviously blend in with every-body on the street. The only thing that made her stand out was her brown skin, but in Berlin there were so many non-native Germans now, she probably didn't get a second glance, except for when somebody noted her striking features.

Blanca Sanchez smiled as Eliza introduced her to Bruner, who came around the desk long enough to shake her hand and show her to the chair before the desk. As Blanca sat, Eliza quietly exited once more. By the time Bruner sat down again, he was alone with the woman.

He smiled. "What brings you to my office today, Miss Sanchez?"

Blanca Sanchez did not return the smile. Her face was serious. "We have a mutual friend who said you can help me acquire some needed items."

Bruner nodded. He knew the friend from Eliza's back-ground check. Despite Eliza's snide remarks, Bruner did pay attention to the information she brought him. But he pretended he didn't to get Blanca to tell him. "Who might that be?"

"Fasil Mahlik."

Bruner smiled. "Ah, yes. He's been a good customer."

"I need enough C_4 to level a city block. Fasil says you can provide that."

"Fasil has purchased enough from me that he could possibly sell you some himself," Bruner said.

"I asked him," Blanca said, "but he tells me it's all spoken for."

"Funny how that works."

"Can you get me some C_4?"

"I can get you enough C_4 to level as many city blocks as

you want, it's not hard to come by. It's all a question of money."

"Name your price. I'll do you the favor of not trying to negotiate, but don't take advantage of me, either."

Bruner tapped the left arm of his chair. The woman's dark eyes didn't leave his face, and her red lips remained a flat line. He wondered what was on her mind. He wondered what she wanted to do with the C4. Obviously, blow something up. A city block, for instance. As long as she didn't intend for Berlin to be her target, he didn't care where she used the stuff.

"Leveling a city block is going to take quite a bit of power," he said, reaching for a pen and some scratch paper. "Let's do a little math and see just how much you need."

"Can't you just sell me six bricks and call it a day?"

Bruner raised an eyebrow. Six bricks could knock down the building across the street and allow him to see the Brandenburg Gate again. He still used the pen and paper, but this time only to write down a number. He passed the piece of paper across the desk to her. She glanced at the number, back to Bruner.

"That's acceptable. I can wire the money to any account you wish."

Bruner said, "Once I have the items, you can transfer the payment."

Blanca rose from her chair, Bruner following her to the door. He told her Eliza would escort her back to the street. They said good-bye. Bruner shut the door and returned to his desk, where he picked up the telephone and dialed an international number to reach his supplier in Greece.

It wasn't a huge sale, but it sure beat a poke in the eye with a sharp stick.

· · ·

Blanca Sanchez pushed through the revolving entrance and out onto the sidewalk. She buttoned her overcoat against the still-falling drizzle and started up the street. She didn't lower her head to avoid the drizzle, and she wasn't going in any particular direction. She just wanted to get away from Bruner's building while sorting through the thoughts in her head.

She had a plan, and it seemed like a good plan, and with Fasil's help it would be a successful plan. She hadn't written anything down. She didn't want to leave a paper trail of any kind, unlike that fool Bruner. Fasil had said not leaving a trail was important. Some trails couldn't be helped, like transferring money, even though she had a dummy account with a fake name with which to pay Bruner. Worst case, if somebody looked really hard, they could trace that account to her, even Fasil had said that might be unavoidable, adding that by the time it happened, their mission would be over.

The meeting marked the end of her time in Berlin. She was bound for the United States next. While she reviewed recent steps and future steps to make sure she didn't miss anything in between, she indeed missed something she should have seen. Two men in a delivery van across the street. The driver snapped her picture as she exited the building, and again as she started walking.

CHAPTER 5

USS Louisiana
  North Atlantic

The submarine surfaced with a crashing roar, stirring the ocean, creating a wake that surrounded the long tube and slowly dissipated.

A midship hatch squeaked open, salty sea mist flying into the hole as John "Reaper" Kane and SEAL Chief Borden Hunt climbed a small steel ladder. If Kane thought the rest of the submarine hadn't been built for tall guys, the same idea applied to the hatchway, but times twenty. He banged his shoulders and elbows in ways he didn't think shoulders and elbows could be banged, and when a sailor reached down to help him onto the flat top of the submarine deck, he breathed a sigh of relief, even though he was still on the ocean.

"Be careful," the sailor said. "The deck is slippery."

Kane stepped aside carefully and made room for Hunt. The sea stirred again, more salty water assaulting Kane's fane, as a Blackhawk helicopter swooped down, hovering over the submarine, the rotor blast threatening to knock them right off the deck and into the ocean. A little more water in his face wasn't going to hurt, but Kane certainly wanted to avoid a swim. The chopper crew chief threw open the side door and lowered a rope ladder. Kane and Hunt slowly, agonizingly slowly because of the rotor blast rocking them back and forth and the constant assault of the sea, climbed the ladder and rolled into the chopper.

A final wave at the sailors on the sub as the crew chief slammed the side door, and they were away, now locked within the confines of a warm chopper.

The crew chief handed out towels and Kane and Hunt did the best they could to dry their faces and clothes, but they'd have to sit in the wet things until they reached the U.S., and, hopefully, a change of clothes and other necessary gear for whatever happened next.

Kane had a feeling that things were about to get really rough.

He and Hunt settled into their seats, typical military-issue steel-framed seats with canvas for support, strapping in as instructed by the crew chief, who returned to his own seat behind the pilot and co-pilot. He brought back a pair of headphones. Once Kane and Hunt had the headphones properly positioned, the crew chief spoke into the microphone of his own pair.

"ETA five hours. I'm afraid we don't have an in-flight movie or any whiskey."

"What am I paying you for?" Kane asked

"So you can see my fabulous ass," the crew chief said. "Not just anybody gets the view you're getting." The three men laughed. The crew chief took his seat and buckled up.

John Kane let out a breath. Hunt didn't look interested

in talking, so Kane didn't try to start a conversation. What would they talk about anyway? The various flavors of the Power Bar?

The only thing on John Kane's mind was that Blanca Sanchez remained free and on the loose, and they could only guess wildly at what she had in mind for breaking her father out of jail.

If Jorge Sanchez had been confined anywhere but Manhattan, John Kane knew he could break out without a sweat.

He'd done so once already, in Mexico, where anti-drug forces who were not corrupt and taking cartel payoffs executed a flawless arrest of the man when he left his well-guarded hacienda and ventured to a meeting with other cartel kingpins. They had him in jail for a few months preparing to go to trial, but then Sanchez broke out, with the help of cops on the take, and led authorities on a year-long chase. Team Reaper only became involved when he reportedly crossed into the United States for help getting to Canada and ultimately a hideout in Europe. While Reaper pursued Sanchez, U.S. and Mexican forces wiped out his empire, destroying labs, growing fields, homes, anything they could to render Sanchez's operations moot. Associates not arrested scattered to hide from the unrelenting drug agents who were armed to the teeth and ready to shoot on sight. There had been too much talking, too many procedural delays, corrupt DEA agents aiding Sanchez, and the debts had to be paid in blood. After more months of searching, many missed opportunities, and clashes with Sanchez associates involved with moving the man throughout the U.S., Team Reaper finally grabbed their quarry.

He had charges to answer for in the U.S., too. Several

contract murders had been traced to him, but the killings were barely a blip on the radar compared with his other charges which included production, smuggling, and distribution of Mexican methamphetamine, marijuana, ecstasy and heroin throughout the US.

Sanchez and his cartel had managed the feat of flooding more drugs to the United States than any other cartel, for a total of five hundred tons of cocaine alone over a period of ten years. Just cocaine. Kane didn't want to think about how much of the other drugs Sanchez managed to get into the U.S. He knew the destruction of the drug first hand, the misery of addicts desperate for a fix, the smaller crimes of violence committed to get that fix. Drugs spread nothing but misery and death, and Sanchez needed to answer for his crimes. Big time. That's why Team Reaper existed: to bring men like Sanchez to justice, one way or another. Most of the time, Kane preferred "other." It was more final.

Since Mexico proved unreliable in prosecuting him on their own warrants, and the U.S. had him in an iron grip, and finders' keepers and all that, the U.S. got the first real opportunity to put Jorge Sanchez in a proper courtroom, where a Manhattan federal grand jury had already indicted him in absentia. The U.S. Marshals dropped him first into the Tombs in New York City, in general population with the rest of the worst the streets had produced, to really make him sweat, then moved him to the Manhattan facility to await his formal trial. None of his usual tricks would help him this time.

But now there was his daughter to deal with. The one they thought would never be a threat. It was a mistake Kane didn't want to make again.

If Blanca Sanchez thought for one minute she'd succeed without a fight, she had another thing coming.

Big time.

Team Reaper HQ
El Paso, TX

Hunt said, "Gotta love door-to-door service."

If anybody in the neighborhood of the nondescript warehouse that housed Reaper headquarters thought it was just another boring building where a company stored overstock, watching a military helicopter land in the mostly-empty parking lot certainly put to bed that idea.

The pilots didn't turn off the engine as Kane and Hunt piled out to be met by General Mary Thurston and Luis Ferrero. They hurried into the building as the helicopter ascended and flew away. Not even a farewell wave from either party. There wasn't time for that.

"You two need to get cleaned up," Thurston said as they entered the building, "and get ready to go to Berlin."

"What's in Berlin?"

"It's the last place Blanca Sanchez was seen."

Kane smiled.

Time to move in for the kill.

A hot shower, change of clothes, and steaming coffee and sweet rolls in the operations room. John Kane was feeling just fine. Hunt's grin showed the Navy SEAL Chief wasn't in a bad mood either.

Thurston conducted the briefing while Ferrero stood to one side to contribute now and then. A picture on the large-screen monitor mounted on the forward wall showed a man in his fifties, bald, narrow face. Shirt and tie, looking respectable outside a Berlin restaurant.

"That's Gunter Bruner," Thurston said. "He's an arms dealer. CIA says he moves not only small arms, but large caches of equipment, tanks, airplanes, stuff like that. All legitimate. But he's also suspected of selling weapons to unsavory types, including terrorists, so German BND has him under occasional surveillance."

Thurston clicked a remote and the picture changed. The new photograph showed a Hispanic woman in a dress, donning an overcoat, and walking along the sidewalk, blending in with the crowd. Almost. She was beautiful, a real Sofia Vergara-type. She'd never go totally unnoticed. She had an appeal that had made her very popular on the European party circuit.

"Bruner keeps an office in that building, using an engineering firm as a front. Blanca Sanchez visited that office only a few hours ago," Thurston said.

"He risked meeting her there?" Hunt said. "Sloppy."

"Bruner has a woman do a thorough background check on any new client," Ferrero said. "With her not being on the radar anywhere, or wanted for any crimes, or even suspected of any, he probably thought it was safe to see her there. But we told our friends we're looking for her, so BND rushed this to us as soon as she was identified."

"Did they keep following her?" Kane said.

"No," Thurston said. "They took a bunch of pictures of people going in and out of the building, just to see who might be visiting Bruner, and the alert for her popped up when they sorted the pictures. She could be long gone by now."

"Unless she's taking delivery personally of whatever she ordered," Hunt said.

"Or she'll have people in Berlin to do it for her," Kane said. "I doubt Jorge's little girl knows how to play in this sandbox."

"Don't sell her short, Reaper," Ferrero said. "We did that once already."

Kane admitted he had a point. He'd thought the same thing in the chopper coming home and reminded himself to not think that way again. Blanca Sanchez, as far as was concerned, was their fiercest opponent yet. *Get that through your head, dummy. Don't get careless.*

"But Bruner is still there," Hunt said.

"Exactly," Thurston said. "Your job is to pay him a visit and see if you can make him talk."

"No holds barred?" Kane said.

"The clock is ticking," Thurston said. "Do what you have to do. We'll back you up. Just don't cause an international incident. We don't need that kind of hassle."

"Hell," Hunt said, "that kinda takes all the fun out of it."

Thurston and Ferrero didn't crack a smile.

Kane finished his sweet roll and swallowed a mouthful of coffee. "Anything else?" he said.

"Wheels up in 45 minutes."

Kane and Hunt hustled to grab their gear.

General Mary Thurston wandered back into the operations room where the computer techs were busy at their work stations, the tapping of keys and quiet phone conversations barely intruding on her thoughts.

And she had many.

Her team was once again in harm's way, and once again she wished for their success while knowing that, maybe this time, somebody wasn't coming back. You can't constantly put your life at risk without, one day, the odds catching up with you. Would that day be today?

Sam Swift, the red-haired expert hacker, saw her and raised a hand. "General?"

She went over to him. "What have you found?"

"Something disturbing, ma'am."

She didn't like that at all. She braced herself for the news, looking at three faces on Swift's computer screen.

"Tell me."

"Facial recognition at three ports of entry have picked up these three men," Swift said. He pointed at the faces.

They didn't mean anything to Thurston. They were Hispanic males, casually dressed, with carry-ons and the usual tired faces of travelers who had just stepped off a long flight. There was nothing significant about them, except maybe a hardness around the eyes. Thurston knew the look. She saw it in her own people sometimes. Eyes that never quit the danger scan, and saw even the slightest movement, detecting the smallest threat. These were men who reacted quickly to such sensations. They might look perfectly normal, but they weren't.

Swift said, "We've identified each one as freelancers for the Mexican cartels. Guns for hire. They don't have any loyalty to one group or another."

"So?"

"They're assassins, ma'am."

"Okay."

"New York, New Jersey, and Connecticut. They've all arrived on different airlines, and they've made no attempt to hide their faces. Passports show other names, of course."

"Who are they?"

Swift pointed at each one. "Miquel Gutierrez, Christopher Ruan, and Fernando Arriola."

"Can we track where they're going?"

"No, ma'am. These photos are several hours old."

Thurston let out a sigh. Great. The connection was unmistakable. Blanca Sanchez obviously had the funds to pay for three elite killers, but who was their target? Would they be converging on Manhattan?

"Why are they infiltrating this way?"

"No idea, ma'am."

"They'd have to know we'd spot them," she said.

"Could be the point."

"Meaning?"

"Decoy? Get us to spend resources looking for these guys while Sanchez does something else?"

"Maybe. But doubtful. You don't use assassins as decoys."

Sam Swift said nothing, looking between Thurston and his screen.

Thurston said, "It does suggest a direct strike against the Manhattan facility."

"I doubt three men could pull off a raid there, ma'am."

"Could be the last of a bigger team already here."

Swift agreed.

"We need to alert Cara and her team," the general said.

"Yes, ma'am."

"I'll make the call," she said. "Keep scanning. See what else might come up."

Thurston pivoted and returned to her office. She'd have to make other calls, too, to General Hank Jones, her commanding officer, and President Carter, whom Jones answered to. They were aware of the situation but holding back other agencies until Team Reaper figured out what was happening. She wasn't sure they'd want to hold back any longer with this new information. The situation was getting worse by the minute.

She entered her office, closed the door, and picked up the phone.

CHAPTER 6

Manhattan

Cara Billings had wanted a relaxing evening prior to the start of the trial the next day. She told Brick and Arenas that she wanted to be left alone in her hotel room with room service and a movie after her nightly call to her son.

Then the phone rang.

When she saw Thurston's name on the caller ID, she paused the rom com on the television that so far hadn't been either rom or com and answered. Nightly check-in, no big deal.

Instead: "We've identified three cartel assassins entering your area," the general said.

Cara swung her legs over the side of the bed and sat up. "Already?"

"They've come in through New York, New Jersey, and Connecticut," Thurston said, providing a further rundown of her conversation with Sam Swift. "We have no idea what they might have in mind, other than linking up with a squad that's already there. Have you noticed anything suspicious?"

"Nothing at all, ma'am," Cara said. "We've practiced the route, noted possible ambush points, worked out decoys and back-up plans. I've seen nobody watching us. I don't think the marshals have, either. They certainly would have said something."

"How are you coordinating with the local cops?"

"They're going to block traffic along the two routes we've selected, one for real and one for the decoy. They'll sweep the area first to get everybody out of the way. I think we've taken just about every precaution we can. Now we just have to make sure the enemy doesn't sneak into the perimeter somehow."

"Well, we know they have three for sure."

"They'll need more."

"Exactly," Thurston said. "That's what doesn't make sense. We've kicked around the idea that they're a distraction, but nobody's really convinced of that."

"I can prowl around a little."

"No. Stand down. You have your orders and I need you to stick with them. Do not investigate this matter on your own."

"It's our necks on the line, ma'am."

"And if anything happens to you, Arenas, or Brick, heaven forbid, it will make even more trouble. Don't make trouble for me, Billings."

Cara sighed. "Yes, ma'am."

Talking to Thurston was like talking to her mother sometimes.

"We have people on the case," the general said, "and I will keep you informed. Meanwhile, stick to your assignment."

"We will."

"Billings?"

"Ma'am?"

"I'm not kidding."

"Yes, ma'am."

"I'll check in again tomorrow."

General Thurston killed the connection and Cara placed the cell phone on the nightstand beside her. Hell with her. Cara turned off the television. She'd have to see if the boy got the girl another time. At the corner table, she powered up her laptop and remotely logged into the Team Reaper servers using John Kane's username and password. She knew the tidbit she'd picked up during an overnight visit with him would come in handy someday. She executed a search for the New York area for any known drug dealers, Mafiosi of the local syndicate, somebody shady and on the street that she might be able to talk with. Somebody who might know where the cartel trio were going. They'd have to clear their arrival with the syndicate and pay a "tribute" to be let alone. No crooks just waltzed into somebody's territory uninvited, unless they wanted to leave that territory in pieces.

But she had to hurry. Sam Swift and the other techs in the operations center wouldn't notice Kane's login so long as it was a quick visit, but if she hung around too long, they might raise an eyebrow.

She speed-read information on various individuals who might fit the profile of who she was looking for but discarded most of them. She needed the jack-of-all-trades, the guy who knew a little bit about everything, somebody non-threatening to the major players who could act as a go-between for the necessary transactions of letting the cartel killers have safe passage through a protected area.

Assuming such an arrangement had been made.

The unintended benefit of alerting such an individual to the presence of the cartel meant a whole other group would be searching for those people, to politely ask them why they were working without permission. It might take the heat off her team and the marshals as they moved Sanchez back and forth.

Finally, she found a name that seemed promising. Once she finished his file, noting his regular hangouts, she knew she had her man. She logged off, traded her pajamas for street clothes, clipped her SIG-Sauer M17 to her belt, and left the room.

Cara had no intention of going out alone. She needed Arenas and Brick, too. Luckily, their room was only a few doors from hers.

"Brick" Peters lived up to his name as he stood in the doorway looking down at Cara. The big man *really* filled the doorway.

"Come on, let's go out."

"What?"

"Let's go out."

"You said—"

"Let me in, Brick."

With a grunt he stepped back, Cara entered the room, and Brick shut the door behind her.

Carlos Arenas, lounging in a chair in front of the television, muted the sound as she approached.

"Getting lonely?" Arenas said.

"We have a problem," Cara said, then recounted her conversation with Thurston.

Brick took the news with a quiet sigh.

Arenas said, "Oh *fuck*."

"I found the name of a guy we can talk to and see if he knows anything."

"No way," Brick said.

"We can't just sit here."

"The hell we can't," Arenas said. "I do believe those are our orders. I'm not doing anything that puts my position at risk, Cara. I got a family."

"And I don't?" Cara said, her son Jimmy flashing through her mind. "Our job is to make sure Sanchez is in court every day. If there is something threatening that mission, it's our job to stop that threat. I think it's pretty clear what we have to do."

"What did Thurston say?" Brick said.

"Not *exactly* yes," Cara admitted.

"We're staying put," the big man said.

"You seriously want to sit here and kill your braincells with the television?"

"We're watching the MMA fights," Arenas said. "It's educational."

Cara's eyes widened. She'd heard a bunch of garbage lines in her time, but that one was a whopper. "How?"

"We pick up new ideas on how to bust heads."

Cara snapped her gaze to Brick. The big man shrugged. "True story," he said.

"I'm going with or without the both of you," she said. "Buh-bye."

She turned for the door, shut it behind her, and casually walked down the hallway to the elevator. They didn't follow.

Cara reached the elevator and pressed the call button. She looked back down the hall.

Three...

Two...

One.

The door opened and Arenas and Brick, big coats covering their artillery, hurried to catch up.

"I knew I could count on you two," Cara said.

"Under protest," Arenas said.

"Hey," Cara said, "if anything bad happens, Brick is a trained medic, remember?"

They stared at her with disapproval. She smiled and ignored them. The elevator doors rumbled open. The trio stepped inside.

Felix Lovoso sat at the back-corner booth of his favorite hole-in-the-wall Italian diner, Luigi & Bella's, on East 41st Street. The small restaurant was sandwiched between two other shops, with more of the same across the street, the neighborhood barely visited by tourists, which the locals liked very much.

He sat alone. At a table near his booth, quietly discussing the football game displayed on a wall-mounted big screen and sipping espresso, sat his two bodyguards. Lovoso needed the protection. He wasn't a big man; maybe five-five, slight build, dark hair and eyes. The Syndicate called him The Mouse, but there was no malice in the nickname. He stayed quiet, did his job, and stayed hidden and thus caused no fuss. Lovoso was the go-between for criminals not connected to the Syndicate, and the Syndicate itself. You wanna pull a payroll robbery in New York City? You better fix it with Lovoso and fork over some cash so the Syndicate doesn't have you killed. Nothing happens in their territory without permission. Lovoso was there so guys could get their permission, whatever the cost was, and carry out their caper. They'd only have to look out for the cops, not a Syndicate killer who'd snuff them out with as much emotion as cleaning a toilet.

His job often made him the target of police detectives looking for information, but the Mouse never gave them anything. The last thing he needed was one of those killers coming after him.

Lovoso dug into the spaghetti and meatballs with gusto. It was the signature dish at Luigi & Bella's. With a fork in his right hand and spoon in his right, Lovoso pressed the fork into the spoon to wrap noodles round and round and stuff the generous portion into his mouth.

Life was going pretty good for Felix. He had a nice pad uptown; no trouble with any of his regular lady friends. When he passed tribute money to the Syndicate, they reliably gave him his three-percent cut, and the money provided a nice lifestyle. He could sit comfortably without a target on his back and enjoy his spaghetti.

The restaurant door opened. A woman and two men entered. They didn't exactly look like cops, but Lovoso knew they were there to see him. When the woman scooted into his booth, he felt a chill up his neck.

"Uh oh," he said.

"What do we tell the marshals?" Arenas said.

"Forget the marshals," Cara said. They reached their rental car, parked in the hotel's underground garage. Fluorescent lights above flickered annoyingly and snapped. "They're at the bar or in bed already."

"Maybe watching the fights," Brick said.

"You can ask them for tips in the morning," Cara said. She climbed behind the wheel and started the car.

"Where are we going?" Arenas asked from the back seat, behind Cara. Brick took shotgun, scooting the seat back as far as it would go so his long legs had room under the dash.

Cara plugged an address from memory into her cell phone's GPS. Turning up the volume, she dropped the phone in a cup holder.

"Little Italian place that has great reviews on Yelp," Cara said. "If anybody asks, we went there to try the lasagna."

She started the car.

"I prefer chicken parm," Brick said.

"It's overcooked," Cara said.

She put the car in gear.

Cara Billings recognized Lovoso right away based on his file photo. The slight man sat alone in a booth, with two body-guards at a table close by. Only another pair of customers occupied a table, one close to the window. The smells from the kitchen were wonderful, and Cara wished they were indeed there to eat instead of brace the man known as The Mouse for information on the cartel killers who were in town.

During the drive over, she'd called Thurston to send pictures of the three cartel assassins. She hoped, if they had checked in with Lovoso for the required tribute money, that he'd recognize them.

Cara and Brick and Arenas walked into the restaurant and zeroed on Lovoso right away. The man sat in front of a large plate of spaghetti.

"Uh oh," he said.

The bodyguards moved fast, rising and reaching under their jackets for hardware.

Arenas and Brick moved faster, snapping out SIG pistols from shoulder leather and telling the bodyguards to put down the guns and sit quietly.

"I don't want any shooting," Cara said. "I don't want any trouble at all. We just want to talk."

The bodyguards were doing what they were paid to do, but even they knew when they were outmatched. They did as told and returned to their seats, placing their hands on the table palms-down.

"Put 'em away," Cara said. Arenas and Brick complied with the order, but remained standing, watching the other two.

Somebody shouted from the kitchen.

Cara dropped into the booth in front of Lovoso.

"Hi," she said.

"What do you want?"

"Keep your hands where I can see them, Felix."

"Hey, I don't got no gun, lady. I'm here minding my own damn business and you come in here showing more artillery than I've seen all week. What do you want?"

Cara showed him her cell phone and one of the pictures of the cartel assassins on display.

"We're looking for three cartel assassins that have come into the area," she said. She told him their ports of entry and that they might be in the city to derail the Sanchez trial. "Know them?"

"Never seen that guy before."

She swiped right.

"This one?"

"Nope."

Another swipe.

"Get out of here, lady, I don't know what you're talking about, who these guys are, or anything like that. Go on, split."

The head chef ambled out of the kitchen, shouting in Italian. Lovoso turned around, not leaving the booth and shouted back. Whatever he said was enough to calm the chef down, who retreated to the kitchen once again.

Lovoso faced Cara.

"I told him not to call the cops, that we've had a misunderstanding, and if you don't get the hell out of here, I'll tell him to call them and then you'll be in real trouble."

"We are cops."

"I know the cops who work this area. Ain't nobody new joined the force."

Lousy ploy anyway.

"Would these three men be operating here without permission?" Cara said.

"If they are, I want those pictures, because I'll have to find these jerks and ask why they aren't paying their tribute. Otherwise, it's *my* ass. I don't want the Syndicate thinking I'm falling down on the job."

"Or cutting them out."

"You see what position I'm in? Actually, I should be *thanking* you for telling me they're here."

Cara let out a sigh and glanced at Arenas and Brick. Arenas raised an eyebrow. She'd get an earful from him on the ride back to the hotel. This whole effort was for nothing and could have gone badly, too. But she couldn't just sit at the hotel and not do anything when gunmen might be targeting her and her team for death. Part of her job was protecting her team. This visit certainly qualified.

"Good luck, Felix." Cara stood up.

"Hey, what about those pics?"

"What's your number?"

He told her; she sent him the pictures via text.

"I'll call you if I find them," Lovoso said.

"Don't call me for anything else."

Lovoso cracked a lecherous grin. "I give great city tours, you know."

"You can do better than that, Felix. Let's go, boys."

Cara headed for the door. Arenas and Brick followed her, but not without a quick danger scan of the rest of the place.

They started driving back to the hotel.

"So we know nothing," Arenas said.

"We know they haven't cleared their presence with the local crime lords," Cara said. "What does that tell you?"

"They're cheap?"

"It means they don't expect to be here long enough to be found. It means they could hit us as soon as tomorrow."

Brick said, "I'm beginning to think we don't have enough troops."

"There is one good thing about this," Arenas said.

"What?" said Cara.

"We have a second pair of eyes working for us. Problem is, he'll probably want a date in exchange for what he finds."

Arenas and Brick chuckled.

Cara cursed.

CHAPTER 7

Mexico City

The whirr of the telephone woke Pete Traynor from a deep sleep.

He fumbled for his cell phone on the night stand. The caller ID flashed RICO RAMIREZ and he answered groggily.

"Too much tequila last night, amigo?"

"I don't think I've slept this hard in a month," Traynor said. He wasn't staying in Mexico's City's most exclusive hotel, but the bed was quite comfortable and he hated the idea of getting out from under the covers. "What's going on?"

"I'm picking you up in an hour. There's an informant we need to see that will have some information for us."

"You've already asked him?"

"He came to me."

The words sent a shock through Traynor and he swung

his legs off the bed, sitting up. Who needed coffee when great news like this was coming through?

"I'll be ready. Bring breakfast."

"McDonalds?"

"Good heavens, no."

Rico laughed.

Traynor hung up, climbed out of bed with a grunt, and started for the shower.

"Who is this guy?" Traynor said through a mouthful of breakfast burrito. He figured the item had migrated from the United States, but at least it wasn't full of mystery meat. The full flavor of the eggs, sausage, cheese, hot sauce, and onions filled Traynor's mouth.

"Pedro Tellez," Rico said. "He used to work for Sanchez. And when I say *work*, I mean he was the second lieutenant. He buried the bodies the other guys say they know the locations of."

"Why is he talking to us?"

"He got out. His wife got sick, so he said the hell with it. He's one of the few people to quietly leave a cartel. Almost never happens. His wife is still sick, and Tellez keeps a low profile, but every now and then he pops up with a morsel of information or so, on everybody except Sanchez."

Traynor swallowed a bite. "He didn't help us out when we were chasing Sanchez?"

"No."

"Then why is he offering now?"

"We'll have to ask him."

"I can't wait to hear."

Presently they turned into a neighborhood full of

dwellings seemingly smashed together without thought to appearance. They were nice homes, obviously packed together to make the most of the space, but their white concrete exteriors and dark pink roofs made them all seem generic, as if they'd been prizes out of a box of cereal.

Both sides of the street were too crowded to park, cars packed tightly bumper-to-bumper, so Rico drove another two blocks before finding an adequate place to leave the unmarked car. Traynor and Rico walked back to the address Rico wanted. A brown door sat atop a small set of concrete steps.

Rico knocked, a series of taps, a pause, and a few more taps. Traynor didn't ask why he needed to use a code. The pattern probably let Tellez know it was Rico knocking and not the mail man.

A short and stocky man in a white shirt and dark trousers answered, the lines on his sixty-something face indicative of experiences Traynor couldn't begin to imagine. He didn't say hello as he stepped back to allow Rico and Traynor to enter, closing the door behind them. The living room was crowded with furniture and knick-knacks, and not very well lighted. Traynor's eyes had to adjust to the sudden cut off.

"My wife's sleeping," Pedro Tellez said. "We have to talk quietly. Come outside."

Traynor followed Rico and the older man through the narrow passages, passed the kitchen, to an enclosed patio in back where Tellez had beer in a cooler under ice. Sure, it was early, but what the heck. Traynor twisted off the top of the offered bottle and took an appreciative gulp of the Mexican water. They sat around a rickety metal table. The white paint was peeling in several spots.

Rico started the conversation.

"You know we're looking for Blanca Sanchez."

Tellez nodded, his eyes tired. Traynor wondered what ailment his wife was sick with, and how much care he was providing her. The strain on his face made Traynor think the lady was hanging onto life with one finger.

The older man said, "She is trying to rebuild the cartel forces. She came to me to ask my help, thinking that my presence would rally the others and convince those reluctant to come out of hiding to do so. I refused."

"Why?" Rico said.

"This is the last thing Jorge would want."

"His daughter getting involved?"

"Yes. He did not want his daughter taking his place. That's why he never made a fuss about her trips around the world. It got her away from his business."

"We think she's going to try and break her father out of jail sometime during the trial," Traynor said. "Did she mention the plans to you, or how she thought she could pull off a rescue?"

Tellez shook his head after a small sip of beer. "She did not."

Rico said, "I'm not sure if I believe you, Pedro."

"Why lie?" the older man said. "I'm telling you that Jorge would not want his daughter involved, and the best way to keep that from happening is to tell you."

"But you haven't told us anything we don't already know, Pedro," Rico said. "Give us something we can work with. We need to find her."

Pedro Tellez drank another gulp of beer.

"When I worked for Jorge," Tellez said, "my job was to organize and train the soldiers."

"Uh-huh."

"She wanted my help doing that again, with new recruits, and some others she'd made an alliance with."

"Another cartel?"

Tellez shook his head. "No, something worse."

Traynor and Rico waited.

"She's made a deal with al-Qaeda, and her troops are being trained at their camp here in Mexico."

Pete Traynor about fell out of his chair. He lurched forward, almost spilling his bottle. "Their what?"

Rico shrank back in his chair.

Tellez frowned at Traynor. "You do not know?"

"That jihadists have a camp in Mexico? Certainly not. I need to know more."

Tellez let out a chuckle. "We've heard that your CIA wants to keep the camp a secret so nobody panics about terrorists a stone's throw away from the Texas border. We didn't think it was true."

Traynor dropped back in his chair. He turned to Rico. "You know about this?"

"There are rumors of a camp," Rico said, "but nobody's made the effort to try and find it."

"Why?"

"Orders."

Traynor scoffed. Corruption. Always. All over Mexico's government and law enforcement. The jihadists, via the cartels, were probably paying a huge amount of money for the Mexican government to protect them from any inquiry.

Tellez said, "Check the northern part of the country, in Sonora. She wanted me to go there and help train her soldiers."

"How many does she have?"

"I don't know. I just know that somebody needs to stop her."

"Among other things," Traynor mumbled. He looked at the amber fluid in the beer bottle and wished it were a little stronger.

He wasn't looking forward to calling headquarters with the news.

"When did the rumors of the AQ camp start?" Traynor said.

Rico Ramirez was behind the wheel of the unmarked car once again, oddly silent after their conversation with Pedro Tellez.

"Do you know more than you're telling, Rico? About this camp?"

"No."

"You wouldn't lie to me, would you?"

"Of course not," Rico said. "Nobody's ever been able to look for the camp because we'll be sacked if we do. We haven't had any tips from informants, either."

"That you know of," Traynor said. "Those reports might have been intercepted."

"Very true, but what about your side?"

"Oh, my side would bury this so deep nobody would know about it until al-Qaeda bombed Texas, then it would be a national scandal. I understand keeping it classified. I don't understand letting it remain when we're more than capable of blasting it off the map."

They rode in silence a moment, Rico watching traffic as he drove, Traynor burning up with the new information. If Blanca Sanchez linked up with the jihadists and brought them into her plan, it might be more than Team Reaper could handle.

"I need to see this so-called camp," Traynor said.

"No way."

"I'm going with or without you, Rico."

"Sonora is a big area."

"Help me."

"How?"

"Let's get back to my hotel. I have an idea."

Rico took the next exit.

Back at the hotel, Traynor spent an hour updating General Thurston on his progress so far and went into detail about the conversation with Pedro Tellez and the alleged al-Qaeda camp in Sonora.

"I've never heard of a camp," Thurston said.

"We need to see if it's there, ma'am. Tellez mentioned it for a reason. Can you get a satellite scan?"

"Better, we can fly a drone over the area. If I order satellite coverage, and we start setting off alarms in Washington, it might get blocked."

Traynor squeezed a fist. Of course, she was right. They didn't have time to deal with interference from the Pentagon, CIA, or whoever else wanted to keep the lid on any information regarding a jihadist camp at the front door of the United States.

"While you're doing that, I'll keep poking around," Traynor said.

"Try and find out how Blanca hooked up with the jihadists," Thurston said. "I'll see also if there's anything in her background suggesting a prior connection. Maybe she met somebody during her party days that made the introduction. Stay in touch, Pete."

"Yes, ma'am."

Traynor ended the call and looked at Rico.

"What's next?" Traynor said.

"My office. Let's see if the surveillance team watching the other Sanchez strays have turned up anything."

The two men left the room.

Berlin

John Kane and SEAL Chief Borden Hunt sat in a corner booth at the Berlin Capitol Club Bar & Lounge looking for a woman.

Eliza Schenk, specifically, the go-between for contact with arms dealer Gunter Bruner, whom Blanca Sanchez had visited earlier. They didn't know what Blanca and Bruner had talked about, or what Blanca wanted to buy. That was the question they needed to answer. They also needed to know if the purchase had taken place. Hopefully, they could intercept Blanca prior to taking delivery of her items. That would solve a ton of problems in one stroke.

"Too bad we're here on business," Hunt said. "This is a nice place."

The seating area was a mix of tables, booths, and couches, multiple big screen televisions on the walls, and bright lighting, which Kane appreciated. There was nothing worse than a bar where they kept the lights dim. He liked to see things. He especially liked to see potential threats before they became reality.

Most of the patrons' attention was on the big screen televisions, watching a late football match. The long bar along the left wall as you entered was also packed, drinkers not paying attention to the game either locked in conversation or attempting conversations with the opposite sex.

Hunt drank some beer while Kane sipped a whiskey and water.

Intell from the German BND stated that Eliza Schenk nightly held court at the Capitol Club, where she sat alone and had to rebuff approaches from men who had other things in mind than business.

"Stick to the plan and we'll be fine," Kane said. "You can come back here on vacation some time."

"Top of my list," Hunt said, taking in the environment with a long look.

Neither of them was armed. They'd left the hardware at the hotel for a reason. They didn't want to get mixed up in a problem that would involve the Berlin police. Engaging with Eliza shouldn't be something that led to violence.

Kane would do all the talking. He'd posed as an arms buyer for rebels in Africa once before while following a cartel connection in Johannesburg, and the cover had never been blown. It was still useful as long as the red-head hacker Sam Swift back at Reaper headquarters had done his part to update Kane's record of activity. Eliza and Bruner would undoubtedly do a background check prior to allowing any meeting to take place.

"There she is," Hunt said.

Kane turned his head. Eliza Schenk entered with purpose, her business attire clashing with the overall casual look of the other patrons. She carried a purse and leather briefcase and took a seat on a couch up against a wall. A waitress approached and she ordered a drink. Opening the briefcase, she produced a laptop and turned on the machine. The glow of the screen lit up her face, highlighting her heavy makeup.

"Give her a minute," Kane said.

When the waitress returned with the glass of white wine, Eliza smiled and handed her a bill. The waitress retreated to the bar.

"Now," Kane said.

Kane left the table first, Hunt following, and Kane felt a butterfly sensation in his stomach as Eliza looked up at him without an ounce of friendliness.

CHAPTER 8

"I already have a drink," Eliza Schenck said.

Kane sat down opposite the couch, Hunt beside him.

"We're not here to talk about wine," Kane said. He kept his face impassive. If she wasn't showing any emotion, he wanted to emulate her as a way of building a connection.

"What are you here to talk about?"

"Guns. Lots of guns."

"Who are you?"

"John Ellison," Kane said. He didn't make a move to shake hands. "I have clients in Africa that require a few crates of small arms and I'd like to talk to Mr. Bruner about supplying the equipment."

"If you know that much," she said, "I suppose you're serious, but it takes a little more than that." She added, "*Mr. Ellison.*"

"I'm not hiding anything. Feel free to look me up. Need me to spell my name?"

She scoffed. "Stop it. I'm not an idiot."

"Of course not. But you also have to be careful. We all do."

"Where can I reach you?"

Kane produced a slip of paper from a jacket pocket with his name and cell phone number. He handed it to Eliza, who took it. Her fingernails were long and blood red, as if the nails were claws and the polish the drippings from a fresh kill. Her dark eyes surveyed Kane's face a moment. He held her gaze.

"I'll get back to you."

"How long?"

"Could be a day, could be a month, could be never."

"My clients are in a bit of a hurry."

She paused a moment, not breaking eye contact. Then: "Which war, Mr. Ellison?"

Kane didn't miss a beat. "Northern Mali. The rebels and all that."

She shook her head. "There's been a cease fire for a few years."

"Talks have broken down. They're starting again," Kane said. "You can look that up too."

"I will. You may go now."

Kane stood. She was the Alpha bitch, and he was happy to let her hold the title. Hunt remained seated until Kane tapped his shoulder. A little resistance didn't hurt at all. They went back to their original booth and didn't look her way again.

"She better not take that long," Hunt said.

"There's always Plan B."

"Which is what?"

"Find Bruner and stick a gun in his mouth."

"Why aren't we starting there?"

"Because the boss doesn't want an international incident," Kane said. "Plus, it will take two weeks to study

Bruner and learn his routine and security arrangement. A formal introduction gets us in the front door."

"You better be right, Reaper," Hunt said.

"I hope I am."

Kane finished his drink in one long swallow. The clock was ticking, and he didn't know how much time they had left.

Direct action against Bruner might be inevitable, but he wanted to try the soft probe first.

Manhattan
Manhattan Jail Facility

Jorge Sanchez paced in his cell, the close confines more of a burden than he thought they'd be. He could only take a few steps in either direction. He remained stoic, though. It wasn't good form to make a lot of noise, and such behavior held no benefit anyway. They had him caged.

The marshals were coming to collect him in fifteen minutes. Today his trial started. The beginning of the end for *el Tigre*, the Tiger, as he'd been called throughout his life. He'd earned the nickname and was proud of the title.

Sanchez grew up the oldest of three kids in Zapopan, and it was a hard life. His family was poor, his father a laborer and drunk who couldn't hang onto jobs, who made a habit of beating his kids, too. That lasted until Sanchez turned fifteen. As a birthday present to himself he stabbed his father in the neck.

The police arrested Sanchez and put him in jail while they worked the case and filed formal charges, but he didn't sit in a cell for long. A man in a white suit, who told Sanchez to call him Henry, showed up and escorted him out the front door. None of the cops at the jail interfered. Some didn't even look at him.

Henry worked for the Chologos drug cartel, he explained, and they were impressed with Sanchez's talent. It takes guts to kill your father, even under the circumstances in which Sanchez found himself. "Your family will stay poor," Henry said, "unless you come to their aid. You're the man now. You have to be *el tigre* that keeps them fed every day."

"How?"

"I have a job for you. If you do it well, there will be more jobs."

Thus, Jorge Sanchez began as a runner for the Chologos cartel, working his way up the ranks, earning the respect of the cartel leaders. Sanchez made sure his family had the best, moving them from their ramshackle home into a much larger domicile, providing his mother and sisters with nice clothes and other material items they had only previously dreamed about. They didn't ask where the money was coming from. Sanchez always thought they'd figured out the source of the income, but they also never objected.

Through a series of violent coups within the cartel, Sanchez eventually assumed leadership, and ran the organization with an iron fist, working his men hard in whichever aspect of the business they occupied. He built the Chologos cartel into the largest and most productive out of all the others. He was feared, respected, looked to for guidance. He'd gone from having nothing to having everything— almost too much of everything—and realized his own dream of providing a better life for his wife and only daughter, Blanca, than he'd ever had.

And all because he'd buried a knife hilt-deep in his father's neck.

It wasn't his last murder, either, but it was the only one that didn't intrude on his thoughts in quiet moments. Nobody, not even the most skilled assassin, talked about the ghosts of the dead who visited in the night. If you could withstand those visits, you might live on to be a legend among assassins. Not everybody reached that plateau. Most cracked and went mad, drowning themselves in booze or the very drugs the cartel smuggled, dying by their own hand, or by the next up-and-coming killer.

And now, he'd reached the natural conclusion of a wild and violent life, and Jorge Sanchez had no regrets. There would be no escaping American custody—they weren't as corrupt as law enforcement in Mexico, very dedicated to their causes. The only way out was the coward's way, and Sanchez had no intention of giving the Americans the satis- faction of killing himself, nor would he tarnish his name and legend with such an act. If this trial was the ending of all endings, Jorge Sanchez planned to take it like a man. The legend of *el tigre* would live forever.

A heavy door thudded open down the hall from his cell. Sanchez stopped, turned, and faced the bars with his chest out and chin up. He was just shy of six feet and stocky, his gut having become more pronounced in recent years, but you'd never think he was soft. His chest and arms and legs showed hard muscle.

A man and a woman and a jail guard stopped in front of the cell. The man was Wayne O'Neil, one of the federal marshals; the woman he knew as Cara Billings, part of the strike team that had arrested him. O'Neil was tall and trim, with a freshly-shaved and alert face, perfectly-combed blond hair, the woman almost matching his height, her long hair tied back. The last time he saw her, she'd been decked out in combat fatigues, body armor, shoving an automatic rifle in his face. The muzzle had remained steady. She was a warrior. He could respect that.

The guard opened the cell and Sanchez turned his back to them, allowing the guard to handcuff his wrists. Without a word of greeting, the trio led him down the hall and presently into the underground garage where a black Suburban waited, the engine already running. Two more of Billings' team sat up front. Billings and the marshal shoved him in back, in the middle seat, and sat on either side. More jail guards, armed, scattered around, let the Suburban exit the garage and pull out onto the street.

Sanchez glanced back to see two more similar SUVs following.

So, a convoy. Other marshals probably rode in the accompanying vehicles, all armed to the teeth. The people he was with only had sidearms. He was well-guarded indeed.

Let the ending begin.

Cara Billings hoped she didn't look nervous. The decoy convoy had left the jail fifteen minutes earlier and should have arrived at the Moynihan Courthouse by now. The marshals had the area covered as best as possible, along with the cops blocking traffic along the transport routes. Helicopters patrolled overhead, other marshals looking for snipers and any other signs of trouble. The armored Suburban had enough plating to withstand a rocket strike and machine gun fire, but that didn't provide Cara with one-hundred-percent peace of mind. Even tanks had weak spots. How would the Suburban stand up to sustained fire?

A glance at Sanchez showed her a man stoically facing his situation, no fuss or drama. She didn't think he believed anybody was coming for him. He was on his own. Alone.

Cara began her morning with a video conference with General Mary Thurston. She had made no mention of her team's extracurricular activity and listened attentively as Thurston told her what Traynor and Kane were up to on their various ends of the case. Cara was glad they were on the job. It made her feel less anxious. If they could catch Blanca Sanchez before she implemented her rescue operation, so much the better.

She hadn't heard a word from Felix Lovoso, the local fixer. Not even for a date. She hoped the little man found the three cartel killers sent by Blanca before they initiated their own plans.

She couldn't help but feel like a sitting duck. The only thing she, Arenas, and Brick could do is keep their eyes open, and take solace in the fact that they had enough marshals with them to hopefully overwhelm any front-on attack.

She had to maintain her confidence in that what they'd planned was enough to protect them.

Because if not, this could very well be her last mission. If Blanca really wanted her father back, she'd have to go all the way, and that meant an assault of such a scale it would make Normandy look like a walk in Central Park.

And the muggers would have machine guns.

She couldn't stand that thought.

The convoy made the final turn for the courthouse. The big gray building loomed ahead.

Mexico City

. . .

Pete Traynor's morning also began with a video conference with General Mary Thurston, as she forwarded to his laptop a series of pictures taken by several Reaper drones flown over the Sonora region. The crystal-clear photos impressed Traynor a great deal. There seemed nothing those drones weren't capable of.

The General Atomics MQ-1 Predator was a sleek, small aircraft that looked like something a large-scale model builder might assemble in his garage, and remote controlled by expert operators like Brooke Reynolds at Reaper head-quarters. The firepower each Predator packed made even the biggest skeptic a believer in its capabilities.

Missile pylons under each wing contained two AGM-114N Hellfire II missiles, an air-to-surface weapon with a high-explosive anti-tank warhead. When the Predator wasn't flying a combat mission, cameras mounted in the bulbous nose provided excellent aerial shots, clear enough to spot a pimple on a cartel soldier's nose.

Traynor carefully examined each picture. Headquarters had counted six camps within 50 kilometers of each other in Sonora. There was no way to tell which camp might be operated by al-Qaeda, and which was a standard cartel camp, either associated with the Sanchez organization, or another cartel.

Traynor decided they were playing a game of pin the tail on the terrorist camp. The pictures were nice to have but didn't help them get closer to Blanca Sanchez or her jihadist allies.

A knock at the door. Traynor left the table and let Rico Ramirez inside.

"Did they arrive?" Rico said. He held two paper coffee cups and carried a leather case across his back.

"They did, but I don't see much that's going to help us."

Traynor took one of the coffees and led Rico to the table where the recon photos were displayed on his laptop screen. Rico bent down and scanned each one.

"Can you tell one from the other?" Traynor said.

"Not like this."

Ramirez set his coffee on the table, then placed the leather case on the bed while he popped the lid. Taking out his own laptop, he placed it beside Traynor's and powered up.

"What do you have?" Traynor said, as Rico began accessing a map file.

"We note the cartel camps, always," he said. He further explained that they knew the camps existed, but there hadn't been any priority in shutting them down. "They're barely monitored," he added, "because the head honchos are bribed to not pay them any attention. It's a source of frustration."

"That's putting it mildly."

"If we can eliminate which ones are noted cartel camps, the one left over might be al-Qaeda."

"Unless they noted that, too, as a cartel camp."

"I'm not sure they would. If they want to keep it hidden, it would be best to make no note of its existence at all."

Traynor shrugged. That made sense. It also made sense to note it as a normal cartel camp. There was only one way to find out. He sipped the hot coffee.

"Thanks for the joe," he said.

"We'll need it," Rico said.

Presently they cross-checked Rico's map with HQ's pictures, eliminating one camp after another until, indeed, only one remained, that was not noted on the official Mexican government map.

Traynor focused on that photo and enlarged it.

"Looks like barracks, a mess hall, even some construction in the south corner," he said.

"Uh-huh."

"I don't see any goats, though."

"What?"

"You'd think jihadists would want goats around, in case they get lonely at night."

"Don't be a bigot, Traynor."

The American chuckled.

After some more study, with Rico in the chair in front of the laptops, Traynor leaned against the wall and folded his arms.

"How are your surveillance crews doing?"

Ramirez had assigned several agents to watch any stray Sanchez operatives known to be in Mexico City as soon as Traynor had arrived in the country.

"Not much," Rico said. "The cartel people are laying low, going about their business. Phone taps haven't revealed any contact from Blanca Sanchez, nor has anybody approached them for secret meetings. The loyalists are just existing right now."

"Of course they are, because she knows we'll be watching them."

Rico shrugged.

"She doesn't know we found out about her new training camp," Traynor said. "I suggest you keep the surveillance active so she thinks we're working in the dark, and you and I take a trip to Sonora."

"It'll be dangerous, just the two of us."

"You got a date tonight or something?" Traynor said.

Rico Ramirez admitted he did not.

"If you don't mind a parachute jump," Ramirez said, "I know a pilot who will fly us out there and keep his mouth shut afterwards."

"Tell him to name his price, it's on Uncle Sam."

Rico nodded and took out his cell phone. He reached his pilot friend on the first try, and it only took a few minutes to make the flight arrangements.

CHAPTER 9

Cabo San Lucas, Mexico

"Who is the VIP?"

"Two of them. You'll get that information when you arrive in Mexico."

Diego Moreno kept playing his conversation with Blanca Sanchez over in his mind, the mystery VIPs mentioned by Blanca the most often repeated line. Their meeting in Berlin continued to empower him. The cartel was coming back; Jorge was coming home; the United States would pay dearly for what they had done to him and his friends. In the end, that's what they all fought for. Sure, the cartel sent drugs into the U.S. and other countries, profit above all else, but in the process, bonds were formed that were hard to break. The occasional backstabbing traitor always lurked somewhere in the mix, ready to kill anybody to advance, Moreno was certainly no fool on that fact, but his life and the lives of the people close to him had been upended by the U.S. assault, and the Americans had to be held accountable.

Moreno was happy to present the bill. And expected his enemies to pay with their lives.

Waves crashed mere feet from him as he sat in the outdoor patio area of El Farallon, a coast-side restaurant in Cabo San Lucas, with the port a stone's throw, or a short drive, away. He still didn't know the identities of the VIPs he was to intercept from a cruise ship that was due to arrive in less than a day. He had a contact on the way, another dear friend from the cartel, to provide the information, as Blanca had promised.

The wooden floor below him had been built into the rocky cliffside, the remainder of a rocky outcropping serving as a backdrop to the restaurant, with its indoor and outdoor seating areas, the outdoor covered in some areas, the rest uncovered. Moreno sat under the sun, the clear blue sky above. It was a huge improvement over dreary Berlin and the drizzly rain. And the loneliness. Especially the loneliness. It had taken considerable will-power for Moreno not to drown his sorrows in booze. Never again, he'd promised himself years ago, and he meant to keep that particular oath.

The gentle breeze went with his refreshing cocktail, a gimlet, the mixture of vodka and lime juice spot on, and what one could expect at El Farallon, where "only the best" actually had meaning.

Ahead, across the shimmering water, was another rock formation that the locals liked to point out to the tourists. Up close it was rubbish, but from far away, one could see what looked like the long neck and head of a dragon drinking from the ocean water. Up close it was just a cluster of rocks that showed nothing specific.

"Diego."

Moreno looked right. He smiled and rose, extending a hand. Sebastian DeSoto matched him in height and wore a straw hat to compliment the rest of his clothing. They sat down. A waiter hurried over and DeSoto ordered a drink. He gazed out at the view.

"Never gets boring," he said.

"No."

"Good to see you again, amigo."

"It's been too long," Moreno said.

"No trouble for you overseas?"

Moreno shook his head. "Berlin was ... well, it was Berlin. I wasn't there to see the sights."

"I headed for Canada," DeSoto said. "Found a cabin as far from civilization as I could find. Worse thing was the snow."

"How did Blanca find you?"

"Same way she found the rest of us."

"But you, apparently, have more information than she gave me."

The waiter brought DeSoto's beer and departed. DeSoto took a long drink.

"Indeed, I do, amigo." He pulled a cell phone from inside the pocket of his white coat, tapped the screen, and passed the device to Moreno.

"Scroll through the pictures," DeSoto said.

Moreno scrolled slowly, noting as much detail as he could about the two women featured. They were both young, perhaps late twenties, and most certainly related. Both had long blonde hair, and their smiles were nearly identical. No way they weren't sisters.

"Who am I looking at?"

"Our VIPs."

"Never seen them before. How can they be VIPs if I don't recognize them?"

DeSoto laughed. "They aren't television stars, Diego. You are looking at the daughters of Arizona Senator Ted Warner. The oldest one is Peggy, the younger is Britney. They are your typical American girls, with the blonde hair and blue eyes, the girl-next-door look that will make Americans freak out when they realize we have taken them hostage. Everybody notices when Barbie is put in danger."

Moreno handed back the cell phone. The two women didn't exactly resemble Barbie dolls, but he understood DeSoto's meaning. Endangered white girls always received the media attention; other ethnicities didn't fare as well.

"Why them?"

"Because Senator Warner," DeSoto said, "has never met a war he didn't want to fight. He loves America's military might so much, he wants the whole world to see it. He especially wants us to see it, not only in Mexico but Colombia. In other words, he likes war, and he especially likes the so-called war on drugs."

"So, this is a direct assault on him," Moreno said. "Do we expect he'll have influence on the president? Will he fight as equally hard for Jorge's release?"

DeSoto shrugged. He swallowed some beer. "Maybe." He looked out at the sipping dragon.

Moreno followed his gaze. A cruise ship, a floating hotel with towering decks, overloaded with tourists ready to spend American dollars in the city, appeared around the side of the rock formation. The ship, like the two others already anchored in the bay, would unload passengers via shuttle boats as there was no harbor for the big ships in which to dock.

"They'll come off a ship just like that," DeSoto said.

"Grab them at the pier?"

"Why not?" DeSoto said. "There is nothing but confusion there. You have line after line of tourists navigating hustlers trying to get their money before they even reach the first bar. They'll be so excited it will be easy to pull them out of line."

"Where are we taking them?"

DeSoto smiled. "Sonora."

"That far?"

"It's the perfect place. Wait till you see it."

Moreno laughed. "You're not going to tell me?"

"Surprises, amigo. We can't spoil all the fun at once."

Moreno wanted to argue, but part of him enjoyed the mystery. He was back in the game in a big way, and nothing and nobody would take it from him again.

After a light lunch, Moreno and DeSoto took a ride over to the pier to see if what they'd discussed was feasible.

Not only was it feasible, there shouldn't be any trouble at all.

The line of tourists coming off the shuttle boats contained an excited bunch of folks from all over the world, passing vendor booths and "surprise" photographers, stopping for a bag search before finally moving on past the pier to where the restaurants and bars awaited.

"Every passenger has an identity card from the boat," Moreno pointed out.

"Good," DeSoto said. "The ship will know when the women do not return."

"They'll raise an alarm."

"The search will be contained to this area," DeSoto

said, gesturing to the waterfront entertainment spots. "Once we deliver our notice, I'm sure the crew will have no trouble leaving port to head back to the U.S. as fast as possible."

"Uh-huh."

"The ship will be docked for two days, we'll have all the time we need."

Moreno let out a sigh and took in the activity around him. He wished he were there to enjoy himself, but business came first.

Fun time would arrive soon enough.

Berlin

Gunter Bruner said, "Do they check out?"

Eliza Schenk, her legs crossed, sat in front of Bruner's desk while he stood looking out the window, night time Berlin aglow, what he could see of it, anyway. The building across the street was mostly dark, with only a few windows lit.

"They check out," she said, "but I don't like them."

"Why?"

Eliza didn't like talking to his back and window reflection but she soldiered on. "Soon after the Sanchez visit we have two Americans asking to see you? Do I need to explain why that sets off my crap detector?"

Bruner finally turned. "The wind sets off your crap detector. Your thoroughness isn't always an asset, Eliza."

"And your greed isn't one of yours, Gunter."

Bruner raised an eyebrow and turned his back to her once more. "You think we should kill them?"

"I'd feel better."

"They'll have friends. They probably told friends they'll be here to see me."

"That doesn't mean anything. Crime is a big concern in Berlin. Unfortunate events happen all the time. Such as American arms dealers getting mixed up with nasty people."

"Like us?"

"Like whoever else they deal with," Eliza said.

Bruner let out a sigh and fogged the glass in front of him.

Eliza examined the red nail of her left index finger. She'd chipped it slightly getting into her BMW for this meeting. She examined the rest of the nails. The polish was beginning to flake on her pinky finger, too. Might as well have it all redone, she decided.

She knew what Bruner's decision in this situation would be. He liked money, he liked doing business, but he was also very cautious when trouble stared them in the face, and Ellison and his friend were trouble.

"Why don't we just turn down their business?" Bruner said. "If they are American agents here to extract information about Blanca Sanchez, they will be replaced by more agents. We can't do anything to make it look like we're anything more than upstanding gun dealers."

Eliza laughed. She knew an oxymoron when she heard one.

"The Americans will have to prove we did something," Eliza said. "The time that takes will give us time to make sure we can prove otherwise. If we simply turn them down, they'll visit you at home and stick a gun in your neck."

Bruner removed a handkerchief from the back pocket of

his slacks and wiped the window where his breath had caused condensation. The fog had faded, but left residue behind.

He turned to her. "Do it."

Eliza smiled and left the chair.

CHAPTER 10

Team Reaper HQ
El Paso, TX

General Mary Thurston stepped away from the coffee machine with the steaming paper cup in hand, blowing on the black liquid. At the kitchen counter, she added creamer and a little sugar and hoped the elixir would propel her through the next several hours while waiting for news from either Traynor in Mexico or Kane and Hunt in Berlin.

She leaned against the counter. She wasn't sleeping well. She may not have been under as much stress as the teams in the field, but she couldn't deny how much pressure she was under too. Capturing Jorge Sanchez had been a victory for Team Reaper; now they had to protect that victory by making sure his daughter didn't cause a major disaster.

Thurston didn't blame Blanca for wanting to free her father. It was a perfectly natural wish. What Thurston *did* mind was the danger Blanca now posed to her crew and the public. How many was she willing to kill? How much damage was she ready to cause?

What bothered Thurston the most was that Blanca Sanchez was a party girl. How had she gone radical so fast, organized an operation that included sending three cartel freelance killers into US territory within days of beginning her plan?

She frowned, sipped the coffee, and returned to her desk where she spent almost a half-hour going through the files on Jorge Sanchez, and then his daughter. She sat there thinking that the daughter had no experience, she wasn't a strategist or tactician, so she'd probably defer to her father's associates and simply do what her old man had done when he needed leverage on somebody—something the associates were already good at. No re-inventing the wheel.

She found it on page four of Jorge Sanchez's file. He excelled at kidnappings, targeting friends and family members of those he needed to get the better of. Sanchez had contributed to a horrible trend in Mexico, where citizens, rich and poor, became kidnapping targets of the cartels who demanded ransom and, once collected, disposed of the victims anyway. In a lot of cases, bodies were never found.

A quick look-up online showed Thurston that the State Department already had active advisories telling Americans not to visit five Mexican states. Sinaloa, Colima, Michoacan, and Tamaulipas—which wasn't far from the Texas border—because tourists were often caught in the crossfire of cartel and gang violence and Americans made for good kidnapping targets too.

She couldn't help but notice that Mexico City, where Traynor was working with his federal drug contact, was on the State Department's "no go" list too.

There was a chance, though, that Americans in Mexico would not be Blanca's targets. She was last seen in Berlin, after all. Could she be scouting targets in Europe?

Thurston left her desk and hurried to Ferrero's office.

"We need to call the State Department," Thurston said.

Ferrero frowned.

"Why?"

"Americans overseas might be Blanca's targets," Thurston explained her theory.

"Where should we focus?"

"Europe, Mexico, for sure. A general alert everywhere else."

"You think that's how Blanca will get the president to release her father?"

"What else you got?" Thurston said.

Ferrero shrugged. "Indeed." He started dialing. Thurston sat in front of his desk to listen to the conversation on the speakerphone.

Berlin

Kane's cell phone rang while he and Hunt were eating dinner in the hotel restaurant. The wait while Eliza Schenk and Gunter Bruner investigated the "Ellison" background seemed to stretch on forever, but only because the Reaper pair were so anxious to get some action going.

Kane answered. "Yes?"

"Meet me on the southwest corner of the hotel," Eliza Schenk said without identifying herself. "I'll be in a black Mercedes GLC. Five minutes."

Kane ended the call and wiped his mouth. "Let's go."

"But—" Hunt's disappointment was palpable as he'd spent their mealmaking plenty of eye contact with their sexy blonde waitress.

"Let's go, Chief."

Hunt looked around for the woman for one last smile, but she wasn't visible. Kane left money on the table. His jacket was zipped to hide the SIG-Sauer automatic under his left arm; Hunt was similarly armed. They departed the restaurant and stepped into the chilly night.

The back of the hotel was quiet, far enough away from the busy streets at the front and side entrances to where they could still hear the sounds but not feel a true sense of Berlin's heartbeat. Loading docks, Dumpsters, staff parking lot, lamp posts casting shadows here and there.

Kane unzipped his jacket for easy access to the SIG-Sauer M17.

Their shoes scratched on the pavement as they turned every which direction, scanning for danger. Seeing none, Kane checked his watch.

"This is a trap," Hunt said, his back to Kane.

When the red dot of a laser sight landed on Hunt's back, Kane shouted, "Down!" and tackled Hunt as a rifle shot cracked. The high-caliber slug whined off the blacktop. Kane rolled away from Hunt, both men drawing their SIG-Sauer pistols. The sniper was easy to spot. The rifleman looked over the edge of the third level of the hotel's backside, the terrace-like area a perfect shooting nest. Kane lined up the SIG's night sights and fired twice, but the sniper dodged back, the shots only kicking up bursts of concrete as they impacted with the wall.

Headlights flashed over them as the promised Mercedes screeched into the staff parking lot, rapidly bearing down on Kane and Hunt. The two men scrambled to their feet, Hunt firing twice to keep the sniper down, as he and Kane ran. There was no cover to speak of, just the open parking lot of the building behind them. Kane powered forward, across the lot, Hunt behind him. Whatever lay beyond was better than being a sitting duck.

The Mercedes put down more rubber as the driver made a wide turn, the engine growling as the vehicle went the same direction. The back-passenger window rolled down, a gunman leaning out with a Glock-18 machine pistol. A long magazine extended from the grip. Flame flashed from the weapon as two full-auto bursts left the muzzle, but none of the 9mm stingers found their targets.

Kane ran hard, his lungs burning. Midway across the parking lot, getting closer to what looked like a dark warehouse beyond, he shouted for Hunt to find some cover at a lamp post. The Mercedes was gaining fast.

Kane dropped and rolled, staying flat behind the wide concrete base of a lamp post as he steadied his aim. The SIG flashed, rounds smacking the hood and cracking the windshield. The gunner on the passenger side couldn't get to him, so the passenger window behind the driver rolled down. Before the gunner with the machine pistol could fire, Kane took his head off with a single round. The man's body dropped, half in, and half out of the Mercedes, before finally slipping all the way out and hitting the blacktop with a smack.

The Mercedes veered left, away from Kane, but right into the gunsights of Hunt. The Navy man's SIG cracked, a line of bullets popping holes in the driver's door and window. The car started to slow, still turning, until it finally came to a natural stop by bumping into a lamp post.

Kane jumped to his feet, Hunt meeting him at the Mercedes. They wrenched open the driver's door and the driver's side passenger door. Hunt hauled out the driver's dead body and took the wheel.

A rifle shot cracked, hammering through the roof, the slug barely missing Kane's head and continuing through the open back door as he slid into the car.

Hunt screeched the tires backing up, then charged forward, back to the hotel. They couldn't leave the sniper alive. But the clock was ticking. The exchange of gunfire surely had the police on the way. Entanglement with Berlin cops was specifically what they wanted to avoid.

Hunt slammed the brakes, stopping the Mercedes close to the building. He leaped out, Kane following. Kane triggered covering shots at the sniper while Hunt moved like an insect up the wall, using a drain pipe.

It was an old SEAL trick, part of standard BUD/S training where potential SEALs learned how to use whatever means necessary to scale a wall. With his gun holstered, both hands gripping the pipe and scraping painfully against the jagged outer wall, Hunt pulled with his hands and pushed with both feet, and eventually swung over the lip of the back terrace, landing on a pile of smelly cigarette butts. He rolled, hearing the sniper as he adjusted his aim to Hunt's arrival, drawing the SIG, coming up on one knee with the pistol braced in both hands. Before the sniper had his weapon lined up, Hunt fired. The slug bored through the sniper's left eye, punching a cloud of bloody mist and bone fragments out the back.

Getting down the drain pipe was easier than going up. Hunt shimmied down, quickly stepping back onto the pavement and running to the Mercedes as Kane waved him over. Jumping into the back, Hunt pulled the back door shut as Kane drove out of the lot, onto the street, going very fast.

"Where are we going?" Hunt asked.

"Wherever Bruner and his woman are waiting."

"How do you know?"

"The home setting on the GPS."

Kane and Hunt had split up during the "background check" period to note the habits of both Bruner and Eliza Schenk, but if they were hiding at a common point awaiting news of the assassination, it would make it a whole lot easier for Kane and Hunt to get them to talk.

Both of them knew what Blanca Sanchez wanted to buy, and where she'd collect the package.

If it wasn't too late, Kane wanted to be there when she picked up the items.

"Where's the spot?" Hunt slapped another magazine into his SIG. "I sure wish we had more firepower."

"We'll be fine," Kane said. "The GPS shows a location east of the city. Hoppegarten area. Out in the country. Should be pretty quiet."

"Then activate the afterburners," Hunt said. "We got bad guys to kill."

"On it," Kane said.

He steered the Mercedes onto the next on-ramp to the autobahn.

The GPS directions took them along a two-lane road with open country on either side, but they couldn't see it. There was more than enough dark to go around. Kane felt encircled by the blackness, the total absence of light other than the headlamps slicing along the roadway; danger lurked everywhere. Kane knew Hunt felt the tension, too. The Navy SEAL whistled quietly, tunelessly, and Kane didn't tell him to stop.

The GPS announced their destination on the left. Kane

cut sharply to the right, easing to a stop on the shoulder. He switched off the lights and stopped the motor. Without a word, the two men exited the vehicle, pistols in hand, and advanced into the brush off the side of the road.

The ground beneath their shoes was grassy and soft and a little wet. They stayed low. The house ahead, surrounded by a low brick wall, was dark in front, but lights burned in the rear of the house.

Kane reached out and touched Hunt's left shoulder. They stopped and dropped flat.

"Wire on top of the wall," Hunt said in a low whisper.

"Think it's electrified?"

"We can find out the hard way."

Kane suppressed a laugh. "There are easier ways. We'll use my jacket to cover the wire and hop over."

But Kane and Hunt did not move straight away. They let a few minutes tick by.

"No sentries," Hunt said.

"Which means they aren't expecting trouble. Maybe they're only expecting the gun crew to come back."

"We can fool them a little then. Bring the Mercedes into the driveway."

"And if they aren't expecting the crew?"

"We'll be neck deep in trouble no matter what."

Kane examined the driveway. No other vehicles occupied the space. From the driveway, they'd have to go up a set of steps to the porch and then the front door. The porch wrapped around the side of the house facing them, stopping midway.

They froze as the front door opened, and a man stepped out. The automatic porch light bathed the man in brightness long enough for them to watch him light a cigarette. A stubby submachine gun dangled on a strap over his right shoulder. The porch light blinked out. The glow of the man's cigarette marked his position.

"Forget the Mercedes," Kane said. "He'll see us right away and know we're not the gun crew."

"My kingdom for a suppressed rifle right now," Hunt said.

"Play the hand you're dealt," Kane said, "not the one you wish you had."

He started forward. Hunt followed. Stopping at the wall, Kane jammed the SIG in his belt and slowly removed his jacket. The night's chill bit through him.

They stayed below the wall, listening. When the porch light snapped on again, and the door opened and closed, they peeked over the top. The sentry had gone inside. The porch light flicked off. Kane draped his coat over the security wire, and Hunt leaped over, running to the porch, then quietly up the steps. Kane followed, putting his jacket back on. Best not to leave any evidence behind. The porch light came on again as Hunt approached the door, and he smashed the light with the butt of his pistol.

Kane waited while Hunt tried the doorknob. Locked. Hunt stepped back, lifted his right leg, and threw a hard kick into the door that smashed the deadbolt and sent the door crashing into the opposite wall.

They entered the front room, guns out. Commotion from the back of the house. They faced a hallway, the room cluttered with furniture, paintings on the walls, thick carpeting. From the hallway came the sentry with the short submachine gun, but as he lifted the weapon, Hunt planted a shot between his eyes. The man dropped. Now there was yelling from the back of the house. Kane and Hunt charged forward, Hunt holstering the SIG to recover the subgun. Kane fired into the room ahead as two more gunners approached, taking one down, while the other dived for cover.

Hunt took the lead, charging forward with the subgun in front of him, firing short bursts. The last gunman cried out as slugs stitched open his chest.

TV room to the left, kitchen to the right, back patio doors ahead. The doors were open, one man already out, the woman, Eliza Schenk, halfway out, turning only to raise a small pistol. Kane fired twice. The rounds punched through her stomach, and she fell in the doorway, her gun flying from her hand.

"Get Bruner," Kane said. He and Hunt moved ahead, Hunt leaping over Eliza while Kane pulled the woman back inside, a trail of blood beneath her. She screamed and tried to slash with her long red nails. Kane straddled her, knees on either side and batted her hands away and smacked her on the head with the SIG. The fight left her.

"Where's Blanca Sanchez?"

Eliza, not unconscious but her eyes glassy and fading, screamed and struggled beneath Kane. He jammed the hot barrel of the SIG into one of her cheeks.

"Tell me, and I'll get a doctor. You don't have to die from being shot in the belly."

"She's gone!"

"What did she want?"

"Explosives, you pig! Enough to blow up a building!"

"Where is she now?"

"I told you!"

"Then I might as well leave you here."

Kane stood up and aimed at her face.

Eliza's right hand flashed behind her back, and she brought out another pistol, a Beretta 950BS .25. Kane's finger twitched on the trigger of the SIG and split her head open.

Hunt swung left, right. Bruner was running to the right, heading for the wall.

Hunt fired once. Bruner yelled and dropped, hitting the grass, sliding a little. He started crawling toward the wall. Hunt reached the arms dealer, shot him in the ass, and flipped him over.

The light from the back window highlighted Bruner's face, which was twisted in pain, as Hunt put a knee in the man's stomach.

"Blanca Sanchez," he said. "Where?"

"You'll never find her."

"Has she taken delivery yet? What did she buy?"

Bruner moaned. "C4. A lot of C4."

"When's the pick-up?"

"Tonight," Bruner said. "But you're too late. They're gone by now."

Hunt cursed. He stood up and shot Bruner in the head.

Back inside, he found Kane in the kitchen. He glanced at Eliza's body.

"Anything?"

Kane told him.

"Bruner said the same but that the pick-up was tonight."

"Tear this place apart," Kane said. "Maybe we'll find something that can lead us to them. If we're not too late."

CHAPTER 11

In a room down the hall, they found Bruner's office. Desktop computer. Notes and papers. Hunt sorted through papers while Kane tapped a button on the desktop's keyboard and called El Paso.

"Yes?" Thurston asked.

"I need Swift, is he there?"

"Just back from a break, hold on."

Kane waited a moment, listening to Hunt rustle papers. There was a painting on the right wall, the only one in the office, and Kane suggested Hunt see if the painting hid a wall safe.

Swift came on the phone.

"I'm here, Reaper."

"I need to hack a desktop."

"Is it on?"

"It's on, and I'm getting a password prompt."

"You expect me to crack it without being logged in?"

"Dammit, Swift—"

"Find the password. Maybe there's a note somewhere."

Kane scanned the mess of papers. He mashed his teeth.

The night was getting worse, and they were falling further behind than when they started.

The painting indeed hid a safe, and swung out on hinges, as Hunt discovered. He was already working on cracking the safe, ear to the door, slowly turning the combination dial.

Kane skipped the papers and opened drawers, bottom first, looking for notes of any kind that might suggest Bruner's password. Perhaps he kept the list here, crossing out old ones every time he updated. Kane had gotten lucky that way before, so there was no reason to think Bruner's security was any better than other foes, and bad guys always left evidence lying around because they always assumed they couldn't be caught.

"Anything?" Swift asked after a moment.

Kane gave up with a curse. "I got nothing, Swift."

"Okay, let's try this. Look at the bottom right corner, and you should see some icons."

"Got 'em."

"Find the shutdown option."

Kane used the mouse pointer to hover over the three icons, each one announcing their function with a word bubble. He clicked on "shutdown" and watched the machine go through the process. When the screen went black, and the CPU lights went out, he said, "It's off."

"Turn it back on and press escape."

He complied, pressing the "Esc" several times. "I'm getting a prompt with options."

"Does one of them say 'safe mode'?"

"Yes."

"Click that."

Kane complied. "New password prompt."

"Type exactly what I tell you," Swift said. "All lower case. Controluserpasswords2."

Kane typed out the command. "Now what?"

"Press enter."

"Now it's asking if I want to change the password."

"Type in whatever you want and then get me an IP address."

Kane nodded. He typed 'BlancaSucks' as the password, hit enter again, and the computer continued the boot-up process. Presently, the monitor presented Kane with a screen full of various icons.

"I'm in."

Swift talked Kane through finding the computer's internet provider address and then told him to not touch anything while he tore down the computer's firewall defenses.

"What am I looking for?" Swift asked.

"Anything related to what Blanca Sanchez purchased, and where the sale is taking place."

"What if it already has?"

"Then we're a day late and a dollar short."

"I'll get back with you."

Swift killed the connection.

Kane let out a breath as he put his phone away and watched Hunt some more.

"How you doing?"

"Waiting for one more tumbler to drop," Hunt said.

Kane checked his watch. They couldn't stay in the house much longer. Luckily, they were isolated from other homes, but Bruner might have other crew members showing up. The butterflies in Kane's gut told him the odds were falling fast.

"Hurry."

"I can only go so fast, Reaper." Then: "Got it!" He pulled the handle on the door safe and swung it open.

Kane jumped up and looked. Stack of ledgers and a tablet computer.

"Take it all, we gotta get out of here."

Hunt grabbed the bundle, and the pair began their exit. They found a BMW in Bruner's garage that didn't have bullet holes in it, so they used that car instead of the Mercedes.

Kane sat in the passenger seat while Hunt drove, sorting through the ledgers, dreading turning on the tablet because of another password issue.

The glow of the interior lamp let Kane read the ledgers well enough, and the entries weren't in code, but they told more about Bruner's other sales-related activities than anything about Blanca Sanchez. He did notice names that would for sure pop up on various terrorist watch lists, so he figured the notes were related to Bruner's less-than-upright clients. On a hunch, he checked the back page of the third ledger and found the last page.

There she was.

Kane cursed.

"What?"

"Blanca Sanchez took delivery of six pounds of C4 explosive two hours ago."

Hunt said nothing.

"Next time," Kane said, "we're shooting first and to hell with sparking an international incident."

Hunt remained quiet. Kane placed the ledgers and tablet on the floor in front of his seat and took out his cell phone again. He called headquarters. General Thurston answered again.

"You ever sleep, ma'am?"

"Every other Friday," the General said.

"Berlin is a dead end," Kane said, updating Thurston. "All we know now is that Blanca has enough C4 to build a bomb, and I can't say we didn't have that idea already."

"I'm afraid Swift hasn't found anything so far that's encouraging, either."

Kane asked, "Do we have any other leads? We're in the third quarter and falling behind."

"I need you in Mexico. Join Traynor there. He's found something that will require our full attention shortly, I'm sure."

Thurston explained her theory on Blanca targeting American tourists for kidnapping and trying to use them as leverage to bargain for her father's release. She also mentioned that Traynor was keeping an eye on a suspected al-Qaeda camp in Sonora, near the Texas border, and how Traynor had learned of the camp's existence and its relation to Blanca.

Kane gripped the phone tight as he listened to the news. A cartel/jihadist alliance was often put up as a "what if?", and the idea that an agreement had been made between Blanca and the terrorists meant Blanca wasn't just a party girl. She had the same ruthless streak as her old man, using any means necessary to achieve a goal.

"We can be in the air tonight if you get a plane ready."

"Way ahead of you, Reaper."

Kane ended the call and updated Hunt.

"We're like a bouncing ball," the Navy SEAL said.

"Hopefully in Mexico," he said, "we finally stop bouncing."

Hunt drove on.

Kane propped an elbow on the doorsill and clenched his right fist against his mouth. He felt utterly useless. First, he'd failed to keep Casiano alive in Brussels. Whatever the informant had had was gone, perhaps information that might have saved them the current wild goose chase on which they found themselves.

Now, he was powerless to stop Blanca from getting her hands on C4. He knew the kind of damage C4 was capable —who didn't? In the hands of somebody who intended harm to civilians, either in the US or abroad, it didn't matter to Kane, the effects of the explosives would be more than devastating.

The hopelessness reminded Kane of how he felt whenever he saw his bed-ridden sister, seemingly forever unconscious, trapped within her own mind.

Almost as dead to him as their parents.

The thought boosted Kane's attitude. He was not going to think himself into defeat. If he could be strong for Mel, because she needed him to be, he could be strong for the rest of Team Reaper in their current fight, no matter how terrible the situation looked.

They needed some luck. Not just Kane, but Traynor and Cara and Arenas and Brick, too. They'd faced incredible odds before and had come out ahead.

Kane wouldn't rest until he produced the same result this time.

The fact that he wasn't fighting alone furthered his resolve.

"Can't this crate go any faster?" he asked

"Why not?" Hunt asked. He floored the pedal.

Sonora, Mexico
Somewhere in the Desert

. . .

The automatic weapons fire echoed up the valley.

The suspected al-Qaeda camp sat nestled in a green valley between Aqua Prieta and Las Barras in northern Sonora, not far from the Texas border. Either side of the valley was dotted with green while the camp had been built in a flat section, the green stuff obviously cleared away to make way for buildings and two water towers.

The terrain was harsh, dry and rocky, mostly mountainous with jagged peaks. Pete Traynor and Rico Ramirez, decked out in desert camouflage and armed for war, occupied a natural dugout on one side of the valley, overlooking the camp.

Both Traynor and Ramirez examined the camp through a pair of high-tech binoculars with 50mm objective lenses, the lenses covered with Steiner anti-reflective honeycomb units that would make sure the cartel or jihadi troops below never saw a hint of sunlight flashing off the lenses.

Traynor wore a Motorola com unit that kept him in touch with Reaper HQ in Texas via satellite.

"How many guys you count?" Ramirez asked.

Traynor scanned the line of men firing Kalashnikov-pattern rifles at stationary targets. They had watched the men practice with the weapons unloaded, and now they were shooting, with instructors nearby watching quietly.

"Fifteen," Traynor said.

But that wasn't the full force of the camp. Among the various buildings were a trio of barracks, lined up almost side by side, similar to any barracks layout anywhere in the world. Traynor figured one hundred men per building. The rest of the trainees were out marching or seeing to duties around the camp. There was a large area that needed to be maintained.

Traynor keyed his Motorola. "HQ, are you getting this?"

"Full video," said General Thurston. "We're trying to capture as many face photos as we can and match up any voice recognition."

Traynor pulled the binoculars away from his eyes long enough to scan the clear blue sky. The heat wasn't terrible, but he was sweating beneath the BDUs. Somewhere above flew a Predator drone, its powerful camera gear getting close-up video of the camp better than he or Ramirez could ever hope to obtain. But they needed real eyes on the camp, too. If Thurston was correct and Blanca Sanchez was planning to kidnap Americans, the camp made the perfect spot to keep them.

And he thought he knew just where hostages might be placed too.

Most buildings in the camp were completed, but a crew on the south side of the camp, farthest from the hide site, was in the process of constructing a new building. Square, new windows. Flat roof. Just the basics. It didn't match the pattern of any other building. If somebody wanted a place to put hostages and keep them from seeing the sun and subject them to sensory deprivation, that new building would be the perfect spot.

But the building wasn't done yet.

Which meant hostages had not yet been taken.

Traynor wasn't sure whether that was good news or bad.

CHAPTER 12

New York City
Moynihan Federal Courthouse

Cara Billings settled into the hard wooden courtroom seat, and for the first time all morning, felt like she could relax.

For such a high-profile trial, Cara was surprised the courtroom was so plain. Whoever designed the room had a surplus of wood paneling, because it was everywhere on the walls, brightly polished, but boring. The earth-tone carpet inspired no confidence, and the benches in the seating area matched the walls, as did the desks for the prosecution and defense. The space between those desks and the bench, where the judge sat above everybody, was made up of off-white tile. The whole design was wonky. But Cara figured the atmosphere in the courtroom didn't matter. This was where trials were held, fates determined, and, in the end, nobody cared what the walls looked like or if the earth tones clashed with the tile.

Arenas and Brick were elsewhere in the room, but close,

they could make eye contact with her. The marshals were spread out as well. The press occupied most of the spectator seats, while the prosecutors and defense team quietly plotted while seated behind their big polished tables.

Cara looked at Jorge Sanchez. He sat at the end of the line of his defense team, staring straight ahead, not blinking.

The drive to and from the jail over the last two days had been quite uneventful, but not without a few false alerts. Cara wasn't turning her paranoia off yet. The three cartel killers were out there somewhere, waiting.

She'd heard nothing from the street fixer, Felix Lovoso, regarding his search for the three, but, then again, he probably decided the hell with it after all. She didn't expect to hear anything from him, not without a big price tag attached.

The bailiff, unarmed, but his uniform tightly creased, his badge shining in the overhead fluorescent lights, said, "All rise!"

The armed federal marshals were already standing, but at the bailiff's command everybody else stood up. The bailiff announced the judge, who emerged from chambers and directed everybody to retake their seats. Once the commotion had settled, the judge addressed the prosecution.

"Is the prosecution ready to continue?"

"We are, Your Honor," said the lead attorney.

"Proceed."

Cara watched the man rise and call his first witness of the day.

The trial had been hectic, not just with moving Sanchez back and forth, but watching the lawyers go at each other with claws, mostly because of the ill-will regarding pre-trial shenanigans. Prosecutors were under direct instructions of the judge not to try and convict Sanchez for the over twenty murders he was accused of. Their instruction was to try the case as drug smuggling/conspiracy to murder and get a conviction on the major charges. The prosecutors wanted all the bases covered so Sanchez would go to prison for *something*, as they didn't want him slipping through on a technicality, but the judge forced them to zero on the major charges, and the lawyers had told the media they were more than up for the challenge.

And, privately, they admitted the judge was right because to try the smuggling and individual counts of murder meant a trial that would last until the next millennium.

The witnesses called and cross-examined on the first day presented a terrific opening salvo, as former Sanchez associates turned informants told their stories, admitting to organizing some of the murders, explaining how Sanchez smuggled drugs into the U.S. and helping Sanchez directly carry out two killings on U.S. soil.

The prosecutors didn't have just any witness to talk about the two killings; they had the man who pulled the trigger each time.

Carlos Juan Espinoza took the stand, but he didn't wear the face he had been born with. After Sanchez's arrest, Espinoza had gone on the run as well and hired a plastic surgeon to reshape his face.

But while the disguise fooled many, his voice remained unchanged, and during surveillance on another Sanchez crony, Espinoza showed up, and the DEA agents on the detail ran a voice check to see if they could figure out who the new arrival was.

When the voice prints matched Espinoza's, they put together the story, finding the plastic surgeon as well, and finally slapping the cuffs on Espinoza, who was stunned they'd caught up with him. He quickly turned state's evidence in return for immunity. The federal prosecutor said nuts to that. You'll turn state's evidence, and we won't put you on death row.

Espinoza said OK.

He described how Sanchez would send him to the United States, usually somewhere in New York or elsewhere on the East Coast, to take care of problems with the local pushers. These problems, he explained, sometimes consisted of people talking too much, stealing, or trying to undercut Sanchez somehow and pocket the difference. Espinoza admitted to ten such visits, but only two killings. The other visits consisted of "beating some sense" into the individuals involved, who were then given stern warnings, and promptly shaped up, so Espinoza did not require a return visit.

But some people don't listen too good, Espinoza said, and on two such occasions, when a beating failed to make the point, he said Sanchez ordered him to return and make use of their "final solution" to such problems—two bullets in the back of the head.

Espinoza went on to describe the shooting of a young woman who tried to rip Sanchez off on multiple occasions while running a drug house, and shooting another man for bragging about selling drugs, which was attracting unwanted attention from the local police.

The prosecutors presented into evidence a notebook used by Espinoza, which contained detailed notations of each trip to the United States, along with what he was paid. He admitted that the notebook contained notations on the murders and told the prosecutor which page to find them on.

It was lurid, it was sensational, the jury sat with rapt attention, and the press ate it up.

Cara and the federal marshal sitting next to her, Wayne O'Neil, the hunky dude who sparked her carnal imagination, exchanged bored looks. The details were nothing new to them. They'd seen the results of such activity first hand.

Cara only wanted to keep her team, and Sanchez, of course, alive until the trial finished. She wasn't interested in the press nonsense or the gossip on television. Let somebody else fight over the attention and the eventual casting of the movie.

As the day dragged on, and the defense cross-examined Espinoza, trying to suggest the notebook was fake despite the killer's protests to the contrary, and the hard wooden seat made her bottom uncomfortable and breaks more than welcome but few and far between, Cara cast glances at Arenas and Brick. They looked bored, but their eyes maintained an alertness that was unmistakable. If the three cartel killers were planning a strike, of course, they'd wait until the Reaper team and the marshals became lulled by a false sense of security. Cara would make sure she and the lead marshal addressed the security team about not falling into that trap. She knew they knew, but it never hurt to remind even an expert about the basics.

Cara watched Sanchez. The man didn't react to the accusations from the witness stand. He didn't react to anything. He let his lawyers run the show. He sat in his seat, properly dressed in a nice suit, unshackled, and stared. She followed his gaze; he wasn't looking at anything in particular, maybe a spot on the tiled floor. He wasn't there. He was outside his mind. A happy place? The thought made Cara laugh. But then she started getting an idea.

She didn't get to follow-up on the idea until after they'd

returned Sanchez to the jail for the night. With U.S. Marshal Wayne O'Neil beside her, she tapped on the bars of Sanchez's cell. She'd had to clear the idea with O'Neil, who insisted on being there, but figured her idea was correct, too, because he'd been getting a similar vibe.

Jorge Sanchez's suit and tie were gone, replaced by the ubiquitous orange jail jumpsuit with a stenciled number on the right side. He wore a grimace but looked at her blankly.

Cara decided her idea was correct. He didn't seem defiant, or hopeful, or expecting any kind of break-out. He only wanted to defy his captors until the very end.

"I have a question for you, Jorge," Cara said.

"I don't have to answer any questions. Go away."

"It's about Blanca."

His head turned sharply.

"What about my daughter?"

His voice had a lift in it proving the mention of the young woman's name alarmed him.

"She's organizing what's left of your cartel, Jorge. She thinks she's going to break you out of here."

"She can't."

"Why not?"

"She's not a fighter. I specifically—"

"You haven't been in the picture for a long time, Jorge. Blanca has been making friends. We hear some very dangerous friends, too, such as al-Qaeda. Did you know al-Qaeda had a camp in Mexico, Jorge? Anyway, they're helping her. She's bought plastic explosives from an arms dealer in Berlin and may be targeting American tourists overseas for kidnapping. Remember kidnapping? You were very good at it, weren't you? She's been a busy lady, Jorge."

Sanchez approached the bars. Cara stood still, even

though she wanted to step back. He couldn't bust through the steel, but her instinct was still to run for cover. *The warrior's life*, she thought, and not without a sense of bitterness.

Sanchez grabbed the bars with both hands. The look on his face changed.

He wasn't mad.

He was scared.

"You have to stop her," he said.

Cara folded her arms. She wasn't letting down her guard one iota. "Tell me why."

"I specifically, as I was trying to say, pushed Blanca away from my business. She was never cut out for it. I wanted my family to have a better life than I, and I provided that, but now it's time for them to forge their own life outside of my business. I told her that when she grew up. She wanted to party around the world, and I did not stop her, because it was the only way to keep her out of my affairs."

Cara shrugged. "Well, she thinks this is what you'd want."

"Exactly!" Sanchez pushed his face closer to the bars, his eyes widening. Cara's right foot moved a little, but she disguised the movement with a shift in weight. Sanchez looked like he was pleading. "She knows *nothing* about what I want in this situation. You *must* intercept her. I don't know anything about al-Qaeda. I know the same rumors you do; my attention was always elsewhere, not what terrorists might be doing in Mexico."

"What do you want, Jorge?"

"The tiger does not fight death."

"And you're *el tigre*, aren't you? Is this jail cell the cave you've chosen to die in?"

He blinked at her. Cara let it go. She had him on the hook, and now it was time to reel him in.

If she couldn't run around New York busting heads looking for a trio of killers, she could deliver, from the horse's mouth, everything Team Reaper needed to know to find Blanca Sanchez and put a stop to her plans.

"I need to know where we can find Blanca, Jorge."

"I don't know. We didn't communicate much while she was out spending my money."

Cara raised an eyebrow.

"But I know a man who might."

"Who?"

"She had a boyfriend. He worked for a television station in Mexico City. Armando Santiago. Talk to him. He'll know where to find Blanca, one way or another."

"A party girl with a boyfriend?"

"He was always waiting for her when she came back home."

Cara laughed. Of course, he was. He was probably her little puppy, and she treated him thusly.

"We'll check it out."

Sanchez took a deep breath and let it out slowly. "You may not believe I'm a good man, but even drug dealers love their children. Find my daughter. You *must* stop her. *Please.*" His grip tightened on the bars for emphasis.

Cara blinked. This was nothing like she'd expected. She was too stunned to say good-bye. O'Neil stepped in, ending the conversation, and escorting Cara out of the cell area.

"You okay?" O'Neil asked as the heavy door to the cell block slammed shut behind them.

Cara let out a breath. "Wow," she said. "I didn't expect to have anything in common with him, but he has a daughter, and I have a son, and for a moment we were two parents who'd do anything for their kids." She shivered. The concrete walls around them gave off a chill, but her reaction came from deep inside her. "Isn't that strange?"

"We're all people," O'Neil said. "We just make different choices. Sanchez doesn't see himself as a bad guy. You heard him. He was providing a better life for his family than he had."

"That's crazy. It's just—"

"Hey," O'Neil said, "you're gonna blow a gasket trying to figure it out. Want to grab coffee?"

The idea sounded very good to her. And O'Neil was looking quite hunky tonight indeed.

Down, girl.

I have to have a little fun, right?

Behave yourself.

"Great idea," Cara said. "I can report this to headquarters on the way."

O'Neil smiled. So did Cara.

American Airlines Flight 3703
Somewhere over the Atlantic
En route to New York City

Blanca Sanchez had worn a disguise to fool any facial recognition cameras at Berlin's airport, and she left the make-up on as she sat in first class absently paging through the inflight magazine.

Her tray table was down in front of her, a vodka and tonic with a slice of lime barely touched. She paged through the magazine, but there were other things on her mind than the ads and written content.

The bricks of C4 she had purchased in Berlin were below in the cargo cabin of the plane, safely tucked away in an X-ray proof case that displayed an entirely different image on the airport scanners when it passed through.

Thanks to Fasil Mahlik, the seductive and charismatic Saudi Arabian she'd met overseas, she knew exactly how to behave as if she had no knowledge of the C4. Blanca couldn't wait to reunite with her lover and join his cause once hers was finished and her father was home.

She knew Mahlik was part of a resurgent al-Qaeda, working under the radar of the western intelligence agencies who were focused on active threats. She'd learned the art of misdirection from him. Start something somewhere other than where you were actually planning, and steer prying eyes away.

Until it was too late.

The cartel assassin trio she'd sent to the East Coast and ordered to enter through separate points was the start of her misdirection. She wanted their faces captured; she wanted U.S. authorities to believe she was behind their arrival. The informant killed in Brussels, Casiano, she felt, may have communicated something to the U.S., and she needed the assassins anyway, so having the Americans search for them thinking they'd lead to her was a ploy she didn't mind using. She wasn't planning on the assassins killing anybody, and she certainly wasn't going to have them stage a commando raid on the jail where the Americans were holding her father.

She had something else in mind for them.

They'd balked a little at the assignment. It was outside their usual activity. But the money helped. And Blanca had her own ways of persuasion that ended any other argument.

She figured the Americans were going nuts trying to track them down, and that suited her just fine.

As soon as she brought them the C4, they could begin their phase of her operations.

Diego Moreno, whom she'd met in Berlin at the start, had communicated his plan for snatching the two American girls, the daughters of the Senator from Arizona. Her deal with Mahlik secured a place to keep them, to do with as his men pleased until she was done using the women for whatever leverage they provided.

Her plan was coming together perfectly. Her landing in New York was timed to coincide with Moreno's mission in Cabo San Lucas. Once the women were in custody, her hell would finally be unleashed.

CHAPTER 13

Mexico City

"Much better than Berlin," said Hunt.

John Kane agreed, tipping back a bottle of beer.

He watched Hunt's eyes dance back and forth between the scantily-clad waitresses at Senior Frog's, while his eyes scanned for the arrival of Pete Traynor and Rico Ramirez. The crowded bar with its sweaty atmosphere and loud music provided the perfect spot for their meeting. Kane wanted to know all about the al-Qaeda camp Traynor and Ramirez had found. He wanted to know what the cartels planned to do with the connection to the jihadists, although he had a pretty good idea.

The meeting with the TV reporter, Armando Santiago, who, Kane heard from headquarters, might have a lead on Blanca, was also scheduled to take place at Senior Frog's. If the man could indeed provide actionable intel, it would erase the sour taste in Kane's mouth from the failures in Brussels and Berlin. But especially Berlin.

Traynor and Ramirez appeared through a parting in the crowd, and Kane and Hunt rose to shake hands and say hello. Hunt flagged down their waitress and ordered two more beers.

Kane scooted close the Traynor.

"Tell me about this camp."

"It's there," Traynor said and explained their insertion into the area, and their observation. He had pictures to show them both later.

Kane sat back, stunned. Whatever else happened with Blanca, they needed to blow up that al-Qaeda facility and send a message that the jihadists faced more than the usual blunt force of the U.S. military should they try a stunt like that again. He'd find a way to communicate his displeasure with the classification on the U.S. intelligence end later but knew the folly of such an act before he finished the thought. He could yell at them all day, but he might have better luck pouring a glass of water into the ocean to try and raise the sea level.

"Where's this reporter dude?" Hunt asked.

Ramirez waved down a passerby. "Right here."

The young man named Armando Santiago wore a white button-down shirt and black slacks. His hair was a little long, and he looked just pretty enough for television.

He awkwardly shook everybody's hand—his palm felt like a wet fish to Kane—and wiped his sweaty forehead. It was warm in the restaurant, but not enough to make somebody sweat the way he was sweating. Kane also noticed his hands trembling.

"We're friends here," Kane told the reporter. "You don't have to be nervous."

"I'm nervous," Santiago said, "for my *life*. I could be killed if they find out I'm talking to you."

"Tell us about Blanca," Kane said after Santiago refused a beer.

"We dated off and on," Santiago said. "It started going bad once she came back from the Bahrain and started talking about breaking her father out of jail."

"Bahrain?" Kane asked.

"Twenty-four-hour parties for the jet set," Traynor said. "Makes sense."

"Well," Santiago said, "what didn't make sense is Blanca suddenly talking like she wanted to build an army and invade the US. But then I caught her on Skype with somebody."

"Who?"

"Does the name Fasil Mahlik mean anything to you?"

Kane shook his head and looked around, the others negative as well.

"He's with al-Qaeda."

"There's your connection," Traynor said. "This whole thing started with a party in Bahrain where she meets this guy, and pretty soon she's a full-blown radical."

"Radical is right," Santiago said. "She became obsessed with breaking out her father. It's all she talked about. She researched the jail where he's being held, read every news report. She vanished for weeks at a time, and I think she was with Mahlik at the camp nobody wants to talk about."

The frustration finally hit Kane the wrong way. He snapped, "Why does everybody else know about that place yet we didn't until now?"

Nobody answered. The following silence felt a little awkward.

The reporter swallowed a lump in his throat and continued. "I tried to report a story on the camp, but I kept getting closed down."

"That's familiar," Rico Ramirez added.

"Eventually Blanca came back and dumped me and said she was going to stick with Mahlik," Santiago said. "Whatever she's doing, she learned it from al-Qaeda, and that puts both of our countries in danger."

"No kidding," Kane said. "Where is she now?"

Kane's cell phone vibrated in his pocket. He held up a hand and asked Santiago to hold the thought as he answered.

It was General Thurston.

"I'm with the reporter now, ma'am," Kane said.

"Tell him to go home if he doesn't have anything concrete."

"Why?"

"Blanca has struck. Senator Ted Warner of Arizona is reporting his daughters have been kidnapped in Cabo San Lucas by the Chologos Cartel. We're watching the al-Qaeda camp. I think that's where they'll be taken. I'm sending Axe to you with a C-130 and your gear."

Kane glanced around the table. All eyes were on him, but only the reporter didn't fully grasp the nature of the call or interpret the other end of the conversation. The eyes of the Reaper operators and Rico Ramirez were focused. They knew the time for talking had ended. Now it was time to act.

"We'll be ready," said Reaper One.

CHAPTER 14

Port of Los Angeles
  Southern California
  24 hours earlier

Peggy and Britney Warner couldn't help but laugh with excitement as they entered their cabin on the Princess cruise ship.

"Wow," said Peggy.

"It's a little smaller than I thought," said Britney, noting the narrow space between the beds and the wall in front of them, as well as the very tiny bathroom where her tall body was sure to be uncomfortable. The toilet had a note above: Do not flush tampons. Thanks, Your Princess Crew.

The rest of the suite resembled a cheap motel room. The TV was on a shelf high in the corner. Desk and chair between the second bed and the balcony doors.

Peggy pulled back the curtains covering the patio doors and stepped out on the balcony, which was hemmed in by two walls on either side separating their cabin from the neighboring two. Britney joined her. There wasn't much to see. The port of Los Angeles was mostly full of commercial ships, cargo container yards, and large cranes scratching the blue sky.

"When will they bring up our bags?" Britney asked.

"In a while. Let's go eat something."

Britney followed Peggy out into the narrow hallway where they had to press up against the wall to let a couple, both of whom were quite large, pass. Britney grumbled quietly. Lack of space was going to be the thing for the next week. Peggy caught Britney's frown and said, "Will you *try* and have a good time, please?"

"Will you get off my ass already?" Britney asked.

Peggy rolled her eyes, and they made their way to the elevators, a much more open space with the elevators on one side and a set of stairs going up and down on the other. Britney shook her head at the faux-gold of the banisters. So far, this boat wasn't anything like *The Love Boat*. The members of the crew she'd seen so far spoke with foreign accents. There was no Gopher, no Isaac. And probably no Captain Stubing. Britney was feeling more ripped off by the minute.

Britney wasn't any happier with the overly-crowded buffet on the 15th level of the ship, where the food lines moved at a snail's pace and everything looked awful from having sat under heat lamps for several hours. Peggy managed to assemble a salad, while Britney hoped her stomach would forgive her for trying some fried fish filets and very dry potato wedges. The tartar sauce she added for the fish looked simply like a dollop of mayo mixed with dill relish. She and Peggy snagged a window table and looked out on the water around the port.

"I saw there's a singles dance tonight," Peggy said between bites of wilted lettuce.

Britney picked at her food. How much had they paid for this cruise?

"So?"

"We should go! Check out the hotties."

"I don't know, Peg."

"You can't keep moping over Frankie. Come on, this trip is supposed to help us start a new chapter!"

"Okay, we'll check out the singles dance."

"I knew you'd come around."

Britney didn't think she was so much "coming around" as she was placating her excitable sister, who always seemed to smell the roses without ever catching a finger on any thorns.

All Britney ever found, she often felt, were the thorns. They hurt. And the pain lasted a while.

A klaxon alarm interrupted their snack, as somebody over the speaker system announced, with a British accent, a "safety briefing" and that all passengers were to proceed to their designated lifeboat areas. Peggy and Britney crowded into a large room with a bunch of other passengers, packed elbow-to-elbow as they listened to a video lecture from the captain, who sounded Jamaican, explaining the ins and outs of a vacation cruise, which included not flushing tampons down the vacuum-operated toilets (*A recurring admonition*, Britney thought), and a demonstration on how the life vests worked carried out by several crew members, who then handed out the bulky and quite unfashionable life vests to everybody for practice. The lady who helped Britney properly zip her vest spoke English dusted with a Romanian accent.

As the ship left the port, Peggy and Britney stepped out

to the port-side walkway to watch the port grow smaller as the ship sailed for the open sea. The wind had picked up, but it was still warm.

"What happened to the crowd?" Britney asked.

"Like on TV?"

"Yeah, the confetti strips, waving, cheering."

"Post 9/11, Brit. If you're not a passenger, you're not getting by the metal detectors."

"That sucks," Britney said. "God, everything *sucks*."

The cruise to Cabo San Lucas had been Peggy's idea, and Britney had to admit she needed the break from the hectic events of her life in recent weeks, not only the break-up with Frankie, whom she'd been dating for almost a year, but the reshuffling of the teaching staff at her school which promptly left her *without* a school at which to teach. She'd told Peggy she couldn't afford the cruise; Peggy had countered that she couldn't afford *not* to go, she had to recharge, get her head together, and return home with a new game plan.

Britney was always making a new game plan. She'd left Plan B behind years ago. What was she on now, Plan W?

She let out a sigh, and her shoulders sank.

Peggy rubbed her sister's back. "It will be okay, Brit, just give it some time."

The ship's horn blared as the floating hotel cleared the port exit. Elsewhere on the ship, passengers let out a cheer.

"I need a drink," Britney said.

Somewhere on the Pacific Ocean

. . .

Peggy and Britney Warner had to take turns in the bathroom, putting on their make-up and getting dressed for the dance because the space simply wasn't big enough for the two of them, and certainly wasn't big enough for Brit's near-six-foot frame. She had to hunch to get a full view of her face in the bathroom mirror.

While Britney waited for Peggy to finish, she stood on the balcony watching the endless length of ocean meet the horizon far in the distance. It was windy, and not just because of the forward momentum of the ship. This time, the wind carried a sharp chill. Goosebumps covered her arms from the cold, but she wasn't ready to grab her wrap just yet. She stared into space, wondering what she was going to do with her life. Did she even want to go back to teaching? Was there something else she could do that wasn't as unstable?

But she'd loved her kids and loved teaching freshman high school history. What else was there for her to do? It's not like she minored in architecture. Frankie had been a welder, with union guarantees and a wage that dwarfed what Britney would make over the next ten years.

When Peggy announced she was ready to go cut the rug, Britney left the balcony. *Enough of this. Seriously.* She was tired of being a sourpuss. She decided she was going to have fun tonight, whether or not she met somebody to help pass the cruise with. Wasn't she supposed to have a good catch-up with her sister anyway? It's not like they saw each other very often, as both lived on opposite sides of the country. If nothing else, they could reconnect without the pressure of visiting home for the holidays.

They'd always been close, along with their mother, Heidi. With their father Ted being in Washington, DC, so much in relation to his work with Congress, the three

Warner women had no choice but to hold the home front together while Dad was gone. The bonds forged between the young Warner women were quite solid, and they knew each other well enough, as all siblings do, to push all the right buttons when they wanted to get under the other's skin.

The singles dance was way up top on the 18th level of the ship, a "nightclub" that offered a panoramic view of the ocean and nighttime sky. Britney's first remark, as the women picked up their drinks from the bar, was that between the black sky and the utter lack of light from the ocean below, it appeared as if they were traveling through a dark void. The long void to nowhere.

"You've decided not to have a good time, haven't you?" Peggy asked.

She had to shout over the thump-bump electronic dance music permeating the club. The dance floor was already full of sweaty bodies gyrating to the beats.

"Look out the window and tell me I'm not right," Britney said.

"It looks like we're in space," Peggy said.

"Great, maybe we can land on the moon instead of Cabo."

"Are you a *Star Trek* fan?"

Peggy and Britney frowned. Neither of them had asked the question. Then the fellow who uttered the words sat at their table to the left of Britney, who immediately shifted toward Peggy.

"I heard somebody say we were in space," the man said.

Britney felt Peggy nudge her with an elbow.

"She's the space cadet who thinks she can live on Mars," Britney said, jerking a thumb at Peggy. "I'm the one who'd rather stay on earth."

"You don't want to get kidnapped by aliens?" the man asked.

Peggy jumped in. "Depends on what they're probing her with." She laughed. Britney glared.

The man said, "I'm Aiden."

"Hi, Aiden," Britney said, shaking hands. Aiden reached across the small tabletop to shake with Peggy too.

"Are you traveling alone?" Britney asked.

"Sure am," Aiden said. "I needed a getaway. Thought it would be fun to go somewhere nobody knows me."

"Are you from LA?" Peggy said.

"San Francisco," he said. "I flew out of SFO to LAX. My Uber driver couldn't find where the ship was docked, and we wound up on the wrong end of the port for a while."

Britney said, "So you came aboard alone, and you're hoping to hook up with somebody to make the trip less lonely?"

"No. I heard somebody mention space. I work at the jet propulsion lab in Silicon Valley, so I *literally* build rocket ships."

Peggy started asking a ton of questions which gave Britney a chance to catch her breath and cover her nervousness by sipping her drink. Peggy kept nudging her to get her back into the conversation, and eventually, Britney did so, and Aiden danced with both women in turn before moving on to mix and mingle some more. He promised to see them as the cruise continued and buy them a drink at when they finally landed in Cabo.

"We'll never see him again," Britney said.

"Will you stop? He was totally into you."

"Maybe."

"I saw it all over his face."

"Even when he was talking to you?"

"He was only talking to *me* to get to *you*, dumdum."

Britney wasn't so sure.

But they indeed saw Aiden around the ship, and he seemed to have no problem making friends with either sex, but he also specifically sought out Britney and her sister, always favoring Britney when he sat with them, but never neglecting Peggy either. When he invited them to accompany him to shore for the promised drink at the bar of their choice, the Warner sisters said of course.

The cruise ship docked in the bay just off the coast of Cabo San Lucas and passengers partaking in shore excursions loaded into "shuttle boats" for the ten-minute ride to the docks. Britney, Peggy, and Aiden crowded into a corner on their shuttle, which was nothing more than one of the ship's lifeboats lowered into the water from, in their case, the starboard side. The boat rode the rough water less than smoothly, the passengers taking it in stride as the swells knocked them side-to-side and against each other, with an accompanying blast of salt water from the open portholes.

The shuttle boat finally docked at the pier, and the passengers stepped off, showing a small greeting party their ship identification before lining up for another checkpoint where their bags and purses were briefly searched.

While in the line for the search, Britney, Peggy, and Aiden kept up their conversation, Britney's guardedness easing off a bit the more she got to know Aiden. She tried not to think about the fact that they lived in separate parts of the country—her in Iowa, him in California. All she knew was that she liked the guy and wanted to be around him more and more as time went on.

When two men wearing sombreros and serapes approached the trio and asked if they wanted a picture, nobody said no. Aiden posed between the two women with his arm around each. One of the men lifted a camera. The flash snapped. The other man then shoved Aiden with a hard push to the center of his chest. Aiden staggered back, letting out a yell as he fell. The two men in serapes grabbed Britney and Peggy, jamming needles into their arms. The women went limp. The two men carried them away. Aiden sprang up, shouting, grabbing one of the men from behind. The Mexican pivoted and struck Aiden in the face with an elbow, but Aiden didn't let go. All eyes on the dock turned to the scene; people shouted for help. Aiden clawed for the Mexican's face, who deflected the American's hand, and then the second Mexican drew a pistol from under his serape and shot Aiden in the stomach.

The crack of the pistol sent panic sweeping through the dockside crowd, and as Aiden fell, the Warner sisters were carried into a waiting van, which quickly sped off into traffic while the scene of chaos and confusion behind them continued.

"You weren't supposed to have a gun!" Diego Moreno shouted.

Sebastian DeSoto, Moreno's partner, steered the van around slower traffic.

"What else should I have done? The man was interfering."

Moreno bit off his reply. DeSoto had a point, but there was nothing they could do about the situation now. Worse case, the Americans were alerted to the abduction sooner than Blanca wanted, and that might make her upset, but, like the shooting, there was no way to fix the problem now. The girls were in custody, unconscious in the back of the van, and that's what mattered. That's all Blanca would care about. But as the man in charge of the mission, it was on Moreno to explain the problem and take the responsibility. Moreno had to admit he wasn't sure what he'd have done had the American male kept at him. He couldn't hold onto the woman and fight at the same time.

Moreno, sitting behind DeSoto, let out a breath and settled himself. They had a long drive to Sonora, with several vehicle changes planned along the way. It was best to try and relax and enjoy the ride.

Blanca's vengeance had begun.

New York City
Blue Moon Hotel

Blanca Sanchez liked the cute hotel called the Blue Moon. It wasn't huge, sandwiched between buildings on either side, the small lobby a preview of the coziness of the rest of the place, including the rooms.

She paced the room with the phone to her ear as she listened to Moreno's report on the mission in Cabo San Lucas. His voice betrayed the overall concern he felt over the shooting. Blanca took the news quietly, processing what Fasil might say in such a case as this. She assured him such complications were inevitable, and that as long as the Warner women were now at their mercy, the other details didn't matter. She told him she'd send her communique to Washington as soon as the women were secured at Fasil Mahlik's camp in Sonora.

She hung up the phone and wandered back to the table by the window where an open suitcase sat, the interior not packed with clothes, but six bricks of C4 explosives, wired together with a remote detonator propped in the upper right corner of the case. She'd assembled the bomb based on Fasil's instructions, and, comparing the results with the notes he'd written, she didn't see any errors.

The rest of her team, the three cartel assassins she'd hired specifically for Phase Two, were still pouring over the secondary target, the recipient of the bomb, plotting the operation to the last detail. There was no doubt in her mind that the Americans faced no choice: they had to comply with her demands. The Warner sisters Blanca planned to dangle as a threat; the bomb would show them that she meant business, and if they didn't want the blood of more young Americans on their hands, they'd release her father. Americans didn't have a strong stomach when it came to "the girl next door". The Warner sisters were a prime example of that. With their pictures on television, and the sob stories sure to follow as the family reacted, public pressure would force the US president to do what she wanted.

Just a matter of time now.

CHAPTER 15

New York City
  Moynihan Federal Courthouse

Cara Billings and her team made a point of always standing
in a different spot within the courtroom every day, less they
get lax always seeing the same view. She was in the back
near the door today, away from hunky US Marshal Wayne
O'Neil, but that was all right with her. Their coffee get-
together was full of awkward pauses and stumbles, and the
guy might have been hot, but he wasn't able to carry on a
conversation very well. Cara wasn't sure if she was disap-
pointed or happy with the result because John Kane was
never far from her thoughts.

The current witness on the stand, being taken carefully
through his testimony by the lead prosecutor, told the story
of how Jorge Sanchez evaded arrest and capture for so long
prior to his first escape. Cara shook her head as she listened.
The corrupt DEA agents they'd encountered during the
pursuit came up during the questioning, and the witness

described providing cash, prostitutes, and money to the agents to get them to look the other way.

The agents in question had been arrested earlier and would be tried separately from Sanchez. Cara didn't want to be there for that proceeding. She might leap across the bench and attack one of the agents. She expected the enemy to be dirty; when the so-called good guys betrayed their oath to join the enemy, she felt no mercy.

There would always be corruption in law enforcement, Cara knew, and it made her job harder in the long run, but agents who took a bribe often put good cops in a crossfire they didn't survive.

What made her job tough now, though, was knowing Blanca Sanchez had taken her hostages.

The news from HQ had her, Brick and Arenas, and the marshals on edge. They expected an attack any second as the convoys moved from point A to point B. She wanted action so badly that she almost hoped Blanca's gun crew did try and attack the convoys. She *really* wanted something to shoot at.

As the witness continued answering questions and his deep voice filled the courtroom, Cara decided she was pissed at John Kane for having all the fun.

She knew from General Thurston's update that Kane and Borden Hunt were already in Mexico with Pete Traynor and one of Traynor's Mexican contacts. Axel Burton, the only member of Team Reaper still in Texas, was on his way south of the border in a C-130 Hercules loaded with gear so Kane and Company could rescue the hostages.

Meanwhile, she was stuck playing babysitter.

She'd actually received a call from Felix Lovoso, the street fixer known as The Mouse, the night before, but the conversation lasted only long enough for him to tell her he was still coming up dry on any Mexican assassins, and nobody else had heard any rumblings about them, either.

She wasn't sure what to think about that. Headquarters wouldn't have made up the story of their arrival, but where the heck were they?

Cara's stomach grumbled. Somebody in the press pool glanced her way. Cara only offered a weak smile in return.

Mexico City
Mexico City International Airport

John Kane stood outside a large private hangar on the south end of the Mexico City airport, watching a sight that never failed to impress.

The C-130 Hercules transport plane, all four engines on the high wings roaring as the aircraft taxied toward the hangar, was as familiar to Kane as his pajamas. He'd flown in countless variations of the old beast, jumped out the back more times than he cared to remember, and the big plane always filled him with a sense of pride.

The Hercules stopped just outside the hangar, the engines powering down slowly.

Behind Kane stood SEAL Chief Borden Hunt, Pete Traynor, and Rico Ramirez. Kane had wanted a squad of Mexican Federal Drug Task Force operatives to assist, but the request was denied. Attacking the AQ camp had to remain hush-hush. Too many cooks in the kitchen meant somebody might talk and spoil the whole party. They wanted the party in Sonora to stay as private as possible as they blasted an al-Qaeda camp out of the sand and brought back a pair of American hostages as a prize.

Thurston's orders had been explicit, and Kane didn't argue one detail. The best stroke of luck they'd had during the entire Blanca Sanchez affair, after all the missteps and errors, was the information leading to the AQ camp. Surveillance from overhead drones, controlled from HQ in El Paso, showed the Warner sisters arriving by vehicle and, tied up, carried into a small, newly constructed building outside the main perimeter of the camp that had been earlier noted by Traynor when he and Ramirez first investigated the camp.

The fuselage door behind the left wing opened, steps lowered, and a lone figure moved across the tarmac and into the hangar. John Kane smiled and greeted Axel "Axe" Burton with a heavy handshake.

"It's about time you got me involved," Axe said. "I can drive a boat too, you know! You had to pick the Navy guy and leave me sitting on my ass waiting for the phone to ring?"

Kane and Axe laughed. All joking aside, Axe was not the kind of person to sit by a telephone, or even sit for long. The tall and solidly-built former Recon Marine Sniper (there was no such thing as *ex* in the Marines) was single and too good-looking and loved the ladies too much to stay in one place too long, especially if there were no ladies present. He and a member of Team Bravo, Brooke Reynolds, had an on-again-off-again-currently-off relationship same as Kane and Cara Billings. It was a complication Axe didn't like to discuss; Kane didn't blame him.

"Did you bring the toys?" Kane asked.

"Small arms and your favorite mode of transportation," Axe said. "All loaded in the back."

Traynor and Borden came forward to greet Axe, and

Kane introduced Ramirez before the crew walked up the rear ramp of the C-130 into the cargo hold.

Three Desert Patrol Vehicles, lined up back to back, waited in the hold, along with heavy Pelican cases containing weapons for Kane, Traynor, Borden, and Axe. Kane and Borden already had their standard-issue SIG pistols, and it would feel good to finally add the Heckler & Koch 416 5.56mm carbine to their ensemble. The ultra-reliable weapons had saved both their lives countless times.

After unloading the small arms, Kane climbed back aboard to inspect the Desert Patrol Vehicles. He jumped into the lead DPV and fired up the motor, revving the air-cooled 2.0-liter engine. With two hundred-horsepower on tap, the power plant never failed to thrill. The four-wheel attack vehicle, built by Chenowith Racing Products, had been a staple of US special operations forces, and some regular army units, since the early 1990s. Seating for two. Which meant Rico Ramirez would have his own vehicle. Kane would pair with Hunt, Traynor with Axe. Ramirez could then carry some extra gear.

An airport gas truck came out to refuel the C-130 while Kane gathered everybody in the hangar. They stood around a collapsible poker table with pictures of the al-Qaeda camp spread out for all to see. The thin sheet metal that made up the walls and roof of the hangar rattled with the slightest breeze, and oil spots dotted the cement floor. The bathroom, in a back corner, hadn't seen any cleaning attention in months, apparently, and looked like a science experiment out of control. Kane had used the toilet only once. *Oh, the places you'll go.*

"Rico," he said, "this is your country. Would you like to lead the briefing?"

"I defer to you, Mr. Kane."

"Much appreciated. Here's what we have, guys, a camp full of jihadists and drug cartel shooters, mostly rookies from what our intel has described, but we can't underestimate their fighting ability. We know the American women are being held in this building outside the south corner of the camp. It's a new building, built just for them. Right, Pete?"

"Right."

"HQ has drones overhead taking constant video of the place, so we'll know if the women are moved," Kane said. "We fly in, hit them hard, and get out. Any questions?"

He scanned the faces looking at him. Nobody had any questions.

"Let's go," he said.

The crew jumped aboard the C-130. The engines fired, and the Hercules taxied into takeoff position. Presently, it sped down the runway and lifted off, heading north to Sonora, the hostages, and a chance to bring to a stop Blanca Sanchez's plan of destruction.

The White House
    Oval Office
    Washington, DC

This is going to be a tough conversation, President Carter decided.

Of all the duties of his office as President of the United States, having to talk to somebody when their family members were in danger ranked as the last thing Carter wanted to do. He'd rather be in a war zone, taking fire, than talk to another parent grieving over a family member lost overseas to terrorism or, in this case, a fellow politician, a close friend, whose children were being used as pawns in a very deadly game neither he or Carter truly understood.

Carter paced behind his desk while Warner sat in front of the Resolute desk, made from English oak salvaged from the *HMS Resolute* and presented to the White House as a gift from Queen Victoria to President Rutherford B. Hayes in 1880. The desk, Carter felt, based on its name alone, signified the attitude the person sitting behind it must have in times of crisis. Resolute indeed. Committed. Unwavering. John F. Kennedy had sat behind the same desk during the Cuban Missile Crisis. That oak knew how to take weight, and not from the items littered on the desktop, but the invisible, crushing weight a man sometimes had to carry on his shoulders.

Like now.

He had to give Arizona Senator Ted Warner credit, though.

The man knew how to keep cool in a crisis.

"Team Reaper," Carter said, "tells me a rescue mission has begun. They know the location where your daughters are being held, and I expect we will have some news within 48 hours."

"That long?"

"They're going to land about 15 miles away and go in on whatever fancy all-terrain vehicle they use," Carter said. He stopped to look out the window behind his desk. "How are you holding up, Ted?"

"It's rough," Warner said. "I don't know if I can communicate just how rough."

"I believe you. Do you need to go home, or is your wife flying here?"

"That's part of what I'd like to talk about. She's at home. I should be there too."

Carter turned to the Senator. "You absolutely should, why are you asking me?"

Warner shrugged. "Well—"

"I want you on the next plane home, Ted. There isn't anything as important as your family right now."

Warner nodded.

"Every precaution is being taken by our people," Carter said. "We will not cave into this woman's demands, Ted, you have my word on that. We'll do everything we have to do and get your girls home."

Warner only managed a nod this time. He held his lips together tightly, an outward expression of what was going on inside the man's head. He might be a good poker player, but Carter sensed the storm raging within.

Carter escorted Warner to the door, giving him an encouraging pat on the back as he left. The door shut with finality, and President Jack Carter stood alone in the Oval Office.

Leadership was lonely indeed. He might be surrounded by some of the best advisors the nation had to offer, but in the end, he, alone, made the decisions. Sometimes he was right, sometimes he was wrong. But even when he was right, he wondered if he had made a mistake.

He went back to his desk and sat down. Resolute. Yes. Hopeful? Yes. Nervous? Absolutely. Because Carter knew that, as good as Team Reaper performed, as many victories they had delivered in the past since the start of the World Wide Drug Initiative, sometimes the worst happened. Sometimes even the best failed.

Carter sat and wondered what he was going to do if Senator Warner's two daughters didn't make it home. He was not going to turn over one of the world's biggest drug dealers, no way. He'd take the fight right to them to show his refusal. But there were two civilians in the crossfire, in a fight not their own, and President Jack Carter knew probably better than the women what kind of danger they faced. All he could do was sit behind a big oak desk and wait for news, but there was one thing Carter knew might help. For the umpteenth time as president, he folded his hands in his lap, closed his eyes, and prayed that the Almighty would guide the forces of good to victory.

Team Reaper HQ
El Paso, TX

"Play it again," Luis Ferrero said.

Ferrero and General Thurston stood behind Swift as he started the video for a third time.

The face of Blanca Sanchez appeared on the screen. She stood before what was obviously the comforter from a bed that was draped behind her. They couldn't see what held up the comforter. She spoke slowly, and in English.

"*Attention, America. You have my father, Jorge Sanchez, standing trial for alleged drug crimes. I want him released immediately. My people have taken hostage two American women, Peggy and Britney Warner, the daughters of Senator Ted Warner, who has seen fit to continue funding the harassment and murder of men like my father who are only trying to help their people. This senseless slaughter must come to an end, and it starts by returning my father to his homeland. If my father is not released within 48 hours, phase two of my plan will be put in*

*motion. Release my father now. Do not make me kill more
of your people."*

The video blinked out.

Swift said, "I think this video was inspired by Bin
Laden's old messages."

Thurston said, "Gee, I wonder where she got the idea
from."

"It's a lot of 'poor me' and 'my poor people' garbage,"
Ferrero said. "They do nothing wrong, of course. It's always
the other guy that's the problem."

Ferrero, his arms folded, tapped a finger on his lips.

"What are you thinking?" Thurston said.

"The comforter. It could be a clue. Is there a way to
trace which hotel or motel she's in by the pattern?"

Swift wound the video back to the beginning, freezing
the frame. The comforter was plain white, with a stitching
pattern creating squares in the fabric. No identifying marks
showed on the screen.

"I can try," Swift said, "but then the question is how
many hotels or motels use the same thing?"

"Narrow the search to New York," Ferrero said.

"Still a big area."

"Do you have another idea?"

Swift shook his head. "I tried tracing the source of the
video, but it bounced through several servers around the
world before landing at the White House. That's a dead
end."

"Find out who made that comforter and find out who
they sell it to in the New York area," Ferrero said. "We
might have to ask the FBI to go knocking on doors, but it's
all we have right now."

"No, it isn't," Thurston said.

Ferrero turned to her sharply.

"Kane and his crew will get the women back before the deadline," she said.

"You're sure?"

"I have to be."

"And this phase two? What about that?"

"Probably involves the explosives she purchased in Berlin."

"And we don't know if the 48 hours," Swift added, "is also the deadline for setting off the bomb, or if she'll do that at a later time without telling us."

"I think we better identify that comforter," Thurston said.

Ferrero turned away and left the operations center. Swift cleared his monitor and started typing.

"When was the last time the fate of millions of people," he asked, "hung on the exact location of a bedspread?"

Thurston said she wasn't surprised by anything any longer. It was a stroke of pure luck that Traynor had found the al-Qaeda camp and that they'd kept watch over the site to see the Warner women delivered there.

She hoped their luck continued.

Because the clock was ticking.

CHAPTER 16

Sonora, Mexico
Al-Qaeda Training Camp

Fasil Mahlik, the Eaton-educated Saudi Arabian and now field commander for an al-Qaeda emerging anew from the ashes of defeat, stood outside his hut and surveyed the camp before him.

It was hot out. Not Saudi Arabia hot, but warm enough that the troops engaging in their morning drill weren't sweating under the sun's assault. Sonora sure was pretty country, he reflected, watching the rolling hills and jagged mountain peaks with their patches of green. He could get used to the posting. He figured his association with the Mexican cartels would provide a safe haven for years to come.

When he'd first met Blanca Sanchez at a party atop a Bahrain high rise, which was so tall it gave one the feeling of seeing the entire world in a 360-degree view, he'd recognized her immediately. The jihadist network had, for several years, been trying to form an alliance with the drug cartels. Their smuggling routes, access to weapons and fighters, and organization was exactly what AQ needed to move about the world in secret, and out of the prying eyes of Western intelligence. There was the risk of being spotted by counter-drug agents, but the cartels had so many either in their pocket or dealt with them in a more lethal fashion, that the risk was actually minimal as long as they kept their eyes open and didn't take advantage of their positions.

Blanca, when they met, was already fuming about her father's capture, and wanted to do something to break him out of custody. Mahlik seized his opportunity and worked her up into such a frenzy that she finally asked him to show her how to get even. Thus began a period of not only seduction but subtle radicalization. And then he sent her on her way. It pleased him greatly to see her adapt to the mission like a duck to water.

Now that they had the American women, there was nothing Mahlik didn't get out of the deal. He already had his camp, his connections, the promise from Blanca that once she rebuilt the Chologos cartel, Mahlik would have a permanent place with her. The two women would be sold into the sex slave trade and kept alive for propaganda use. Mahlik grinned at the thought of the shockwaves he might unleash if, every now and then, he sent pictures of the two women in whatever abused condition they happened to be in at the time, to Washington and their family.

Mahlik looked up at the blue sky. Not a cloud in sight. He wondered, as he often did, if there were any drones up there. He had no knowledge from inside sources that the location of the camp had leaked, and he couldn't see anything flying up there, but he always had to assume they were. Too many of his fellow fighters in faith had perished by missile strikes fired by Predator drones that seemed to come from nowhere.

Footsteps crunched on the dry ground. Mahlik watched Diego Moreno, the man who had brought the hostages to the camp, stop short of the hut.

"What is it?" Mahlik said.

Moreno said, "We have something on radar. A Hercules transport plane is coming from Mexico City."

Mahlik shook his head. So much for secrecy. He'd have to kill the government officials they'd paid off to keep the camp hidden. They had failed, somehow. And now the Americans were on their way to try and be heroes.

As always. So predictable.

"When it's in range," he said, "shoot it down. This is a chance to see if our troops are any good. Once the plane goes down, send out a squad to check for bodies, and bring the survivors back here. We'll have a little fun with them."

Diego Moreno nodded and departed.

Fasil Mahlik allowed himself a small chuckle. It never failed. The Americans thought they had the upper hand because of their military might. They never seemed to take into account that their opposition might be as well-prepared as they were.

Kane and his crew held tight to anything they could grab as the Hercules lurched left, the alarms blazing in the cockpit and cabin piercing their eardrums.

Missiles incoming!

The big Hercules wasn't made for combat maneuvers. The evasive action might tear the wings off eventually. The plane had countermeasures, like chaff and flares, but not even those capabilities promised to deflect heat-seeking rockets, especially if there were more than one.

"I think they know we're coming!" shouted Axe as he held onto the frame of one of the DPVs.

Kane's grip on the fuselage webbing above the bench seat began to slip as the plane lurched to the right this time. The strained faces of his fellow warriors showed just how much G-force the sharp turn generated. Ramirez lost his grip and fell headlong to the floor, yelling loudly.

"Are you hurt?" Kane shouted.

Ramirez let out another yell as he tried to crawl back to the bench seat and grab hold.

Then the plane shook, the massive explosion against the outside fuselage ripping a big hole in the aircraft. A violent blast of air filled the cargo hold, and the mighty Hercules tipped downward, Traynor losing his grip next, landing hard on the floor and sliding.

Kane glanced through the hole. Flames licked the outside of the plane. Had the rocket taken out one or two of the engines?

He knew one thing for sure.

They were going down.

The mission might have ended before it started.

The pilot's voice came over the loudspeaker.

"One minute to impact!"

They were still falling, but the G-forces had lightened to where the men could move.

"Grab your gear!" Kane shouted. The team scrambled into their packs and slung weapons tightly across their chests. The act might be foolish, they might all perish in the crash, but if any of them survived, they had to continue the mission and rescue the Warner women before it was too late.

Kane wasn't planning to give up until his spirit left his body; even then he'd still find a way to fight. He had no intention of dying this day. He wanted to die at home, an old man, not in the middle of nowhere in Sonora, Mexico.

Smoke poured from the right side of the C-130 Hercules, thick black smoke mixed with fire. The missile had smashed into the side just under the wing, destroying one of the two engines as well as the flaps closest to the body of the plane. The left wing still worked, as did the second set of flaps on the right.

The nose of the Hercules lifted a little as the pilot steered for a space of flat land. The black smoke left an easy to follow trail in the sky. At the cockpit controls, Captain Greg Macedo and his co-pilot, Lieutenant Mitch Storey, shouted over the multiple blaring alarms the readings from various instruments as the ground rushed toward them. The plane had stopped shaking, at least, but the yoke continued to fight against Macedo's strong grip. He needed to hold it steady until touchdown. If the plane flipped or stalled at this point, they'd have no chance of survival.

The crash-landing procedure included the shutting off of all engines, and Storey handled that chore, having already shut off power and fuel delivery to the engine damaged by the exploding missile.

With the props silent, the C-130 coasted downward, and Macedo thought they had an even chance of surviving if the land was indeed flat and they didn't bounce into any nooks or smash into a boulder.

Macedo activated the plane's intercom. "Brace for impact!"

The ground filled the windscreen. Macedo pulled back on the yoke at the last moment and then the belly hit the ground hard.

John Kane and his team kept their mouths covered as the smoke drifted into the cargo cabin, but their gloved hands couldn't stop the coughing fits some of them experienced. When the pilot said, "Brace for impact," the team grabbed anything they could hold onto, strapping in where possible as well. The plane hit, and each man about bounced out of his seat, the secured DPVs also straining against the clamps holding them to the cargo hold floor.

The plane shook as it slid along the desert floor, dust and debris filling the cabin, mixing with the smoke, stinging Kane's eyes. He shut them tight as they watered against the intrusion, his body shaking with the plane, and, just as the glide to earth had seemed to take forever, the landing was taking equally long. But they could only hold on until the forward momentum ended and hope they didn't fall off a cliff in the meantime.

Presently the plane stopped. The debris in the cabin settled on the floor, but the smoke and dust hung thick. Kane coughed. Traynor, having lost his grip and landed on the floor, cried out. Kane bolted from the bench seat, hand still over his mouth, and put his free left hand on the exit door. He pulled up on the catch and shoved the door open. Sunlight streamed inside; better, the smoke and dust exited like an unwanted houseguest. Kane stuck his head into the fresh air long enough to let out a breath and suck in another. Turning around, he raced to his teammates. He lifted

Traynor to his feet, escorting him to the door and out of the plane. Traynor landed roughly on the ground and staggered to the shelter of the back wing. Kane and Ramirez helped Axe Burton next, and Chief Hunt after that. Kane glanced at the nose of the Hercules but saw no sign of the pilots in the narrow cockpit glass. He went back inside. Hunt followed. They helped the stunned and shaking pilots out of the cockpit and outside.

The C-130 listed to the damaged side, black smoke still trailing, but the fire was gone. Macedo, the pilot, said they'd cut off the fuel. There was no chance of the plane blowing up. Kane pointed to a cluster of trees about twenty-five yards away and suggested they make for those. When every man was in the shade, Kane allowed himself to pause and catch his breath.

"Was that a perfect landing," Kane said, "or what?"

Macedo let out a short laugh.

"What about our gear?" Traynor said.

"Let's take five and go get it," Kane said. "Is anybody hurt? Or just winded?"

Kane watched his team and the pilots, all of whom looked battered and bruised, but there were no serious injuries.

"Just winded I think," Rico Ramirez said.

"We got lucky," Hunt said.

"We need the luck to hold," Kane said. "The DPVs need to run, and our radios need to work."

"We're not turning back," Traynor said.

"What if we don't have coms?" Kane asked.

"We've made it happen with less, Reaper," Traynor said.

Kane nodded. Pete was right. They might only have one chance to get the Warner sisters out of the al-Qaeda camp.

As long as nobody was hurt, they had to carry on. A look at Hunt, followed by his thumbs up, cemented the idea. He wasn't going to be shown up by a Navy SEAL, for heaven's sake.

The desert looked quite desolate, rolling hills, sand, patches of green. Kane didn't know how far they were from the target site. Certainly further out than their intended landing zone.

Five minutes turned into ten, the smoke from the C-130 dissipating, and Kane grabbed Traynor to examine the state of the gear.

"Careful not to slip," Kane advised as they entered through the fuselage door. A layer of dust covered the floor.

The DPVs were in good shape. Bad news: the C-130 rested on its belly. There was no way to open the rear cargo door and get the DPVs out of the plane.

"Looks like we're walking," Traynor said.

Kane and Traynor gathered packs and weapons and carried the gear out. Their load-bearing belts held two canteens each, along with grenades and spare magazine pouches. Each team member claimed his kit, but the pilots carried only their SIG 9mm sidearms, with two spare magazines, and no body armor. The pilots also didn't have extra water, so the team would have to share.

"We aren't going to be much good," Storey said as Kane and the others threw on their packs and secured their HK 416 carbines.

"We can't leave you here," Kane said. "March with us, and when the fight starts, help guide in the pick-up chopper."

"What pick-up chopper?" Hunt asked.

"The one I'm calling in," Kane said. He toggled his Motorola com unit and called HQ in El Paso. The Motorola unit had satellite-link capability, and it took a few minutes to get a reply. Luckily, none of their com gear had been damaged in the crash.

Kane hoped their luck held.

"What's the situation, Reaper One?" Thurston asked.

Kane kept his cap pulled low on his forehead to help block the bright sun above.

"On foot," Kane said, leading the team in a wedge formation. He explained about the missile strike and the crash of the Hercules. "Can you spare a drone? I'd like a flyover of our route."

"Where are you?"

"Approximately 48 klicks south of the target," Kane said, reading off their GPS position by consulting the Garmin Foretrex 601 wrist unit he wore.

"48 kilometers, okay," Thurston said. "If we take a drone away from the camp, we may miss something."

"They must have seen us on radar to fire the missile, ma'am. And that means they know we're coming. I'd like to know if they're sending any troops to collect bodies."

"We'll redirect. You'll need a chopper?"

"A Blackhawk will be a nice sight indeed, ma'am."

"On the way."

"The Hercules pilots will direct the chopper to our back-up landing zone."

"Copy all."

Kane terminated the connection. So far so good. His boots crunched over the ground, Kane moving his head in a constant danger scan. His HK 416 was loaded and unlocked, his finger off the trigger. If the pizza hit the fan, he didn't want to risk losing valuable time by fooling with a safety catch.

"Four trucks incoming, Reaper One."

"We see the dust trail, ma'am."

"Copy. We're going for the shot."

"A drone with two missiles versus four trucks? Can we fix the math a little?"

"We'll do what we can. Out."

Kane cursed.

They'd indeed seen the dust clouds on four vehicles in the distance. Traynor, with his sun-shaded binoculars, identified at least six men per truck, and each truck had a mounted belt-fed Browning .50-cal machine gun. Kane and his team of six found a small hill and scattered along the length of the rise. The gunmen would have to climb a slope to reach them. It didn't promise victory, but it helped, and if they could get their hands on one or two of those trucks, and one or two of those big Browning .50-cals, they might stand a better chance at freeing the Warner women.

A rocket motor screeched overhead.

"Drone above," Traynor said.

Kane watched the Predator swooping down through the clear sky, passing above them at about 33,000 centimeters.

"Trucks aren't reacting yet," Traynor said.

Kane smiled. If they weren't reacting by now, they didn't know what was coming for them.

"Rockets away," Traynor said.

The white plume of the Predator's Hellfire missiles as they left the wings streaking from air to ground.

"Trucks are scattering," Traynor said.

Kane let out a curse.

The impact, at almost 1600 kilometers per hour, shook the ground where Kane and his team waited.

Two of the trucks turned to the right, another continued straight ahead, the fourth moving left. The first Hellfire struck the desert ground, a nice explosion kicking up dirt and debris into a nice cloud, but it didn't do anything to satisfy Kane. The second Hellfire met its target, the truck tumbling end-over-end as it rode the top of a fireball, burning bodies flying from the vehicle only to hit the ground before the bulk of the machine dug a trench into the dirt.

Two trucks still were incoming.

"Stand by," Kane said as the trucks closed the gap. He sighted along the iron sights of his HK 416. The maximum effective range of the 5.56x45mm ammo was six hundred meters. The trucks were still too far away, but once they entered the killing reach of his ammo, Kane intended to let the enemy have some.

Not far from Kane, Traynor readied his 416 as well. He had a trio of fragmentation grenades laid out in front of him.

Rico Ramirez, choosing not to carry his usual standard issue HK UMP for this mission, instead snapped the bolt back on an IWI Galil ACE, and flipped up the rear sight. The ACE chambered the excellent 7.62x39 round, the same cartridge made famous by the Kalashnikov AK-47, and it was meatier than the ammo chambered in the HK 416s, but with a shorter effective range of only five hundred meters when fired out of the ACE. That didn't make any difference to Ramirez. He could hit what he aimed at, and the thirty-round box magazine promised he'd hit plenty.

Closer now.

John Kane lined up the outline of one of the driver's in the sights of his 416. His index finger moved back as if working independently of his brain; he took up the slack, feeling the hammer spring tension as the trigger stopped, then his finger completed the press, and the trigger snapped, and the hammer dropped and the HK spit flame.

The salvo struck the truck's windshield, the first two shots cracking the glass, and the third passing through the opening and striking the driver directly under the nose. The driver's head snapped back, and he slumped forward, his weight hitting the wheel just right and sending the truck careening into a sharp turn. The front passenger wheel struck a rock, the vehicle tipping over, stopping with a violent crash on the driver's side. Gunmen fell from the truck, some not moving once they hit the ground, others scrambling to their feet. A rain of deadly projectiles descended upon them, more of the survivors screaming as the bullets from the high ground pierced their chests and backs, the bodies dropping, the salvos only lessening once nobody else moved.

Then the second truck stopped and six gunners piled out, the driver hopping into the truck bed to grab the Browning .50 and open up.

The big machine gun thumped, and flame licked from the muzzle. Team Reaper dropped flat. The .50-cal rounds chewed the ground around them, Kane covering his neck as chunks of dirt landed on his back.

Pete Traynor, as he ducked, grabbed for the grenades laid out before him. He pulled the pin and threw one, then another, spacing them out, grabbing his HK as the detonations rang out. Over the rise, he opened fire, ignoring the hammering .50-cal for the six gunmen charging them with bayonetted AKMs. The 416 rocked against his shoulder, the light recoil enabling quick engagement of targets. Left, two rounds, right, two rounds, repeat. One gunman dropped and tumbled into the dirt. Another dived for cover.

Ramirez zeroed the Galil on the .50-cal gunner and let a burst go. The salvo whined off the roof of the truck, smacking the armored shielding in front of the gunner's face with a loud clang. The roof of the car covered most of the gunner's midsection, the armor plating the rest of him. They'd have to fire at a different angle to take him out. Ramirez ducked as another string of big .50 rained their way, coughing and spitting out dirt as some landed in his mouth.

Traynor and Hunt crawled to Kane, who was working the trigger of his HK rapidly. Hunt said, "We need to flank the truck!"

"Do it! I'll cover you!"

Traynor tossed another grenade, and Kane changed magazines. The grenade blast thundered; Hunt and Traynor took off. Kane shouldered the HK and fired again and again. Another gunner down. The Browning swung his way. He dropped back as a burst raked his position.

Traynor and Hunt, a few meters between them, stayed low as they hustled around the hill to where it met flat land. Traynor tossed another grenade while Hunt probed with a burst of rounds. The .50 gunner didn't turn their way, the grenade blast peppering the truck with shrapnel and cracking the driver's side window. Hunt crawled a little further. Traynor, his HK now shouldered, covered him. The four remaining cartel gunners were focused on the rise, not looking at the left flank. Hunt fired a burst. A miss. The Browning gunner started to swing the muzzle when Hunt and Traynor fired at the same time. Score. The gunner's body twitched as the 5.56mm rounds stitched through him. He landed hard on the truck bed. Another gunner ran to the truck and started to climb behind the gun, but another burst from the hillside punched through his back, and he landed half-in, half-out of the truck bed.

Three left.

Traynor threw another grenade as a gunner broke for a new position. The explosion lifted him into the air, and he fell back to earth with a plume dust.

More gunfire crackled, the last two cartel shooters hunkered down.

"Let's take the truck," Hunt said. Traynor followed his lead as they closed the open distance to the truck, taking cover on either side. They had a clear view of the last two shooters. Hunt and Traynor opened fire. The cartel guns finally fell silent.

Hunt hauled the first body out of the truck, then climbed into the bed and tossed out the other body. Kane, Axe Burton, Ramirez, and the Hercules pilots joined them.

"Hunt, check that Browning over. Everybody else grab weapons and spare ammo and if any of these guys has water, take it. We're going to need all we can get."

"Two spare gas cans, Reaper," Hunt announced. He checked over the mechanism on the .50-cal. "Browning in good shape."

"Roger that."

Kane called HQ on the Motorola.

"Everybody all right?" General Thurston asked.

"No casualties and we've gained a truck with a heavy machine gun. We might pull this off after all."

"We'll keep you posted if they send out any more. Right now, the camp is quiet."

"They're waiting for a report from the team they sent out."

"Get moving before they send another."

"Copy that. Reaper One out."

Traynor showed Macedo and Storey, the Hercules pilots, how to work the cartel gunners' AK-47s, and helped them load up with spare magazines.

Hunt started the truck's engine.

"We're good to go!"

"All aboard!" Kane shouted.

CHAPTER 17

Team Reaper HQ
El Paso, TX

"What the hell is going on down there?" Ferrero asked as he entered the operations room.

Thurston turned from where she'd been watching the red-headed hacker Sam Swift work.

"The Hercules got shot down," she said. "Then the team was ambushed."

"Anybody hurt?"

"Not yet."

Ferrero cursed. "This keeps getting better. Any news from New York?"

"Sam might have something."

"Sam?"

"I got a few hits on that bedspread," Sam Swift said. He referred to the display on his screen. "A company called BedSoft in California. They are a hotel supply company. Everything from bedspreads to the little soaps."

"They aren't the only hotel supply company, though, right?" Ferrero asked.

"No, sir," Swift said. "But they do supply to hotels and motels in New York City."

"How did you find out?" Ferrero asked.

"I took a screen shot of the bedspread behind Blanca, leaving her cropped out, and did a reverse image search. Found a similar image in the BedSoft on-line catalog."

Ferrero shook his head. "Technology."

"But there's a problem," Thurston said. "We have a list of hotels that BedSoft supplies bedding to, but we have no way of knowing which one Blanca is staying at. Or if she still is."

"I'm working my way through each location," Swift said, "and I'm running a program to sift through their lobby security footage to see if anybody matching Blanca has checked in. Best we can do right now."

"It's a start," Ferrero said, "but we're running out of time. Fast."

Thurston didn't argue.

"I got something," Swift said, his fingers tapping commands. He called up a black-and-white picture that moved to the right side of his screen.

"What is it?"

"Three men matching the description of our three missing cartel hitmen just showed up at a hotel called the Blue Moon."

Ferrero said, "Is Blanca there too?"

"Still checking."

Thurston dialed Cara Billings on her cell phone.

New York City

Blue Moon Hotel

Tonight.

Blanca looked at her reflection in the bathroom mirror and thought that most girls her age, in the city at that moment, were probably looking forward to the end of the workday so they could go home, get dressed up, and go out for a good time.

She was going out too, albeit a little earlier than those other girls.

But her good time included planting a bomb at an elementary school in New Jersey. She finished brushing her hair just as somebody knocked on the door.

She checked the FN-509 autoloader on her belt before answering, but one look through the peephole showed no danger.

Blanca Sanchez opened the door and welcomed the three men who entered, her trio of cartel freelance killers who were there to help her implement the second phase of her revenge plot, the one that would weaken the Americans' resolve and force them to release her father.

Miquel Gutierrez, Christopher Ruan, and Fernando Arriola. Gutierrez and Ruan were the tallest of the three; Arriola, at only five-five, seemed like a child beside the other two. All three were clean-cut and wore street clothes that would not raise any eyebrows in public. They looked like your standard New Yorkers.

"I need somebody to carry the case," Blanca said. She waved a hand at the closed suitcase sitting on the bed. Inside, the bomb she'd so carefully assembled, the blocks of C4 properly wired to explode at the push of a button, the remote detonator in Blanca's purse.

The detonator was in an inside pocket next to her lipstick.

She thought that was cute.

Ruan took the case, and all four left the room, Blanca, carrying an overnight bag, not bothering to check to see if the automatic lock clicked because she wasn't coming back.

The Blue Moon's basement—level garage wasn't big, but big enough for the black Mercedes SUV Blanca and her team piled into, Gutierrez behind the wheel, Blanca in the back seat next to Arriola. She didn't like the look the shorter man gave her as she buckled up. Then again, he was a murderer, so perhaps whatever allowed him to kill without feeling made him look that way no matter what. She faced forward. The case with the bomb, along with her overnight bag containing a change of clothes, make-up, and other necessities, was in the back cargo area. Nothing would jostle the bomb into a premature detonation; Fasil Mahlik had shown her how to secure the device to prevent that kind of accident.

As Gutierrez drove into traffic, their destination south of New York City, specifically Middletown, New Jersey, she thought about Fasil back at the AQ camp in Sonora. They hadn't communicated since her arrival in the United States, though each had a burner cell phone in case of emergency. Total radio silence was important for the mission, he'd told her. But she did not stop thinking about him when she wasn't busy. Before dozing off at night was when she thought about him the most, missing his warm embrace. She didn't think they'd ever have a happily ever after, whatever that meant these days, because The Cause would guide their destiny no matter what. She knew they'd have all the private moments they could spare as they created chaos all over the world, Fasil with his jihad, her with her drugs.

Nobody talked during the drive. Gutierrez left the radio off too.

Blanca leaned back and closed her eyes as they hit the interstate heading south.

Fernando Arriola shifted, so he didn't have to look at the dozing Blanca.

He'd cut her throat if he could. The other two wouldn't care; they'd all been paid ahead of time.

Arriola had killed many people in his relatively short career. At twenty-eight years of age, he'd grown up with violence. The sight of blood meant nothing to him. The people he was hired to kill, who usually deserved it, meant nothing to him.

But Blanca wanted to kill kids.

That's not something Arriola, despite the coldness he relied upon whenever he had a job, could tolerate.

Some lines you didn't cross.

Some lines *couldn't* be crossed.

It was a problem Arriola needed to solve.

Fast.

He hadn't known about the plan for the bomb when he agreed to take the job. All Blanca had told him was to head for Middletown, New Jersey, secure a safehouse, and link up with Gutierrez and Ruan. They were to wait for her to call them with more details. When those details revolved around taking pictures of an elementary school, and finding a spot to put a bomb, the pieces fell into place, and Arriola realized exactly what he'd signed on for.

His colleagues, of course, didn't share his code. They didn't care who they killed, young or old, deserving or not.

If he killed Blanca, indeed Gutierrez and Ruan might

not care, until what remained of her cartel hired them to kill him. Then they'd care for sure. He wouldn't last a week with an open contract on his head, and that's what he faced should he use the knife hidden up the sleeve of his jacket.

Arriola cleared his through and watched the passing scenery.

He'd faced greater challenges in the past.

And he'd overcome all of them. This would be no different.

Cara's cell phone rang. She answered without looking at the screen, listening through her Bluetooth ear unit.

"What is it?"

She expected General Thurston's voice. Instead, she heard a man's.

"Hey, it's the Mouse."

Cara sighed. "Go ahead."

"I found those guys you were looking for."

"Let me guess, Blue Moon hotel?"

"How did you know?"

"You're a day late and a dollar short, Felix."

"That's cool, I'll make it up to you with—"

Cara ended the call. She steered around a corner. The hotel was on the right side of the street, but the road was jammed with cars, ditto any curbside parking.

"This goddamn city," she snapped. "There's never a place to park."

"They're gone by now."

"We don't know that, Brick."

"Garage entrance right there," Arenas said.

Cara turned the vehicle into the garage and slowed down to pass under the low ceiling. Once inside, the tires quietly screeched on the smooth floor surface. She found an empty parking spot and stopped the car.

Thurston's call had come in the middle of testimony, the trial dragging on and on without much forward momentum and transporting Jorge Sanchez to and from the courthouse was giving Cara a new definition of tedious.

But now she had an idea why the trio of cartel killers she, Brick, and Arenas had gone looking for never showed up. Blanca had them in hiding for something else entirely. The Mouse probably had a contact at the hotel who dropped a dime when they arrived. Where had they been hiding all this time?

She dialed Sam Swift at Team Reaper headquarters.

"Where they at, Sam?" she asked as they crossed the garage floor to an elevator. Their shoes squeaked on the floor, and Cara's voice echoed a little.

"Gone," the red-haired hacker said. "They took off in a black Mercedes SUV that we're tracking with street cameras."

"Then what the hell good are we here at the hotel, Sam?"

General Mary Thurston spoke over the line. "Get up to her room and search the place."

"Copy," Cara said, changing her tone a little. The elevator opened and they stepped inside.

"Room 208," Swift said.

"Copy."

"I'm working my way into the hotel's computer system," Swift said, "and I'll trip the override so you can just walk in."

"The what?"

"The override. Every hotel with electronic locks has one in case of emergency. They can lock or unlock any or all of the doors without needing a key card. It's usually done from the server room, so it's an easy hack. Hotels are notorious for lousy network security too."

"I'll keep that in mind on my next vacation," Cara muttered. Arenas and Brick, unable to hear Sam's side of the conversation, looked at her questioningly. She shook her head.

The elevator doors opened, and they stepped into the hall, Cara in the lead. There was nobody else on the floor. Cara took out her SIG-Sauer M17 autoloader and held the gun beside her right leg, finger off the trigger. Brick and Arenas followed in her wake.

"208," Swift said again. "Locks are clear, but I can't keep them that way for long."

"Here we are," Cara said. She turned the handle of the door marked 208 and held it open for Brick and Arenas, then shut the door quietly. "We're in."

"Locking," Swift said.

Cara heard the electronic lock slam home.

Thurston said, "Start looking."

"Way ahead of you, ma'am."

"What do you see?"

Cara, Brick, and Arenas moved about the cramped room.

"Usual women stuff," Cara said. "I have wire clippings, a piece of paper that looks like bomb instruction. It *is* bomb instructions and whoever wrote these writes like a doctor."

"Any sign of the bomb?"

She asked Brick and Arenas, and they said no.

Cara reported that to Thurston.

"There's a laptop," Cara said. She examined the closed computer that sat on the writing table in a corner. "Doesn't look booby-trapped and it's on."

"Did you say *on*?" Swift said.

"Copy that, lid is closed."

"Lift the lid."

"Okay."

"Is the password prompt showing?"

"Yes."

"What about the little icon on the bottom left that shows if it's on WiFi or not?"

"It's connected."

"I'm going in," Swift said.

Thurston again. "Get out of there, Cara."

"She might come back," Cara said. "We can be here when she does."

"She has three known killers with her, and you can bet they'll be armed. I don't want a gun battle in a hotel where innocent people can get hurt. We're tracking the truck and Sam will find something on the computer. Return to your hotel and stand by."

"All I've *done* on this mission is stand by," Cara snapped.

"Would you like to come back and have a conversation about that?" Thurston said.

Cara mashed her teeth together, stifling a nasty reply. "No, ma'am," she said.

"You'll see action soon enough. Get out of there and wait for us to call you again."

Thurston ended the call, and Cara removed the Bluetooth.

"We're out of here," she told Brick and Arenas.

They didn't need any Sam Swift magic to open the door as they left.

· · ·

Sonora, Mexico
   Al-Qaeda Camp

"Britney, stop crying. Please."

"We're not going to make it!"

"Dad won't let us rot here; you have to stay strong!"

"I can't stop thinking about Aiden. What happened to him?"

Now Peggy wanted to cry herself. Or at least reach out for her sister, but she couldn't. Their arms were clamped to the wall of the hut, above their heads. They could barely see each other because of the lack of light. A sliver of light peeked under the crack at the bottom of the door, but that was all.

She had no concept of time or how long they'd been captive, but it couldn't have been very long. A day? Two? Her arms were numb, and she had to fight to remain upright. Letting her legs relax, so she dangled from her arms, was too painful.

Peggy knew terrorists when she saw them. Her father talked about the issue enough when he was home, and of course, she saw all the news footage. She was keeping details in her mind. Anything she could. If and when they got out of there, she'd have a ton of information to share with US authorities.

Britney, though, didn't seem as strong. Peggy's heart ached for her sister.

They'd been kept in a small tent upon their arrival, hands bound behind their neck, ankles tied together, forced to lay on one side. The construction crew hadn't finished building their hut, so they had to wait. And, as she looked around, the building still wasn't completed. There were gaps where the roof met the walls. Dirt floor and all that. Then she laughed to herself. The building wasn't supposed to be the Ritz, after all.

The heat inside was the worst. Their clothes stuck to their skin. Sweat dripped constantly. The only saving grace was that neither had dressed for winter when they first left the ship.

The wooden door opened slowly. Britney stopped crying. Peggy watched a sweaty gunman enter. He carried a rifle. Peggy instinctively glanced at the gun's receiver and saw the safety catch on. The safety catch was always on when a gunman entered. So far, anyway. It meant they weren't going to be shot. Yet. Behind the gunman appeared a woman carrying a tray of food. *Noon or a little after.* The woman fed Peggy first, lifting a spoon from a bowl of soup. Vegetable soup, beef broth. Peggy coughed a little. When the level of soup reached the halfway point, the woman switched to Britney. The gunman leered at Peggy. She glared back. *Do your worst. Your time is coming.*

The woman departed. The gunman lingered, looking Peggy up and down.

"Hey."

The gunman pivoted sharply. Peggy looked at the man behind him. Not an Arab. Hispanic male, fortyish, wearing white. He carried no weapon.

"The women are not to be molested," the man said. "Don't you have a post to return to?"

The gunman muttered something and pushed by the man.

The man looked into the hut a moment, said nothing more, and pushed the wooden door shut.

Peggy swallowed. Her mouth felt dry.

Britney's head hung low.

"Hang in there, Brit. Dad's not going to let them keep us here."

Britney did not reply.

Diego Moreno pushed the wooden door shut and turned his back to the hut.

The gunman he'd spoken too walked away, albeit slowly.

Moreno didn't like the al-Qaeda crew. The soldiers especially. They were undisciplined. They all wanted to die for the jihad, which almost made them useless as soldiers. Moreno and DeSoto and the cartel soldiers mixed in with the AQ fighters had no intention of dying. Death meant they'd be unable to enjoy the fruits of their labor. And Moreno planned to live long enough to enjoy as much as he could until he finally met the bullet that ended his life.

What had Blanca been thinking? *She'd been thinking about Mahlik, obviously.* He didn't mind Fasil Mahlik. The man was a disciplined strategist and knew his enemy well. Moreno had that in common with him. But his fighters? Forget 'em. He wished more of them shared Mahlik's attributes, but you can't make a dumb dog smart.

He didn't have any love for the American women, but also knew damaged hostages didn't make for a very good bargaining chip. The fact that the US had already dispatched a rescue team bothered him, though. It meant they knew about the camp. It meant they, somehow, also knew that was where the Warner women were being held. Moreno didn't think they had a plant inside the organization. But how else had they discovered the location?

And why hadn't the team dispatched to intercept the Americans' returned?

He wanted to feel optimistic about their chances of getting Jorge out of jail, but now he wasn't so sure the plan was as foolproof as Blanca claimed.

He found Mahlik outside his command center--another small building, which also housed Mahlik's living quarters.

"What's on your mind, Diego?" Mahlik asked.

"Our team has been gone too long."

"I know."

"We can't count on them having wiped out any survivors."

"But what shape are the survivors in? Their plane took a direct hit, according to my radar people," Mahlik said. "You don't just walk away from a plane crash, Diego."

"I've seen the Americans in action more than you have," Moreno said. "You'd be surprised."

"If they are still on their feet, they are low on ammo, probably wounded, and in no shape to mount a rescue attempt. If they did survive our teams' attack, they're waiting for a pick-up."

"Then they'll try again."

"How long will it take to get another group of troops here? By the time they do, our work will be done."

"I'm not so sure. I'd like to beef up the nighttime security especially, and have squads patrol the perimeter at least five miles out."

"Do it."

Moreno nodded and departed to organize the security update. He had to admit Mahlik had a point, but he'd seen Team Reaper in action once, and if any of them were aboard the Hercules aircraft, he didn't think they'd be so easily counted out.

CHAPTER 18

Sonora, Mexico
16 kilometers from al-Qaeda camp

Night had finally fallen.

The truck had made the journey from the hill where they'd engaged the cartel troops much easier, allowing everybody a chance to catch their breath, lick their minor wounds, and put their focus on the remainder of the mission.

The Hercules pilots, Macedo and Storey, had learned how to use the wireless com unit Kane wore, and he'd given the gear to Macedo to call for a chopper once the shooting started.

Now Kane and his crew spread out along another rise, taking advantage of the camouflage offered by the night, the light from the AQ camp visible 16 kilometers away. They weren't close enough to observe anything, but the lights burning throughout the camp marked the area just fine.

Kane, Traynor, and Rico Ramirez huddled around a tablet computer Kane had removed from his pack. The image on-screen showed an aerial view of the camp, with plenty of heat signatures dotting the landscape.

The footage came courtesy of high-flying Predator drones controlled by headquarters back in El Paso.

"Two signatures in this building here," Kane said, pointing to a spot on the south corner. "Is this the new building you saw?"

"It is," Traynor said.

"The heat signatures are shifting now and then but not moving," Ramirez pointed out. "Those are the hostages."

"Right."

"I count about thirty troops," Traynor said.

"Whole bunch more sleeping in the barracks here and here," Kane said.

"It would be nice to blow up the barracks first," Traynor said.

"I think HQ can manage that."

"What about this perimeter patrol?" Traynor asked, pointing to the heat signatures far outside the camp.

"About eight klicks out," Kane said. "Watching for us, probably."

"It's just one patrol in orbit," Traynor said. "Shouldn't be too hard to meet them along the way somewhere."

"I like the way you think, Pete," Kane said.

Kane put the tablet away, and the three men moved back toward the truck a little way behind them. Kane quietly whistled for the others, and they rallied around the vehicle.

Kane gave a short briefing and had Traynor update headquarters.

Then they moved out.

Middletown, New Jersey

Miquel Gutierrez steered the Mercedes SUV through a quiet neighborhood. Blanca watched the houses they passed. The suburbs were the perfect place for Phase Two, and she quietly commended the team for picking out the exact kind of target she wanted. Mass casualties weren't the end goal, although bodies in the street were certainly desired. What she really wanted was terror. Sheer terror. Blowing up an area that had zero security would show Americans that not only were they not safe in the major cities, normally the targets of such activity, but they weren't safe in their homes, either. Blanca wanted to create the kind of paralyzing terror that would make the little people *demand* their government cave to her demands.

There was no other way.

Because she didn't think the senator's daughters would be enough. A good start, yes, but not enough.

Gutierrez finally stopped the Mercedes in the driveway of a dark one-story house that badly needed yard work.

The dying lawn wasn't what captured Blanca's eye, though, as she stepped out of the vehicle with the others.

The elementary school across the street had her full attention.

The buildings on campus were dark, the visible lighting in the open walkways between those buildings, and her stomach quivered in anticipation.

"Where are we putting it?" she asked to Gutierrez.

"Building 11A, the center of the school," the killer said.

"There's a crawl space protected by a mesh screen. Arriola is the smallest of us, so he'll crawl in there with the bomb."

Blanca smiled.

"We need to do it right now," she said.

"Let's get inside first," Christopher Ruan said, as he and Gutierrez and Arriola headed for the front door. Arriola held the case containing Blanca's bomb.

She glared at their backs. But then she followed them into the house.

The furnishings were sparse and the kitchen cabinets and refrigerator barely full but that wasn't Blanca's concern. She wanted the bomb armed and in place before midnight. They had less than thirty minutes. Gutierrez and Arriola said they'd take care of it; Blanca demanded to go with them. Arriola carried the case, with the other two following him. They crossed the street to the campus without incident. The neighborhood was quiet, other than a barking dog now and then. No cars drove by.

Fernando Arriola had to change hands on the case because his palms were sweating. He'd agreed to be the one to plant the bomb under building 11A for two reasons. Number one, he was indeed the only person who could fit in the crawl space, so there was no reason not to say no; two, he had a plan. Sabotage the bomb while he was alone with it. He wanted no part of killing children. He still wasn't sure how he'd alert the authorities, but maybe that didn't matter. Maybe all he needed to do was make sure the bomb didn't go off.

They followed the concrete walkways to the center of the campus, where Building 11A waited. The side of the building that faced the quad didn't contain the mesh-screen crawl space. They had to walk around to the opposite side, the one that faced the athletic field, for the access they needed. Midway along the outer wall, Arriola stopped at the mesh screen, and Gutierrez knelt before it with a screwdriver.

It took only a few minutes to remove the four screws holding the mesh screen in place, and Arriola dropped to his belly, pushing the bomb case ahead of him as he slithered into the narrow space.

He used a pen flash to light the way, ignoring the sounds of scurrying critters as he moved toward the center of the crawl space. Reaching that point, he used the flash to highlight the catches on the case. Carefully opening each one by covering the snap lock with the palm of one hand, he raised the lid. The pen flash revealed the C4 and mass of wires. It wasn't a complex bomb. Wires leading from the detonator had been inserted into the C4; when the detonator received the electronic pulse from the remote carried by Blanca, the pulse would run down each wire and set off the C4. To make the bomb useless, all Arriola had to do was pluck each wire end out of the C4, which he did quickly, before lowering the lid without pressing the lock catches a second time.

Arriola backed out of the crawl space. The cool night air felt good on his sweaty face as he brushed off the front of his clothes. Blanca looked at him with a smile. She seemed very happy. The woman was insane.

Gutierrez reattached the mesh screen, carefully twisting each screw back into place. By the time they walked away, nothing looked like it had been disturbed.

Back at the safehouse, each person retired to their bedroom. Arriola sat on his cot and checked his handgun. He might not have a chance to call the authorities, but once Blanca realized the bomb wasn't going to go off on command, he might need the gun to defend himself. She was, probably, just bonkers enough to blame him for the failure. Shooting everybody seemed like the best solution to his problem.

Spartan indeed, Blanca thought, as she lay on the army surplus cot in her quiet room. She didn't bother undressing, laying on her back with the small pillow under her head and hands on her stomach. No matter. Fasil had said that, when on a mission, one had to put up with a certain lack of luxury. To Blanca, it was part of the effort. She'd seen enough luxury in her time that it became boring.

Tomorrow, or the next day, depending on what the Americans did and what Fasil advised, she'd set off the bomb.

Not much longer now.

She wanted to call Fasil and not only tell him the bomb was in place, but she also wanted to hear his voice, and his reassuring advice.

But they had to maintain radio silence. The Americans had perfected the art of intercepting communication traffic over cell phone and even satellite phone to the point where it simply wasn't safe to use either unless the worst happened, and Blanca didn't intend to make an emergency call of any kind.

She slept with Fasil's face in her mind's eye. That smooth face, the sharp jaw, thick black hair, and dark eyes...

Among other attractive attributes.

Their reunion would be magical indeed.

Team Reaper HQ
El Paso, TX

. . .

Sam "Slick" Swift yawned. His eyes itched. He downed a little more of the Monster Energy Drink beside his keyboard but the elixir, usually able to give him a proper boost, was ineffective this night.

They'd all been pulling super long hours trying to track Blanca Sanchez, and now that they had a serious lead on her location, the long hours were beginning to catch up. He had plenty of time off accrued from many long hauls such as this. Once everything settled, he'd take a few days and try to feel normal again.

General Thurston came up behind him.

"Where's the Mercedes?"

The question he didn't want to hear, but there was no way she wouldn't have asked. Now he had to deliver some bad news.

"We lost it on the turnpike," Swift said.

"What do you mean *lost it?*"

"I mean exactly what you think it means," Swift said, adding: "Ma'am," as Thurston folded her arms with a scowl.

"Anything on her laptop?"

"Enough to make up for losing the Mercedes," Swift said.

"Tell me."

"This is the big clue." Swift cleared his screen and called up a screenshot of a map. An area of Middletown, New Jersey, had been circled. "I think she's in this neighborhood here."

"What's the significance?"

"This school. Biggins Elementary."

"You think that's where the bomb is?"

"I'd bet my pension, ma'am. And one of the houses nearby is where she's hiding until they detonate."

"Can we scan the area and try and find that Mercedes?"

"Worth a try."

"I'll call the Pentagon."

Thurston went away. Swift drank down the last of the Monster and yawned again. He pitched the can in the wastebasket under his desk. If he could yawn after drinking one of the most potent energy drinks on the market, he was exhausted indeed.

General Mary Thurston made two calls. The first, to General Hank Jones to tell him they needed a satellite pass over the neighborhood specified on Blanca's computer. Jones promised to tell the president right away and get the pass authorized. With the big man making the call, there would be no problems. There were indeed some perks of having connections at the top of the Washington food chain.

Thurston's second call was to Cara Billings in New York. She provided the location of Blanca's possible strike point and told her and her team to get moving. The satellite scan might give them all they need but, if that failed, they'd need to supplement the information with eyes on the ground, and if everything worked out, they'd hit Blanca and her team and solve the problem once and for all. As Thurston ended the call, she couldn't remember the last time she'd heard Cara Billings so excited.

Thurston eased back in her office chair feeling quite excited herself.

Kane and his team in Mexico were poised to strike the al-Qaeda camp and make a play to rescue the hostages.

They had a ninety percent fix on Blanca's location.

What had started as a chaotic operation was finally solidifying.

Of course, Thurston knew, their good fortune might come undone with even the smallest error or unknown advantage the enemy had. And that meant lives would be lost.

They were close, but the fight wasn't over yet.

CHAPTER 19

Sonora, Mexico
Outside al-Qaeda Camp

The perimeter patrol finally reached pistol range. They weren't the most disciplined troops, having probably grown tired, hours ago, of walking in circles. There was some short chatter among the soldiers, a sharp rebuke from the team leader, all of it audible to Kane, Traynor, and Hunt as they waited at their ambush point. When the patrol was close enough to touch, the trio rose from their hiding spot and opened fire with suppressed SIG-Sauer M17 9mm pistols.

The rapid spits of the high-velocity slugs and the clicking of the automatic actions filled the night. One, two, three troopers down, a heap of arms and legs in the desert sand. The fourth fell as he swung his AKM toward them, and the fifth got off a burst before he fell, the muzzle flash lighting up the area, the bullets skyward, but the sound everywhere. The echo of the salvo stretched across the desert. The burst might as well have been Gabriel's trumpet, and that meant they had to hustle before more armed troops were dispatched to deal with them.

Kane and his men holstered their weapons, Ramirez, Macedo and Storey standing by with their automatic rifles as Kane and the other Reaper members grabbed their HK 416 carbines.

An alarm sounded at the camp.

Kane cursed.

Too late.

"Where are those drones?" Traynor asked.

Kane looked skyward, but the black sky offered no reassurance.

The plan was already going off the rails. What had required quiet removal of the perimeter sentries followed by a drone strike to take out the full barracks buildings and other targets in the camp was now up in the air. They were within sight of the hut where the two hostages were being held, but that didn't mean much if they faced the entire force of cartel gunners and al-Qaeda fighters combined.

Lights in the barrack buildings burned bright as troops assembled in battle dress, with weapons, ready to defend an attack or take off in pursuit of the enemy. Kane and company were within four kilometers. If they tried to run, they'd only be overtaken. The odds were quickly turning against them. If they struck now, they'd be overwhelmed and killed within minutes.

Kane cursed again.

"What are we doing, Reaper?" Hunt asked.

"Give 'em another minute."

"We're running out of time *really* fast, Reaper!"

Then the drones swooped down.

The roaring screech of the General Atomics MQ-1 Predators filled the night. Kane had called for three, armed to the teeth, all controlled back at HQ. The first drone loosed four missiles, and the flaming streaks shined bright in the night sky. The rockets hit their intended target, the barracks. The ground shook from the sudden explosions, Kane and his crew averting their eyes from the blinding surge of light. Debris landed on the hard-packed ground around them with loud thumps.

Ramirez yelled.

"You okay?" Kane asked.

"Just a scratch!"

The flame from the buildings made the whole camp seem like it was on fire, but there were plenty of areas unaffected and wide open where troops were seeking cover at the command of squad leaders.

But that didn't last long.

The second drone swooped down and launched Hellfire IIs on the center of the camp. More heavy blasts. Screams echoed as the force of the explosions ripped bodies apart.

The third drone fired on a cluster of trucks similar to the ones the Reaper crew had faced after the Hercules crash. The missile strike ignited full gas tanks, the spectacular explosion adding to the other fires that lit the night.

"Now!" Kane shouted.

Kane, Hunt, and Axe Burton, per the plan, raced on foot to the hostage hut, their boots pounding on the hard-packed ground.

Behind them, the engine of the captured truck rumbled to life as Rico Ramirez and Pete Traynor followed, the tires kicking up a plume of dust as Ramirez steered the vehicle into the center of the camp, seeking gaps in the inferno to aim the vehicle through. Traynor, behind the big Browning .50-cal, started blasting, the *thump-thump-thump* of the .50

loud and unmerciful, wounded and straggling troopers immediately falling to the fusillade of steel-score projectiles.

Macedo and Storey, the pilots from the C-130 Hercules, armed with their captured AKM rifles, held their ground. Storey scanned their immediate vicinity for threats while Macedo began talking into the Motorola com unit, telling Reaper HQ that the strike was underway and to send the recovery choppers.

"Oh my God what is that?" Britney asked. She bolted upright, having tried to rest her legs by letting her knees bend a little. The move put pressure on her back and shoulders, but so much of that area was numb she barely felt the discomfort any longer.

Something shrieked in the sky, that was for sure. A jet engine, it sounded like, but not like any jet they'd ever heard at an air show of air force demonstration their father had taken them to. The shriek might have been from an enraged animal.

The hut, dark and cold, remained their only shelter as the nighttime temperature dropped.

As the ground started shaking and what sounded like Armageddon began beyond the wooden door, the Warner women looked at each other with a mix of hope and fear.

Peggy said triumphantly, "I told you Dad wouldn't let them keep us here!"

More explosions. The women screamed. Waves of heat blasted through the gaps in the doorway, the wooden door itself shaking against its shoddy lock, and Britney decided it would be an awful trick of fate if the door somehow broke off in the onslaught yet they had no way of freeing themselves.

Typical.

Gunfire. Lots of it. The sharp cracks of rifle fire were unmistakable. Britney's hopes lifted. Maybe they were being rescued. Maybe they wouldn't die trapped in an inferno from which there was no way out.

Then the lock snapped, and the door swung open.

The women screamed again. An al-Qaeda gunman raised his automatic rifle at Britney.

This was the end.

Britney screamed and shut her eyes tight.

Kane had his eye on the hostage hut, as he'd taken to calling the building, as the mad scramble around the camp continued. He was already sweating from the intense heat of the flames, his eyes stinging with the drifting smoke.

The cartel and AQ troops weren't concerned with the fires. The two maniacs in the truck with the .50-cal were their main concern, as Ramirez and Traynor sliced through the disorganized defense, blasting away at anything that moved.

As Kane, Hunt, and Axe closed in on the hut, three cartel fighters rushed their position. Hunt and Axe dropped flat, opening fire. Kane stood his ground, shouldering the HK 416. His first shot took down the gunner in the lead. As he tumbled and rolled, one of his buddies tripped, falling as well. Hunt fired a burst that pierced the second man through the head and neck.

The third gunman dodged to his left, the hut covering him. Kane advanced. The gunman fired a burst that tore apart the corner of the hut, his bullet ricocheting at Kane. Kane stopped short as he felt the slugs pass in front of his face. He brought up the HK. The gunman pulled open the hut's door. Kane ran faster. As the gunman raised his rifle at the women inside, Kane smashed the butt of the HK into the side of his head.

The gunman fell, losing his grip on the AKM rifle, leaping at Kane for a mid-section tackle. Breath left Kane's lungs as the gunman slammed into his gut, and the rush of air around him meant he was falling. He held his breath, landing hard on his back, smoke entering his lungs as he tried to suck some air, retching instead. The gunman didn't waste time using his fists. He grabbed the knife sheathed on Kane's web belt, the long stainless-steel blade gleaming in the light of the fires. The gunman raised the blade with a yell.

Kane jerked his M17 and fired. The suppressed rounds made no noise in the chaos surrounding him, but the +P Hydra-Shok hollow-points did their job, tearing through the gunman's chest and stomach. Blood spilled on Kane as the man started to fall on top of him. Kane's left arm blocked the fall, Kane shoving the man to the side, rolling at the same time. Kane recovered his knife as he rose, keeping the SIG in his right hand and grabbing his HK with the other.

Automatic weapons fire chattered nearby, Hunt and Axe firing on more troopers, Kane low-crawling through the hut's doorway. He jumped to his feet and slammed his back against the interior wall.

"We're Americans," he said breathlessly to the two women shackled to either side. "We're getting you out of here."

Two rounds smacked the doorway. The women screamed. Kane pivoted to face the threat, raising the HK one-handed. He let off a long burst, then more shots with the SIG. Two gunmen fell as two others ran for cover, only to be cut down mid-stride by fire from Hunt and Axe.

Kane jammed the now-empty SIG 9mm back into his leg holster, slapping a new magazine into the HK. Slinging the carbine, he grabbed his knife. The sharp blade made quick work of the ropes holding one of the Warner daughters, and then the other, the razor-edge of the blade slicing through effortlessly, and they collapsed to the ground. One didn't speak; the other sobbed quietly.

Kane yelled for Hunt and Axe. The two men dived through the doorway.

It was hard to see their faces in the dark, but Kane's orders were crystal clear.

"Get them back to the rally point. You'll need to carry them. Don't stop for anything."

"What are you going to do?" Axe asked.

"Somebody's gotta keep Traynor and Ramirez from getting blown up," Kane said. "Plus we have a prime target to remove."

"Don't get killed," Chief Borden Hunt said. He grabbed one of the women and Axe grabbed the other. Kane covered their exit. Most of the threat was beyond the hut now, the .50 still hammering.

Kane waited until Hunt and Axe had cleared the area, then charged ahead. The heat from the flames created a wall he needed to break through. He felt the fire searing his skin. The smoke became thicker.

But John Kane had his mind locked on a prime target, indeed. Blanca Sanchez's remote control.

Fasil Mahlik.

He was somewhere in the inferno. And Kane was going to find him.

· · ·

Rico Ramirez wrenched the wheel left, then right again, then left again, the seatbelt stretching against his upper body as he moved with the turns. The thumping Browning .50 behind his head beat a constant rhythm, punctuated by Traynor's shouts of "Yahoo!" as the .50-cal projectiles cut a swathe through the armed cartel troops and jihadist fighters around them.

Driving around the camp inferno had not been without its challenge, as Ramirez felt the heat in the cabin even with the windows rolled up, which at least blocked most of the smoke. Some puffs did make it through the vent system, and into the cabin, but this minor exposure paled compared to what would come in should he open a window. Most of the troops around the fire were already dead, a few stragglers trying to rise as the truck bore down on them. Outside the perimeter of the fire there were more troops, trying to rally to fight the invaders, and suddenly facing one of their own death machines. The moment of confusion reflected in their faces as they thought one of their own was firing on them was short-lived, and that advantage now lost, but it didn't matter. The merciless Browning ripped away chunks of flesh and left nothing but destruction in its wake.

Ramirez had to keep turning the vehicle rapidly since Traynor had no protection behind him. The shielding in front of the Browning worked well; he could tell from the loud *clang-clang* of AKM 7.62mm bullets striking the metal barriers, but keeping the enemy from getting a shot at Traynor's backside was the priority. All he could see of the American in the rearview mirror were his knees, Traynor shifting his legs constantly to stay upright during the fast maneuvering.

Thump-thump-thump-thump.

"Yeah, baby!" Traynor shouted, his words slightly muffled. Ramirez didn't fight a grin.

Clang-clang.

"Get some!"

Thump-thump-thump.

A gunner opened fire about ten yards ahead of the truck, Ramirez ducking as the salvo stitched a line of holes in the windshield. His foot didn't let off the gas as the truck barreled on, the bumper catching the trooper midsection and knocking his body under the wheels. One side of the car lurched up, down, then settled, and Ramirez turned the wheel again.

Pete Traynor, the muscles of his bare tattooed arms flexing as he tightly gripped the Browning's firing handles, didn't waste time with the front and rear sight. When he saw upright bodies in front of him, he swung the muzzle and fired. The muzzle blast and glare from the inferno left his night vision ability at near zero; the enemy was merely a shape, moving, behind cover, whatever, and everything fell to the big .50.

The air-cooled belt-fed machine gun was a freak of engineering, but it was not infallible. The ammo box connected to the right side, which contained the ammo belt, was something he kept an eye on, and the belt was running low. Ramirez had his rifle in the cabin of the truck; Traynor's HK was strapped to his back. When the .50 ran out, they'd have to go at it with the small arms, assuming there was still resistance.

Enemy troops clustered around a building, opened up on the truck, off to the left, their muzzle flashes marking their position, and suddenly the car stopped moving, the front tires destroyed, the gunners shifting their aim. Traynor spun the Browning their way, firing, Ramirez shuffling out the passenger side with his rifle. The .50-cal rounds knocked down two of the gunners, but then the belt finally ran out, and the gun fell silent. As more enemy rounds came his way, Traynor leaped off the back of the truck, landed hard on the ground, and dropped. Bullets hammered the truck body. Ramirez fired around the front end. Traynor made his way to the back, bracing against the bumper, as the surviving troops broke cover and rushed the truck.

The HK 416 had almost no recoil, the carbine's gas system soaking up most of the energy that caused muzzle flip, and that worked to Traynor's advantage as he gave the light trigger a short pull and listened to the weapon crack its message of death.

He aimed for the trooper behind the first, leading him slightly, watching the 5.56mm slugs impact against his chest and lower body. The gunner tumbled to the earth and stopped moving. As Traynor shifted his aim, he held his fire, the other trooper joining his compatriot, having fallen to the 7.62mm burst from Rico Ramirez.

Traynor left the bumper and joined Ramirez, and the pair ran toward the southern end of the camp to continue cleaning house.

The gunfire came from the front windows of what Kane figured, from the drone photos, was the command center. It seemed the perfect place to try and find Fasil Mahlik.

Inside the command center, AKM rifles in hand, Fasil Mahlik, Diego Moreno, and Sebastian DeSoto hid below the windows, taking pot shots at anything that looked like one of the enemy. The hammering of small arms fire had replaced the booms of the stolen .50-cal, and the flames from the fires cast flickering shadows across the darkened room. One other soldier was inside with them, and two troopers outside behind sandbags to defend the command center from attackers.

"Can you see anything?" Mahlik asked, then coughed, as the smoke coming through the open windows thickened.

It's like staring into hell, Moreno thought. "I think there's somebody approaching," he said. "Alone."

Outside, Kane ran, in the open for a moment, long enough for the troopers behind the sandbags to spot him and open fire. Their AKM crackled, and Kane dropped behind a stack of tires. Bullets thumped into the tires, spraying bits of rubber. Kane, low on the ground, swung his HK around the side.

Rounds kicked up geysers of dirt and zipped through the air around him. Kane fired, seeing puffs from the sandbags as his bullets tore into them, raising his aim to fire again. The head of one trooper popped, spraying his compatriot with blood and bits of bone, but the man didn't notice as he focused his fire on Kane's position.

Kane fired again, stitching a line of slugs from the sandbags to the second trooper's chest, driving him down and out.

Now gunfire came from the building itself as muzzle flashes appeared in the window frames. Kane studied the structure. It had been built with its back against rock, raised slightly off the ground by six-foot stilts. If he could get under the building, he might end this fight quickly.

He noted that the big Browning machine gun had been replaced by sporadic small arms' fire. He hoped Traynor and Ramirez were okay and holding their own. Ditto the hostages and Hunt and Axe. The Blackhawk Kane had requested to pull them out of the combat zone was hopefully on the way. If he wanted to get out of Mexico in one piece, he had to deal with the shooters in the building, and then get to the chopper.

Kane plucked a grenade from his web belt as the gunfire from the building came his way. The frag grenade landed short of the building, blasting a hole in front of it and pelting the outer wall with dirt. Not good.

A cartel trooper ran out of the building, Kane firing twice, but his shots missed as the trooper landed with his dead buddies behind the sandbags and started shooting again.

Kane pulled the pin on another grenade and put some more *oomph* behind the overhand pitch. The gunner's head lifted a little as he watched the grenade sail his way; the explosion cut off his scream, setting the outer wrapping of the sandbags on fire. The smoke started drifting into the building. Some of the shooters in the windows moved back. Kane smiled. He flicked the selector switch on his HK to full auto, and let the magazine go, tracing a line of shots along the wall. Then he jumped to his feet and ran toward the building.

As the sandbags burned some more and smoke drifted in front of the windows, Kane dropped prone and low-crawled under the building. He looked through the small openings between the floorboards and saw three men inside, two Hispanics and an Arab. Fasil Mahlik. He didn't know who the other two were, but undoubtedly, they were part of the Chologos Cartel, and thus on Kane's death list. The three men held AKMs just like all the other troopers in the camp. One of the Hispanics was moving between the windows, looking out, announcing that he no longer saw the man who'd been shooting at them.

No kidding, Sherlock, I'm below you now.

"He has to be out there," Mahlik said nervously.

Kane smiled. He set his HK aside in the dirt and drew his SIG-Sauer M17 pistol.

Inside, Mahlik and Moreno jerked around in surprise. They watched, helplessly, as bullets ripped through the floor and tore into Sebastian DeSoto's body. The cartel terrorist stood long enough to gaze at the holes in his legs and stomach, then his eyes rolled into the back of his head, and he crashed to the floor.

Mahlik and Moreno wasted no time. They aimed their AKMs at the floor and opened fire, sweeping the barrels left and right. Muzzle flashes filled the room and ejected brass hammered the floor, the wood splintering under the impact of the 7.62mm rounds, chips of wood flying up at them.

Mahlik moved further to the back of the room as Moreno's gun ran dry and he jammed home another magazine. He started shooting again. Mahlik let the sound of the AKM cover his movement as he found the spot in the floor he was looking for. He lifted a trap door. Down a short ladder was the beginning of an escape tunnel he'd drawn into the design of the command center, for just such an emergency as this.

Moreno's AKM clicked dry again. He reached for another magazine. His hand did not shake. His pulse raced, he knew he needed to move fast, but he wasn't in a panic. If this was the end, he'd meet it with a blazing gun. He'd been ready for the end at the beginning, but Blanca had given him a second chance—or a third chance, as it were—to return to his former glory. Out of the gutter again. But as he grabbed the magazine and snapped it into the AKM, he knew it wasn't going to happen this time. The only question in his mind was who he was taking with him.

John Kane leaped through one of the windows behind Moreno, raising the SIG pistol in a two-hand grip.

Moreno spun around and screamed as Kane pumped three single shots into his chest. As Moreno hit the floor, Kane swung the M17 looking for his next target.

But there was no third man in the room.

Kane moved through in a combat crouch, carefully examining every nook, the smoke an ever-present irritant until he found the trap door. He didn't hesitate. Jamming the M17 in his belt, he started down the ladder. No bullets came his way. He drew the M17 once again and dropped into a crouch. Darkness ahead. The ringing in his ears from all the gunfire prevented him from having any sense of sound, but he charged ahead anyway, staying to the left side of the tunnel wall, feeling with his left hand while gripping the M17 in his right. The tunnel went straight for a bit, then began to curve, and butterflies began to invade Kane's stomach. Pitch black all around. No sound. He had a flashlight on his web belt but didn't want to use it right away. Against every instinct in his body, he kept going forward. Then one foot hit something hard, and he fell forward, landing hard, breath leaving him.

Automatic weapons fire came his way, the chattering loud in the confines of the tunnel, the 7.62mm rounds chewing up the rock wall and bouncing to-and-fro in all directions. Kane felt several rounds land next to him and around his legs. A sharp sting signified one had nicked his left arm. The gunfire stopped. Kane returned fire with the M17, the muzzle flash leaving his vision spotted with bright dots, but he didn't rise. Grabbing the flashlight, he held it up and shined the beam ahead. The tunnel continued, the light illuminating only so much before the black abyss resumed.

Wherever Fasil Mahlik had gone, he was nowhere in sight. He was either at the other end of the tunnel or had escaped.

And in that case, there were better ways to track him.

Kane worked his way back to the AQ camp, climbing the ladder to the command center, sweeping the muzzle of the M17 back and forth. No threats.

He put his gun away. A quick retrieval and reload of his HK 416 from under the building, and he started running. He had to find Traynor and Ramirez; the three of them had to get to the rally point, and away from the death zone. He needed to call headquarters and get a sat scan of the area. Fasil Mahlik was on the run, on foot, and on his own. With any luck, they could pick up his trail and finish the fight once and for all.

Fasil Mahlik ran as fast as his legs could carry him.

The unforgiving terrain, especially in the dark of night, made him doubt every footfall, but he managed to move without tripping or landing in any holes in the ground. His lungs hurt from the smoke, but the fresher air this side of the camp was welcome. Sweat coated his body and stung his eyes. But he dared not stop. He figured his blast from the AKM had driven back whoever might be behind him prior to hauling himself out of the tunnel via another ladder, but he didn't look back. Just in case there was somebody back there.

The tunnel exit had been created by chiseling through the rock behind the command center, the surface exit itself a narrow nook hidden in the rear of the rock formation and camouflaged with the brush.

The ground began to slope downward as Mahlik headed for his target, a cave dug into the side of the hill.

There were vehicles stashed in the cave, light ATVs, and on one of those he could make a run for the city and vanish into the night.

Mahlik reached the cave and ran inside. He wasn't worried about an ambush here. If the drone aircraft had flown over, their cameras never would have spotted the cave or the gear within. He pulled the cover off a black TaoTao250 Rhino. Tossing the AKM, which clattered hard against the rock wall before falling to the ground, he swung his legs over the seat and twisted the key. The little engine rumbled to life. Mahlik worked the clutch and gear shift and accelerated ahead, turning west, leaving a trail of dust behind him.

"Where's Reaper?" Hunt asked.

"Chopper coming over the rise," Ramirez said.

Pete Traynor remained flat on the hard desert ground, his HK aimed toward the camp, which was still on fire, trying hard to ignore the conversation because, yeah, Reaper wasn't back yet, and he had no radio with which to check in with the team, and the Blackhawk was coming in fast.

They couldn't very well leave Kane behind, but also couldn't sit and wait, either.

The Warner women were behind him with the two C-130 pilots, and Traynor wished they had Brick along with them, because, as a trained medic, he could do a better job of looking them over than he or the others. There were no outward wounds on the women other than cuts and bruises, and they were sucking water out of canteens as fast as the team could pass them over, but they otherwise appeared okay. Traynor wanted greater reassurance, though—they were the daughters of a senator, after all, and they couldn't avoid the extra accountability that went with this rescue.

Movement ahead. Traynor alerted Hunt and Axe and Ramirez, and they trained rifle muzzle in the direction indicated, but soon Traynor heard Kane's voice, and they settled. Traynor rose to greet the out-of-breath John Kane, slapping him on the back. The Blackhawk chopper appeared overhead and came to rest on the ground ten yards away, the whipping rotor blades loud in the quiet night, kicking up a virtual windstorm that forced everybody to raise an arm in front of their eyes. The Warner sisters each let out a scream as the dust flew at them. Kane and Traynor helped the women to the helicopter, loading both into the cabin, then following suit as the rest of the team boarded. The Blackhawk lifted off from the desert floor and ascended skyward. There were no seats, not even the standard army steel-frame-and-canvas seat, so everybody spread out on the floor. The Warner sisters moved against the rear bulkhead while the rest of Team Reaper stayed in the center of the cabin.

The engine throbbed above their heads. Even with the side door closed, it was loud. Kane gestured to the crew chief for a headset. The crew chief retrieved one and handed it to Kane, who traded his combat helmet for the headset and adjusted the microphone in front of his face.

"We need to look for somebody."

"No can do. Our job is to get you and your crew out of there."

"The man in charge of that camp is on the run. On foot. I think I know which direction."

"Not happening, Reaper."

"Dammit—"

"I'm not going outside our mission parameters without

authorization," the crew chief said, leaning close to Kane. "If you'd like to call Texas and get that authorization, we won't stop you."

Kane cursed and ripped the headset off his head, jamming it back in the crew chief's chest. The crew chief glared, but took the headset back, and resumed his seat behind the pilot and co-pilot. Kane sat down on the hard floor. He glanced back. The Warner sisters were next to each other, huddled close, heads on each other's shoulders.

Kane looked away to let them have their moment. At least they were safe. At least that part of the mission had been a success.

As for the rest, he had no idea what to do next.

No matter how close they seemed to get to the prize, it kept slipping away.

CHAPTER 20

Middletown, New Jersey
   En route to Blanca's Safehouse

"I can't believe they left the Mercedes parked in the drive-way," General Thurston said.

Cara felt like a kid on Christmas morning. "I'll take it. What's inside?"

"Four heat signatures and a 3D imaging suggests the house is sparsely furnished."

"We're stuck in traffic."

"We'll keep eyes on the house as long as we can."

"What does that mean?"

"Clouds coming in."

Cara let off a string of curses that would shame even the most vulgar sailor.

"I totally agree," Thurston said.

Cara ended the call. Traffic inched along ahead of her, the bright red brake lights of other vehicles particularly irritating.

. . .

The safehouse

Trust but verify.

Blanca heard Mahlik's voice in her head and snapped awake.

She sat up on the cot and stared at a spot on the carpet. She hadn't seen the condition of the bomb when Arriola left the crawl space; she needed to confirm that all was well. She jumped up, grabbed a jacket, and went out into the hall. The house was quiet. Outside, she started across the street, carrying only a flashlight and the screwdriver Gutierrez had used to remove the mesh screen. She glanced briefly at the layer of clouds above the neighborhood that blocked out the moonlight. Luckily the school had several lights burning on the campus, and they helped guide her to the spot where they had placed the bomb.

She set the flashlight down, so the beam pointed down the crawl space and went to work on the screen, carefully remove each screw and leaving them in a pile in the dirt. She coughed as she removed the screen and disturbed a layer of dust. She grabbed the flashlight, thankful that she was small enough to handle the limited space available as she slithered into the crawl space.

She grunted and huffed as she moved, wiggling her body along, the flashlight beam highlighting the bomb case, and presently she reached the case and lifted the lid. The flashlight beam shined on the hunks of C4 inside, the wires, and—

The wires!

Arriola had pulled the wires out of the C4.

The bomb, in this state, was useless. Why would he do that? With a grimace, she maneuvered her left arm to jam the wires back into the C_4, shut the lid, then crawled backwards out of the narrow space. The cold night air felt good on her sweaty neck and head when she emerged. She brushed off the dust on her clothes, and, with hands shaking from anger, reattached put up the mesh screen and started to partially thread the screws back into the holes the same way Gutierrez had done. She dropped the first screw and started over, dropping it again. She took a deep breath to try and calm herself, but it was no use. The Latina fire was burning hotly. Finally, with all the screws in place, she tightened them and stood. Turning the flashlight off, she made her way back to the safehouse.

Blanca splashed water over his face and neck in the bathroom and returned to her room, where she grabbed her pistol from her overnight bag, a polymer-framed FN 509 9mm autoloader. The sights glowed in the dark room. There was a round in the chamber; she didn't need to check. She didn't stop to think as he stalked down the hallway to Arriola's room, twisting the knob on the closed door, crashing through to the other side.

"Wake up!"

She kicked the cot. Arriola slept on his side, and the jolt shook him from his slumber. Blanca kicked again, slamming the steel frame against the wall. She grabbed the groggy man by the front of his shirt, put a knee in his crotch, which elicited a sharp intake of breath, and jammed the FN 509 into his neck.

"Why did you sabotage my bomb?"

Arriola stared at her wide-eyed.

"Tell me!"

Arriola pressed his lips together and struck. He swung

up the palm of his left hand. Blanca stared at him so intently, her eyes focused, she didn't see the move, and he smashed his palm into the side of her head. She yelped, falling sideways, Arriola bolting from the cot to grab his own pistol which lay on the floor near the cot.

Blanca rolled once, twice, coming up on her side as Arriola lifted his pistol from the carpet. He stretched the gun in her direction. Blanca's finger tightened on the FN's trigger, and the 9mm pistol let out a blast of fire. Arriola's head snapped back, the gun falling from his hand as he sank heavily against the cot, pushing it awkwardly up against the wall.

Gutierrez and Ruan appeared in the doorway, their faces covered with incredulity. Blanca wasted no words on them. Arriola had compromised the entire mission, and now she needed to get out of there and leave no trace behind. As she rose, the FN came up again. She shot both men, and they tumbled into the hallway, leaking red onto the carpet. Blanca stepped over them. She grabbed her bag from her room. She paused a moment to look at the detonator to the bomb she had so carefully built but decided to leave it. She would be too far out of range for the signal to reach the school, and the thought letting the Americans trip over themselves while they tried to locate the bomb amused her. It would show them she meant business and the threat of her striking somewhere else would occupy their attention while she indeed formed her next plan.

Because, luckily, Mahlik had foreseen such a complication, and they had a backup in place. She raced from the bedroom and grabbed the keys to the Mercedes from the kitchen counter. She left the safehouse behind and didn't look back.

. . .

"The Mercedes is gone," Cara Billings reported.

She'd stopped their vehicle across the street from the Blanca safehouse. Brick and Arenas were already exiting the SUV and heading for the back gate.

Thurston replied in Cara's ear.

"We lost the picture because of the cloud cover, but we're still showing heat signatures inside."

"How many?"

"Three."

"There were four earlier."

"I'm aware."

"I don't like this, ma'am."

"Well, it's about to get worse. Those heat signatures are fading, and the bodies aren't moving. They're clumped together in the same area. Get in there, Cara, but use caution."

"We're going to need the locals."

"Alerting them now."

Cara jumped out of the SUV, ending the call with General Thurston. She joined Brick and Arenas at the back of the vehicle.

Brick lifted the tailgate of their SUV. A large case with stacked drawers filled the back of the vehicle. Each drawer contained their gear. HK 416 carbines, body armor, sidearms, and flash grenades. The trio took a few moments to strap up and lock and load and crossed the street.

Cara and Brick took up position near the front door and Arenas kicked the door open. As it slammed against the opposite wall, Cara tossed in a flash-bang stun grenade. Another loud boom. Arenas entered first. Cara and Brick following, all three swinging their weapons left and right looking for threats.

Open living room. No hostiles.

"Down the hall!" Brick said.

Cara moved down the hallway while Brick and Arenas took up security on either side behind her. Cara carefully approached the bodies, mindful of the wet carpet. She shined a light on their faces. Whoever shot them had aimed for the chest, so she clearly recognized two of cartel assassins she'd been wanting to find. A quick peek in the bedroom the first two bodies had fallen in front of revealed the third man, as lifeless as the other two, but Cara did not try to approach him.

"What's it look like, Cara?" Brick asked.

"Three dead. They're the guys we've been looking for."

"Any sign of—"

"No."

Cara wandered into the other bedrooms, noting the lack of furniture or luxury items. She stepped into Blanca's room and immediately knew Blanca had been there. The room retained a faint trace of perfume. Then Cara's eyes landed on a rectangular black box on the floor beside the cot. The detonator. For a bomb.

She yelled for Brick and Arenas, who shouldered their rifles and joined her.

"Where's the bomb?" Arenas asked.

"Slick thinks the school across the street was the target," Cara said. "We'll look there first as soon as the locals arrive."

As if on cue, they heard sirens in the distance.

"Let's get outside and wave them down," Cara said. "Gonna be a long night."

Her hotel room was off limits.

The Americans might not know she'd been there, but she couldn't take the chance. Her laptop wouldn't reveal anything other than the location of the Middletown safe-house, and they could spend all the time they wanted sorting dead bodies and looking for a bomb that may be in the area.

The Mercedes was probably red-flagged as well, but for now she needed the vehicle. She'd ditch it as soon as possible which, she figured, would be soon.

She figured staying in New Jersey was better than trying to drive back to New York, so she drifted out of Middletown and headed south along the Garden State Parkway, easily joining the flow of traffic, and careful to keep to the speed limit less she attract unwanted attention from a state trooper. The last thing she needed was a speeding ticket—Fasil had said her fake identification would hold up to scrutiny, but it wasn't something she was eager to test.

Light flashed into the Mercedes every time she passed under a lamppost. Blanca watched the in-dash GPS show her the region and plotted a course for Tinton Falls, a place that looked small enough to hide in, for a short time at least.

She had the burner phone with which to call Fasil, and all she wanted, after such a disastrous night, was to hear his voice.

She'd been away from him for too long.

Sonora, Mexico

Mahlik abandoned the ATV outside a quiet neighborhood and started walking. He was very glad for the late hour. There was nobody else on the street, except for a stray dog or two, and the animals ran away. He'd straightened his clothes as much as he could, brushing off the desert dust, letting the wind in his hair as he rode the ATV dry the sweat on his skin. But he was glad for the late hour because nobody could see how he looked.

He approached a small cottage on the left side of the street, the windows dark and the place apparently uninhabited. He found the key to the front door under a loose brick to the right of the entryway. The key let him into the cottage and he shut the door behind him, resting his back against it as he caught his breath.

The place was dark. There were no sounds other than Mahlik's breathing. He had to feel along the wall to find the light switches. He'd only been in the house one time, and that was to sign the rental agreement and add furnishings and at least give the neighbors the idea somebody lived there. His main interest was down a short hallway to the master bedroom. As inviting as the bed looked, he needed a shower first and stripped off his dusty clothes to stand under the hot water for nearly twenty minutes. He tried not to think about the failure at the camp. Hostages rescued. His men killed. The cartel people dead, too. If Blanca was still alive, he needed to link up with her, and either run off to fight another day or figure out how to continue the mission.

And, like it or not, his mind was already working out his next move. Blanca wanted her father free. Mahlik wanted to make Blanca happy; he also wanted the advantages her organization might supply. A win for him, and the jihad.

Mahlik finished his shower and turned off the water.

The master bedroom felt stuffy, and against his better judgment, he cracked a window to let some air in, then opened the closet door.

Shirts and pants hung in the closet; baskets on the floor contained socks and underwear. He dressed hurriedly but felt himself becoming drowsy after the relaxing shower. He checked his watch. It was the middle of the night, and there was nothing he could do until his bank opened in the morning. The bed sure seemed inviting. He stretched out and fell asleep as soon as his head hit the pillow.

He'd left his cell phone in his other pants. Had he not, he would have heard the phone ring.

Tinton Falls, New Jersey

Blanca listened to the ring on the other end, what would be Fasil's phone, but he didn't answer. She wouldn't have broken radio silence unless she had to. In this case, she thought she had no choice.

But he didn't answer. Which meant either he couldn't or wouldn't. If he couldn't, did that mean the camp had been raided? Or was there a reason for not picking up?

Blanca sat in a motel room. She'd stopped at the first place she'd found since entering Tinton Falls, and the room was comfortable enough, the heater warming the room. The only light on was the one on the nightstand beside the bed, and she didn't think she had the energy for anything except go to sleep and start over in the morning. She undressed and climbed into bed but remained tense. Was Fasil in danger? Was he even still alive? But why wouldn't he be? How could the Americans have found where her people were keeping the Warner sisters? Certainly, there was no way they found them this quickly.

No. She was thinking paranoid because of Arriola and his treachery. She took a deep breath and finally started to settle down. Then she dozed off.

. . .

Sonora, Mexico

Fasil Mahlik bounced out of bed with a list of activities running through his head. He didn't have a car, but there were plenty of cabs in the city. First, some calls. He dug his cell phone out of yesterday's pants and noticed a missed call. The number displayed was Blanca's burner phone. He leaned against the kitchen counter while his tea brewed in a kettle and called her.

"Fasil! You're alive!"

"Barely," he said.

"What does that mean?"

Mahlik explained the raid on the camp and the rescue of the Warner sisters.

Blanca provided her own update.

"What do we do now?" she asked. "Is it over?"

Mahlik sighed. The despair in her voice was palpable.

"We do not stop," he said. "There are contingencies I did not tell you about because I didn't think we needed them. We need them now. Where are you?"

"Still in New Jersey." She told him where.

"Stay where you are. I'll be entering the US under another identity, and I'll meet you in New Jersey. Before I get there, I will have everything arranged."

"But what—"

"Don't worry about it. What I need you to do in the meantime is research."

"Research what?"

"Find us a suitable target in New York City. A big target

providing, perhaps, plenty of civilian casualties if the Americans do not release your father."

She was quiet a moment.

"Are you there?" Mahlik asked.

"Yes."

"Okay?"

"I'll do it."

"Stay strong. I will be there soon. We will finish this together."

Mahlik ended the call.

The tea kettle began to whistle.

The cab dropped him in front of the bank. Mahlik asked the cab driver to wait.

He identified himself to a teller and asked to see his safe deposit box. The bank manager led Mahlik to a private room where the safe deposit boxes lined the walls. A rectangular table on stilts occupied the middle of the room.

The manager excused himself and shut the door behind him. Mahlik stood alone.

He went to the wall of safe deposit boxes and used a small key to unlock one on the top row. Pulling open the door, he slid the container within out and placed it on the table.

The metal container was the same size as a shoe box, and when Mahlik lifted the lid, he took in the contents for a moment. Multiple passports, cash, identification cards. This was his stash for quick international travel. He didn't have a weapon hidden in the container because if a situation had become so bad that he needed it to begin with, it meant he was on the run, and heading for a place of safety. It meant traveling unarmed. It meant taking certain risks.

But Mahlik's life had been full of risks. He'd always survived.

Not because of luck, but skill.

Skills honed over a lifetime.

He examined the six passports and selected one that identified him as Bento Almada from Portugal. He chose a driver's license that matched and looked at the picture on the ID. He'd need to add a mustache and a mole on his chin. No problem.

Pocketing the passport and driver's license, he returned the container to the safe deposit slot and closed and locked the door.

He left the bank with a farewell wave to the manager, who smiled at him.

CHAPTER 21

Tucson, Arizona

Mahlik rented a car under his Almada identity and drove to Nogales, where he caught a plane to Tucson, Arizona. Sitting in coach, near a window, he kept his head in a paperback, reading but not comprehending, as he calculated his next move. As soon as he touched down in the US, he'd be quite busy indeed.

His disguise not only matched his driver's license, but also fooled any facial recognition cameras, though there weren't any on the Mexican side of the border, and not enough on the US side. For all the talk about such technology, the US wasn't as covered as the proponents of the tech, or the government looking to keep people under control, wanted the general population to believe. That didn't stop him from taking precautions as he entered the US, however. He cleared customs without incident but didn't settle down. He had to watch his step every minute.

Renting another car at the Tucson airport, a big

Chrysler sedan with a powerful engine, he started driving, changing direction several times as he drove to shake any tails. When he was confident there was nobody back there, he settled back for his long journey—and left Tucson. Thirty-six hours to Tinton Falls, NJ, and the soft arms of Blanca Sanchez. He followed I-10 to I-70 to I-54, keeping to the speed limit, staying in the right lane and letting faster traffic go by. The fake mustache itched; he left it on. Despite the easy explanation as to why the mustache was in his photo and not on his face, he didn't want any extra scrutiny.

He took two days to make the trip, stopping twice along the way, sticking to the cheaper roadside motels. His Eaton education served Mahlik well, as he was able to speak almost perfect American English, with appropriate slang, and if anybody wondered about the color of his skin, nobody seemed to notice.

During each stop, he spent some time on the phone—his burner cell—to make various calls to three locations along the East Coast. The calls were short, his instructions brief and to the point, and the party on the other end of the line asked no questions. He was speaking with AQ sleeper cells planted in the US, in some cases, for years, and now he was calling them to active duty. He needed weapons, willing fighters, and explosives. If he and Blanca were to finish their mission, if he were to cement his relationship with her and, in turn, the cartel, he needed help. He and Blanca couldn't do much with only a couple of pistols and a limited amount of ammunition, and no money. One of the sleeper teams had access to "emergency cash" for operatives passing through who needed to escape US authorities. One such scenario had happened more than once already, Mahlik knew. They'd have the funds required for the job.

The sleepers had been in place for decades, waiting for just such a call, and all of them responded with enthusiasm and promised to meet him in Tinton Falls. He had a special request for the cell near New York City, who was closest to Tinton, and able to move quickly to secure an operation base.

He smiled after the last call, thinking Blanca would be quite happy with the news of the extra help. She'd be more surprised than on her 16th birthday when her father presented her with a red Ferrari.

Now they only needed a target big enough to accommodate the eager fighters. He hoped Blanca was busying herself with the selection. He'd kept his instructions vague hoping she'd remember what he'd taught her about target selection. Having to focus on her training during a time of stress would help her forget what was causing the stress. He needed her mind clear if they were going to be successful. He had no doubt she'd perform exactly as he wanted.

While driving through Pittsburg one morning, Mahlik used his burner phone once again, to call Blanca, and tell her to put the kettle on. He'd be there in a few more hours. She said she couldn't wait.

Neither could he. No matter what happened next, whether they succeeded or failed, he'd have Blanca by his side again. Considering his luck so far, maybe he—or both of them—had somebody watching over their shoulder, clearing the path to victory.

It seemed plausible enough.

Mahlik kept driving.

Tinton Falls, New Jersey

. . .

He stopped outside the Tinton Inn and scanned the parking lot, his eye flicking left and right, at a high state of readiness. Since he had no gun, his only recourse was to back up and speed away.

There were no threats evident. A cleaning crew, guests at a vending machine, a lone woman behind the counter in the main office.

No federal agents waiting with handcuffs and pistols. Or worse.

Mahlik exited his car and clicked the key fob to lock the doors. Blanca had said she was on the ground floor, room 102, and he found it in the middle of the bottom row of rooms. He'd promised to tap a recognition code on the door. Truthfully, they hadn't worked out one. But any series of taps on the door would signal his arrival.

He took a deep breath and raised his right fist, but his mind went blank. He tapped SOS instead.

The chain rattled, and the door flew open.

Blanca stood framed in the doorway wearing plain blue jeans and a sweater, her hair, undone, falling like an untidy wave down her back. She looked stunning.

Finally, Mahlik removed the fake mustache from his face. He smiled.

"Aren't you going to invite me inside?"

She couldn't believe it.

There he was, standing before her, after so many weeks apart. A wave of relief washed over her.

Blanca almost felt giddy as she backed up and opened the door all the way, Mahlik stepping inside. She shut the door.

"Are you okay?" he asked.

"Don't you have any—"

"Just what I'm wearing."

"We have to fix that."

"I could use some water," he said.

She filled a plastic cup from the bathroom with tap water. He sat on the bed and drank it down.

"What happened?" she asked, standing before him with folded arms. He looked tired.

He explained in more detail than their previous phone conversation allowed. She began to pace. When he finished, she said:

"I have some ideas for a target, but how are we going to pull off a strike with just the two of us?"

"I have a surprise for you," he said and explained about the sleep cells he activated during the road trip. Her eyes widened.

"That's perfect," she said. "I should have known."

"What's your target?"

"We'll need to look up pictures, but it's a hotel I once stayed at in New York City. Your people will know it. The Liberty Suites."

Mahlik shook his head. "I haven't heard of it."

"Two buildings with a courtyard between them. They've done concerts there, big events like that. Always plenty of people."

"Why do you like it?"

"The main building. Single-level, lots of windows, plenty of people... for human shields."

"I like the way you think."

"When do we meet your sleeper cells?"

He checked his watch. "Few more hours. The leaders of each team are meeting us here."

"At the motel?"

"No, a park here in Tinton Falls. I'd never ask them to come here."

"Nobody's come around," she said. "I go out for food, that's it. There was a big argument in another room down the hall, and the cops came for that, but otherwise, it's quiet."

"Okay," he said. "So. We have a few hours. I need clothes, and some food would be—"

She rushed at him, his arms going around her out of instinct, as she mashed her lips against his. It took a moment, but soon his own lips melted into the kiss. She knew the move startled him but, dammit, she couldn't wait any longer, and all he wanted to do was talk about the mission. The mission, the mission. A girl had needs. She figured he had the same needs.

He grabbed her by the hips and turned her around, back to the bed, and shoved her onto the mattress. Swinging his legs over her, they began pulling at each other's clothes and finally did more than just kiss.

As Mahlik unzipped her jeans, Blanca figured he'd really need to go shopping when they were done.

Team Reaper HQ
El Paso, TX

General Mary Thurston paced the floor while Ferrero sat behind his desk, leaning back in his chair.

"What do we have that's good?" she asked.

"Kane and his crew got the Warner women to a hospital here in El Paso," Ferrero said. "Our Mexican contacts are working their end. The police diffused the bomb Blanca planted at the elementary school in New Jersey. I'd say we've done pretty well."

"Except."

"Yes, except the big fish."

"Swift has been through Blanca's laptop top to bottom," Thurston said. "He told me he can't find anything remotely useful unless we want him to watch all of her bookmarked make-up videos on YouTube to see if there are any clues there."

"Don't give me ideas," Ferrero said. "Stranger things have happened."

"If we can't find her," Thurston said, changing directions again, not making eye-contact with Ferrero, "we can only wait for her to strike."

"And by then it may be too late."

"Right."

"But we know where she might be."

Thurston stopped, locking eyes with Ferrero. "New York. Of course. But—"

"But nothing. Let's redirect Kane's crew to the Big Apple. He can link up with Cara, Brick, and Arenas, and we'll pick up the action there."

Thurston folded her arms and let out a sigh.

"They keep slipping through our fingers."

"I know."

"If we're not quick, thousands of people are in danger."

"Yes, they are."

"How many are going to be dead by the time this is over?"

"Hopefully only the bad guys," Ferrero said.

Thurston wasn't so sure.

. . .

Hospital
El Paso, TX

It felt good to be back in the United States, on home turf. It felt good to be alive. It hadn't been the worse operation, but John Kane figured it could have gone better.

Kane looked down the table at his teammates—Hunt, Axe, Traynor. They were on babysitting duty until the arrival of Senator Ted Warner as his wife, who were flying out from the West Coast. The Warner women, Peggy and Britney, were still under observation, being treated for dehydration and assorted minor injuries. Nurses were in their rooms now, checking up on them, so Kane and his crew had been dispatched to the commissary for coffee and lunch.

Kane and Company had at least had time to change from combat fatigues to civilian clothes before posting to the hospital, and while they didn't have heavy artillery, each of them carried their SIG M17 sidearm. Nobody expected Blanca Sanchez to attack the hospital, but she might. They had to be ready.

It was the kind of "what if" they had signed up for; nobody complained. Kane and his crew were a group of people who only felt at ease when bullets were flying.

The flight out of Mexico had posed no problems. A quick drop-off for Rico Ramirez back at the base they'd departed from and the Blackhawk headed for home with the two American women safe and sound.

Kane had no way of knowing at the time, but as the Mexico fight raged, Cara Billings and her portion of Team Reaper prevented a major tragedy. The difficulty in chasing Blanca Sanchez had been disheartening enough; had that bomb gone off, it would have been devastating.

And Kane had never felt prouder of his crew.

The two Hercules pilots, Macedo and Storey, were back on their own home turf, none the worse for wear.

Kane felt pleased about saving the Warner women but haunted by the fact that he couldn't save his own sister. A man might drive himself crazy trying to sort out the emotions involved, and Kane wasn't about to make the attempt. But it weighed on him still. There was nothing he could do for Mel; there was a lot he was able to do for Peggy and Britney Warner. If nothing else, he owed it to Mel to help whoever he could, whenever the chance arose. And he had the best crew with which to accomplish those goals.

"How much longer?" Axe asked.

Kane laughed. "You sound like a ten-year-old in the back seat of his parents' car on a long trip to grandma's."

"Nuts. At least then we'd have a DVD player or something."

"This plastic seat," Traynor said, shifting, "is making my butt hurt."

"Your face makes my butt hurt," Axe said.

"You keep talking like that, your ass is *really* going to hurt," Traynor said.

"Stop it, ladies," Kane said as everybody started laughing. It felt good to let off some steam. Heaven knows they had enough of it. But the respite wouldn't last forever. Already, Kane knew, Thurston and Ferrero were figuring out where to send them next, probably to New York City, to join Cara and her crew, and see if they can get a lead on Blanca and Mahlik again. No doubt they were heading for New York; it made sense.

It was about the only thing that made sense in all the madness of late.

SEAL Chief Borden Hunt, next to Kane at the table,

nudged his elbow and pointed at the doors to the commissary. "VIP incoming."

Kane followed Hunt's finger. Senator Warner was unmistakable, albeit not wearing his customary black suit, white shirt, and black tie. He might have resembled Mr. Rogers with the tan cardigan sweater and slacks, and he looked to have grown some extra worry lines on his face in recent days.

Kane approached the senator with an outstretched hand. "Mr. Warner."

"You should have stayed at the table," Warner said, pumping Kane's hand, slapping the side of his arm. "Please introduce me to the others."

Kane made the rounds, keeping as low key as he could. Nobody mentioned any details of the mission. Warner certainly didn't need to.

"I can't thank you all enough," Warner said. His wife, behind him, offered only a smile.

"The doctor says they'll be okay," Kane said.

"We just saw them. Yes, indeed, they will be okay, but, you know—"

"Uh-huh. I'm sure you'll get them what they need," Kane said.

"Britney keeps asking about somebody named Aiden," Warner said. "Do you know who she's referring to?"

"Somebody she met on the boat," Kane said. "He was shot during the abduction."

"Is he—"

"No, he'll live.."

"I see."

Kane had to be cordial, but part of him wanted to tell the senator that he might be about to learn what people put through traumatic events had to deal with—like the myriad of soldiers and marines he'd gleefully voted to send into harm's way without thought to the consequences, based only on what reasons the president and other saber-rattlers claimed were for the assorted military action. Kane knew many a Marine with PTSD; he knew some who were never quite convinced they were fighting for the right reasons; others, unaffected, believed they'd done the right thing, and that their country would not do them wrong.

"We had to come and say hello," Warner said, his wife still dutifully behind him. He did step aside to let her shake hands with the team, though she didn't say much above a whisper. Kane wasn't sure if she was deferring to her more vocal husband, or too stunned to really articulate anything. He decided to give her the benefit of the doubt.

The couple left, the commissary door swinging shut behind them. Kane sat down with his teammates once again.

Axe asked, "Can we go home now?"

Kane's cell rang. He glanced at the screen. Thurston. "Yes," he said, "and no." He answered the call.

"Yes, ma'am?"

"Back to HQ right away."

She hung up without another word.

CHAPTER 22

New York City
  LaGuardia Airport

Complain enough, Cara Billings thought, *and maybe you can change something.*

She'd left Brick and Arenas back at the hotel while she drove the SUV to the airport to collect Kane and the rest of their merry band of marauders. She met a private jet at a perimeter hangar and stood waiting by the lowered steps as Kane, exiting first with his pack, followed by Traynor, Hunt, and Axe, each with their own gear, came down the steps.

"Hi, boys," she said. A gust of cold wind whipped at the side of her face. La Guardia was closest to Manhattan, and the chill from the east river cut like a knife through the air. Good news: still not summertime. Bad news: bloody hell, the wind!

Kane stopped in front of her as the rest of the crew loaded into the SUV.

"How you doing?" he asked.

"Fine."

They stared at each other a moment.

Kane nodded. There was still a strain between them. But he couldn't very well ignore her or their past, and neither could she, and Cara at least appreciated his attempt at connecting with her one-on-one. Heaven knew it would probably be the last time they had that chance, considering the workload they had before them, which, she feared, might mostly consist of randomly searching for the proverbial needle in the never-ending haystack of New York City and its surrounding environment. One hell of a haystack.

Kane climbed into the passenger seat while she settled behind the wheel. Strapping on her seat belt, the relief from the wind improved her mood a great deal. She started driving after saying hello to the guys in the back, who looked eager, despite having just returned from battle in Mexico, to whoop it up all over again.

Cara inched through traffic to the Grand Central Parkway, which moved a little better and then took the Robert F. Kennedy Bridge back into Manhattan. Even the mid-afternoon traffic was thick, crossing the span was slow-going, and Cara gripped the steering wheel tightly. She wasn't sure if she was anxious about tracking down Blanca, or because Kane was sitting inches from her.

"How are Brick and Arenas?" Kane asked.

"Probably watching MMA fights on the hotel pay-per-view."

"They think it's good training."

"We've had that discussion, yes," she said. "They're full of shit."

Kane laughed.

"Do *you* think it's good training?" she asked.

"You know what I think. The only good training is *real* training."

"Hey, Reaper," Hunt yelled from the back. "How about we shoot our way out of this traffic jam?"

Kane had a hard time arguing with the idea.

Cara nixed it entirely.

But she had to admit that, after being separated for so long, it felt good to have the whole team back together. This time they'd finish the fight. One way, or another.

But she knew for certain that she and her people had completed their courtroom babysitting assignment. Now they were needed for something more direct, and Cara looked forward to the trigger time ahead. When the time came, she wanted Blanca Sanchez lined up in her sights.

"So what's the plan?" Kane asked.

They were more than halfway across the RFK Bridge, the bumper-to-bumper delay and flaring brake lights as annoying as ever, punctuated by honks and yells from drivers who thought they might speed things along by engaging in such behavior. Traffic, like a stubborn gorilla, refused to move no matter what they attempted.

"Thurston wants us to shakedown Blanca's hotel room again," Cara said. "Maybe we missed something the first time."

"Doubtful. And now that their primary plan has been disrupted, they're either going to try something else, or run."

"I don't think they'll run."

"I agree, but whatever they do next, there won't be a note about it in the hotel room nightstand."

"You got a better idea, Reaper?"

"No, but at least I'm not suggesting something just to keep us busy."

"You think we're going to end up waiting until she makes a move?"

"What else you got?" Kane asked.

"We might have somebody who can help."

"Who?"

She told him about Felix Lovoso, the street fixer.

"Where'd you meet this guy?"

"Don't ask," Cara said.

"Cara—"

"Seriously, *don't* ask."

She heard Kane laugh to himself. He probably knew the answer already; he knew her almost too well, and part of her hated him for that.

Finally, traffic began to loosen up, and they crossed the span into Manhattan.

Kane shut the door to his hotel room—he was three floors above Cara's room—and tossed his gear pack on the bed. He wondered what the hotel staff would do if they saw what was in it. His weapons, tactical gear, and spare clothes—and more weapons than clothes at that.

He left the weapons disassembled in their respective cases and shoved the cases into the closet. He'd long ago decided the best way to travel was to indeed fill dresser drawers with clothes instead of living out of a suitcase; it created stability, even if you were leaving in two days or less.

As he jammed the last of his shirts into the drawer, he went to the window to look out on the cityscape. Manhattan was lighting up, preparing for the nightlife, people making plans and having a good time without any knowledge of the sword of Damocles that hung over them.

If Kane had his way, they would remain ignorant.

Cara drove again, Kane riding shotgun again, but with Brick in the back seat. The rest of the team remained at the Marriott standing by for orders should Cara's street source have actionable information.

"Who is this guy again?" Kane asked.

Cara gave a rundown of Felix Lovoso, also known as the Mouse, who had arrived late with the info she needed on the cartel assassins but might know of other movements in the city if Blanca and Fasil Mahlik were launching a second attack. Something had to be going down, she figured, because Blanca and Mahlik certainly didn't have enough gear to pull off an attack on their own. They'd need help. And that meant, though the word remained unspoken, activating sleeper cells.

Sleeper cells were not a joke in US intelligence circles, they were a real threat, and the jihadists managed to use the States' own laws to their favor. You can't arrest somebody for practicing their religion; you can't put under surveillance somebody practicing their religion, and that's how the sleeper cells were assembling. People within the US, who practiced jihad ideology, may not ever "Activate" for a mission. Instead, they raised money, sent cash overseas, provided points of rest or avenues of communication for active operators, otherwise maintaining a low profile and not doing anything to warrant attention from authorities. Every now and then a jihadist might slip up and make a statement on a jihad-related internet forum that piqued the attention of the FBI—as had happened in several cases, which is why the Feds monitored such outlets—but the arrests never took down large groups, just lone individuals who had no information on other sleepers. The cells tended to remain spread apart, so no one person could be linked to the whole group.

And, of course, there was Blanca, who, while on her own and on the run, would certainly know how to tap into the US drug network and hire out any shooters she might have a need for.

But if Cara was right and her fixer friend might have a clue as to who was coming into the city, they might get their next big break in a mission that seemed to have no end, where it felt like he was banging his head against a wall. The victory in Mexico and the reunited of the Warner sisters with their parents was already a distant memory; might as well not have happened. The wins never stayed with Kane, but the failures did. The failures lingered and haunted. Kane had had enough of those to last a lifetime.

They weren't rigged for war, but neither were they defenseless. Kane, Cara, and Brick carried their SIG-Sauer M17 pistols, with Kane packing a knife sheathed on his right hip. If Cara and Brick had brought any extra toys, they hadn't said anything to him.

Sometimes it was best to be surprised.

"So you changed your mind? Sit down and—oh, you brought friends again.'

Cara grinned. Felix Lovoso's wore a face of palpable disappointment. She slid into the booth in front of him. Kane and Brick held back, Lovoso's bodyguards eyeing them warily, but nobody made any sudden moves.

Cara said, "Don't you ever eat anywhere else?"

"My table is always waiting for me, and the spaghetti is hot, it's never crowded. Short answer, no. What brings you back here? Did you get those three guys?"

"Surprised you didn't hear. They didn't make it out of New Jersey."

Lovoso dismissed the remark with a wave. "Outside my territory."

"We have another problem. The person who brought those three killers here is, we think, in the city herself, and she's planning a new attack. She'll need help."

Lovoso chewed as he listened.

"So we're not talking three people this time," Cara continued, "it will be more than that."

"Uh-huh."

"Any ideas?"

Lovoso swallowed. "One. What's it worth?"

"Your life?"

Lovoso laughed. "That's been tried a thousand times, babe."

A flush crawled up Cara's neck. She dared not look at Kane because he was probably laughing. "What would you like?" she asked.

"Well—"

"It has to be reasonable."

"Yeah, yeah. Look, my kid brother's out on bond, got busted boosting a car. You make the charges go away, and I'll put my resources to your disposal."

"We don't have time for that."

"Help me out, or no deal."

"We'll help you, but we can't take care of your brother first. Maybe you don't understand the situation."

"I understand, don't you worry. You need something from me, and I need something from you."

"We're talking *jihadists*, Felix. The kind of people who knocked down you-know-what."

That made Lovoso stop chewing. He swallowed what was in his mouth and put down his fork and spoon.

"Really? You ain't lying?"

Cara shook her head.

"Okay, you ready?"

"You know something now?"

"Yeah, get this. My people, you know, we sometimes rent office space or warehouses, and keep them empty, to be used only when necessary, for meetings and such."

"Typical," Cara said.

"Well, there's this one office spot that somebody snagged years ago, and it's never been filled, yet it's not been taken by anybody I know, get it?"

"Sure."

"And maybe I've been hearing about somebody showing up and making sure the plumbing works within the last few days."

Cara took out her cell phone and opened Google Maps. "Where is this office?"

"Right across from Washington Square Park."

"Address?"

Lovoso told her.

Kane took over driving chores while Cara navigated via the GPS unit.

It would have been a direct drive, but the Italian restaurant made Kane hungry, and he convinced Cara to allow a stop at a Chick-Fil-A along the way, which was down a block from Washington Square Park. As Kane munched on a waffle fry with a Deluxe Sandwich resting on his right knee, he steered through traffic on Washington Square North heading for to Washington Square West straight ahead. A left turn and he shot into the one open street slot curbside in front of the park.

"It's a Team Reaper miracle," Brick said from the back, sucking down the last of his Coke and setting the cup in the rear seat cupholder.

They exited the SUV at the corner of Washington Square North and Waverly Place, with the Hangman's Elm casting a shadow over the vehicle. The elm was a fixture of the park, a historical landmark, but debate raged about whether anybody was ever hung from that tree. It gave Kane a strange feeling in the pit of his stomach.

They crossed the street to a brick building where, Lovoso said, an empty office awaited on the top floor that may or may not be part of Blanca's next attack plan. Kane had argued that the Mouse's "lead" was weak; Cara insisted they had to check it out because Lovoso knew the intimate comings and goings of the underworld in the city. When Kane joked that he'd obviously known all about the three cartel killers who almost blew up an elementary school, she became quiet.

As long as they didn't go in blasting. Sure, Lovoso's description was certainly curious, even suspicious, if he was right about offices and other such spaces being rented without use until nefarious parties required somewhere to meet. Kane was just nervous about following a rabbit trail that took them down a dead end while Blanca and Mahlik went in another direction entirely.

They had to be in New York. If Blanca wanted her father out of jail, she *needed* to be in New York.

Taking hostages in Kansas and demanding the release of her father didn't seem like a choice she would make instead.

Kane took the lead and he, Cara and Brick climbed the steps of the brick building, careful to maintain distance between them. Kane entered first, followed by Cara and Brick, and Kane consulted the directory looking for the 14th floor where Lovoso had said the rented empty office sat. There was no company name listed for the 14th floor; the line was blank. If there had been space available for rent, he would have expected to see a note about that. Maybe Lovoso was right. Kane pressed a button for an elevator, and the three Reaper operatives stepped aboard when the lift doors rumbled open.

Cara took out her SIG and checked the chamber. Holstering the gun, she glanced at Kane.

"What's on your mind?" she asked.

"I hope we're not making a mistake."

"Don't you trust me?"

"You, yes. Your buddy? Not particularly."

"I still ain't got any chicken parm from that place," Brick added.

The elevator stopped on the 14th floor. The doors slid open on an empty hallway.

They heard music.

Exiting, they turned to the source of the music, what became obviously a Johnny Cash tune as they approached where it was coming from—an open door at the end of the hall. Other office doors lined the wall as they advanced, but the one at the end was the only one standing open.

Kane, Cara, and Brick stopped near the doorway, Kane slightly leaning in to take a look. Open floor plan. No cubicles. There were tables, mostly cluttered with cardboard boxes and other miscellaneous packaging, more strewn across the floor. At a wall, a dark-skinned man with a bald head and a sweater-and-slack combo hung a map on an open wall space. The sweater was a light blue, like the color of the sky on a nice day. He seemed like a normal, conservatively-dressed businessman preparing an office for the opening.

Either it was the perfect cover, or perfectly innocent.

Time to play dumb.

Kane nodded to his teammates and entered the room.

"Hi," he called out.

The man hanging the map paused, startled, and turned to look over his shoulder.

"What do you want?" he asked, with no accent.

"I think we're lost."

The man turned from the wall with the large map in both hands. He placed it across a nearby table that wobbled a little.

"You probably are. The only company on this floor is mine. Where you trying to be?"

Kane almost shot a glance Cara's way. He had been right—this was a nowhere lead. The Mouse was useless—if he was ever useful to begin with because the story Cara had said portrayed him more as a lecher than a helpful informant. He kept his attention on the man in the blue sweater, though, and saw the man's eyes flick to the left. And then two more men joined the conversation. They entered from another hallway, carrying boxes, and one had a pistol sticking out of his belt. The two men paused, startled by the new arrivals.

"I see we really are in the wrong place," Kane said, gesturing to the door. Cara and Brick started to exit, but then the man in the sweater shouted in Arabic. The two newcomers dropped their boxes, one taking out his exposed pistol, the other drawing from behind his back.

The two men carried striker-fired Smith & Wesson

M&P 9mm autoloaders, and the muzzles might have been small, but the men meant business.

"Whoa, hey now—" Kane said. He held up his hands and purposefully stepped in front of Brick and Cara. "There's no reason for guns here; we just got off at the wrong floor."

"Step forward and get on the ground, on your knees," Sweater Man said.

Kane said, "Okay," and as he began to kneel, tucked in his elbows and rolled to the left, clearing the way for Cara and Brick.

Cara and Brick had their SIG pistols, both in a text-book isosceles stance, zeroed on the gunmen. Cara fired first, a quick, two-round burst that hit one gunner high in the chest. A follow-up round punched through his head, knocking him to the ground. His partner also fell quickly, as Brick stitched his own Mozambique Drill to the second gunner's chest and head.

Sweater Man dived for a leather carrying case in the corner nearest him, where he grabbed for a Glock pistol. He was also already in Kane's sights. Kane fired twice. Sweater Man took both hits but didn't fall. As a splatter of red covered his blue sweater, he swung the Glock their way. Kane fired twice more. Cara and Brick fired two. Round after round ripped into Sweater Man and he twitched and danced and finally fell in a bloody heap.

Kane executed a quick tactical reload and jumped to his feet, stepping around the fallen gunners Cara and Brick had shot, aiming down the hallway they'd come from.

No other threats made themselves obvious.

"Reaper," Brick said, "better come and see this."

Kane kept his eyes down the other hallway as he backed

up to where Brick and Cara stood. Near the table where Sweater Man had placed his map.

He looked at the map, particularly at the markings in red made on the paper, around a specific location.

"Did we get it right?" Kane asked.

"I think we nailed it bang-on," said Cara.

"Know where that is?" Brick asked, tapping the circled area.

"I do," Kane said, "and now I'm getting a really bad feeling about this."

Manhattan
Moynihan Federal Courthouse

Getting Blanca's father involved seemed risky, stupid—every negative word Kane could think of—but he had to admit that if Cara was right, and the Jorge Sanchez didn't want his daughter attempting to break him out, then perhaps a few words from Dear Old Dad was exactly what they needed.

Cara, at least, had managed to convince Thurston on the first try.

Stripped of cell phones, weapons, even their wallets, Cara Billings and John Kane followed a jail guard down the cell block to where Jorge Sanchez waited in his cell. He was fresh off another day of testimony, back in his orange jumpsuit. Kane and Cara stopped at the cell door. Sanchez sat on the edge of the bed. His hair was still slicked back. He looked at them with a frown.

"Jorge," Cara said.

"I've been concerned about you," Sanchez said. "You're not with us in the courtroom any longer."

"I didn't think you'd notice."

"I notice everything," Sanchez said.

"We need your help."

Sanchez laughed. "Don't torture me like that." Then his face became serious. "Is it about Blanca?"

"Yes, it is."

"I knew she wasn't dead."

"How?"

"A parent knows. I heard rumors of something in New Jersey, but I knew she wasn't among the dead. Tell me what Blanca is doing."

"Still working with al-Qaeda."

"Uh-huh."

"They're planning a strike on the Grand Hyatt in New York City," Cara said.

Unloading the information on Sanchez had been Cara's idea, as she thought being honest with him was the best way to get the man to cooperate, but Kane was wary. Who knew who Sanchez had communication with, who might say something to somebody on the outside? He didn't think for a minute that Sanchez was as concerned a parent as Cara made him out to be but then checked himself. She'd been right about Lovoso. The men they killed at the "office" had been identified by the FBI—suspected jihadists, living in the U.S. under assumed names. Only Sweater Man had been a New York resident; the other two, the FBI had traced back to Pakistan.

"What do you mean by 'strike'," Sanchez said. He still sat on the edge of his cot.

"We're not sure. A bombing, hostages, who knows?"

"What do you need from me?"

"We have to clear this with the jail, all sorts of other people," Cara said, "before it can happen, but it won't work if you say no off the bat."

Sanchez rose and approached the bars. "Tell me."

"We want you to make a video," Cara said.

Sanchez frowned.

Cara finished her explanation.

Grand Hyatt Hotel
New York City

"They're everywhere," said Blanca Sanchez.

"The Americans found the office faster than I thought they would," Mahlik said, "but it looks like we're okay."

"Their intel was very good."

"Almost too good. If Omar had been a little behind—"

"Omar did his job well."

"And he is being rewarded," Mahlik said, "even as we speak. Tell me what you see."

Blanca sat in the huge lobby of the Grand Hyatt Hotel, in a corner chair, watching the comings and goings. She wore sunglasses to shield her face from the ceiling cameras. She spoke to Mahlik via a wireless Bluetooth in her ear, scrolling through news articles on a tablet computer resting on her lap to look occupied. None of the words registered with her and that was fine. She only needed to play a part. The brightness from the skylight over her head at least made the sunglasses plausible. The glare from the polished aluminum support posts nearby was quite strong.

The lobby impressed her, but the hotel was too ornate to make a good target. Very crowded, as well—not just from registering guests, but daily visitors making use of the bars, restaurants, and meeting rooms. The wide-open lobby with its second level walkways overlooking the entrance would have been a logistical nightmare for a squad to contain. They'd manage to collect hostages, sure, but couldn't cover all the potential exits for those they missed, or the entry points for SWAT teams.

The Liberty Suites had far less problems.

"Several utility vans outside, obvious surveillance vehicles. People in the lobby. Couples, mostly, but they all smell like federal agents."

"They took the bait. Excellent."

"Where are you and the others?"

"Two more hours—we'll be in position on schedule."

Blanca smiled. "This is going to be amazing."

"They will have no choice but to respond. I have to go."

"See you soon, my love."

Blanca ended the call.

CHAPTER 23

Team Reaper HQ
El Paso, TX

Sam Swift said, "Oh no."

Thurston, nearby, hurried over, bracing herself with a hand on the back of his chair. She leaned over his shoulder. "What's happening?"

She spotted nothing of note on Swift's computer monitor, so raised her head to scan the wall-mounted flat screens in front of them, the three large screens offering a perfect view of the Grand Hyatt in New York City, the feed originating from various security cameras inside the buildings. Street CCTV provided alternative views. So far, the footage had been very boring, where they'd spent more time counting undercover police and federal agents than spotting cartel terrorists.

"It's not the Grand Hyatt, ma'am," Swift said. He wore a headset tuned to the NYPD police band. He pressed a button and let the police frequency play over the speakers in the operations center.

The chatter was almost indecipherable at first, but words like "multiple active shooters" and "all units respond" were loud and clear. Thurston frantically watched the big screens. There was no shooting going on at the Grand Hyatt. Activity at the hotel was normal.

"Where are they?"

Swift opened a map on his monitor and pinpointed the location of the emergency calls.

"Liberty Suites, another hotel about six blocks away."

"Grand Hyatt was a decoy?"

"Apparently."

"I need video."

"Coming up." Swift's fingers flew across the keys.

Thurston grabbed a phone from a nearby work station and called John Kane in New York.

Blanca had struck again, fooling them with a sleight-of-hand trick they hadn't anticipated.

Grand Hyatt Hotel
New York City

"Patch me through to everybody, Reaper."

Kane tapped his cell phone screen. "Okay, everybody's on."

"Attention, everybody, we have multiple active shooters reported at the Liberty Suites about six blocks away from your current location."

Kane and Cara sat at a table in the Grand Hyatt's lobby

bar. She perked up with interest at the shocked expression on his face. She heard the call through her own Bluetooth.

"They set us up," Kane said.

Kane spoke in a normal tone of voice. The noise in the bar from patrons and big-screen TVs meant he didn't have to whisper.

"Yes, they did, Reaper. Can you relocate?"

"*We* can relocate. What about the rest of the locals? We put our reputation on the line for this; they aren't going to be happy."

The process of getting the New York Police Department and anti-terrorist elements of the local Federal Bureau of Investigation had required more legwork than Kane or Thurston wanted to admit. Neither felt comfortable with "Team Reaper" running around in the city, insisting that any incident landed under their jurisdiction and they had sole responsibility. And then President Carter inserted himself into the conversation and made sure Team Reaper had a place at the table. But that was when they thought the Grand Hyatt, based on the map recovered from the office front used by Fasil Mahlik's sleeper cell, was the target. Cops and Feds and Reaper had converged on the building to intercept the shooters before they did any serious damage. But the whole scenario had been a fake-out, and now innocent people were in harm's way.

Thurston said, "We'll get the president involved again if we have to, but we're wasting time talking about it."

"We're moving. Team Reaper, all copy?"

The crew responded in the affirmative. Kane knew their approximate positions in the hotel; their vehicles were in the garage, with easy access to weapons and equipment. It was the best rally point for the group.

"Everybody, meet at the vehicles; we're moving."

"We'll coordinate with the locals on this end," Thurston said.

Kane looked around for some of the faces he'd picked out as cops or FBI. Multiple individuals were already sprinting for the exit.

"I think they've been informed, ma'am."

"Get moving, Reaper."

Cara and Kane left their chairs and ran out of the bar together.

Team Reaper HQ
El Paso, TX

"I have visual on Liberty Suites," Sam Swift reported.

"Show us," said Thurston. She and Ferrero stood behind the red-headed hacker.

The wide screens blanked out for a moment, then new images flashed. Security camera footage from the lobby of Liberty Suites caused a collective intake of breath from everybody in the operations center.

Men and women armed with automatic weapons sprayed fire in the lobby of the Liberty, guests screaming, running, falling.

"Patching through a Facebook Live transmission," Swift said.

A center monitor cleared, and this time sound accompanied the video.

Screaming, mostly. Shouting. Crackling gunfire. The shaky cell phone showed a little of the carnage, a woman saying, *"They're coming from everywhere—"* before her cell camera captured the image of a shooter lining her up in his sights. His muzzle flashed, the blast of gunfire over-powering the cell phone speaker. The phone fell to the ground, the camera lens now showing only the ceiling and emergency sprinklers, as the gunfire and yelling continued.

Thurston and Ferrero turned to each other. Neither spoke.

Liberty Suites
New York City

There had been too many guests. Blanca and Mahlik didn't have enough fighters to handle that many hostages, so their first instructions had been simple: *go in and kill as many as possible.*

Once the number of people had been reduced, the troops had orders to herd survivors into the restaurant and put them on the floor.

The Liberty Suites wasn't as elegant as some other New York City hotels, but it had become a "best-kept secret" in the city with those who wanted luxurious rooms and an open-air resort-like experience. The main building, where the check-in desk, bar, and restaurant were located, didn't have any rooms. To get to a room, one had to exit the rear of the main building, cross the promenade, and enter a second, taller building, shaped like an L, that contained the rooms. The promenade featured cobble-stone walkways, grass and trees, a variety of shops, an outdoor bar, and the swimming pool.

Blanca Sanchez entered the main lobby and removed her sunglasses. Dead bodies were strewn about like trash, bullets having ripped them open and apart. The sight did not bother her at all; neither did the odor.

The hostages had been herded into the restaurant to the left of the entryway, and she walked in that direction, stepping carefully around the bodies and pools of blood on the tiles, the men, women, and children. She made a sour face. It was so unfortunate. But if the Americans were to take her seriously, and understand she meant business, it meant there had to be some bloodshed, and a lot of it, because Americans were stubborn. They might have snatched the Warner sisters from her grasp, but there were a whole lot of other dead around her that wouldn't be so fortunate.

And there was weeping and gnashing of teeth, she thought as she stepped inside the restaurant. The hostages, pressed close together on the floor, jammed into booths and under tables, whimpered and sobbed openly. Mahlik's sleeper cell fighters were positioned throughout the dining room, holding their weapons casually, their faces blank. The slaughter had no effect on them. They were truly robotic in their murderous nature.

She found Fasil Mahlik standing in a corner, holding a submachine gun. She went over and kissed him on the cheek, taking a pistol from his shoulder holster. She jumped onto a table and fired three shots into the ceiling. Bits of plaster rained down.

"I want quiet!" she shouted. *"Quiet!"*

It took a moment, but the hostages quietened down, with only a choked sob breaking through now and then.

"My name is Blanca Sanchez," she announced. "You are my hostages. If you cooperate, you may live to see tomorrow. If not, you'll join the fate of the others scattered in the lobby."

She jumped from the table. Mahlik came over.

"They're setting up the video equipment in one of the conference rooms," he said.

"Good," she said. "Show me."

Blanca felt the eyes of the hostages on her back as Mahlik led her out of the restaurant. She still held the automatic pistol casually, as if it were as non-threatening as her purse.

"Are the bombs placed?" she asked.

"Around the base of the guest tower," Mahlik said. "I have the detonator in my back pocket."

"Better not sit down. Wouldn't want to demolish the building too soon."

She laughed.

"What do you see, Slick?" Kane asked into his Bluetooth.

Cara Billings, more familiar with the New York streets from her time there than Kane, drove the SUV, with the rest of Team Reaper filling every seat, gear stacked in the back. Kane sat in the front passenger seat, watching traffic and pedestrians flash by as Cara executed precision maneuvers to avoid delays.

"Hostages have been placed in the restaurant," Swift said. "They left the TVs on—she wants to see the news."

"That will come in handy when we play her father's video."

"Copy, it's standing by."

"What else?"

"There are two ways inside. You can enter through the lobby's rear exit and turn right to get to the restaurant or use the bar door that leads straight to the pool area. They'll see you coming if you use the pool approach because there are wrap-around windows behind the bar."

"Copy. We'll figure it out when we get there."

"There's a lot of dead, Reaper."

Kane took a deep breath. There was nothing they could do for the victims now. They had to focus on saving the ones still alive and prevent more from getting killed while Blanca played her sick game.

"What about outside?"

"No guards. Looks like everybody is inside."

"Are you positive, Slick?"

"I'll amend that to say I can't *see* any guards, Reaper. They might be standing out of camera range."

"Bombs? Traps?"

"They've wired the guest tower. Once the shooting stopped, I rewound the footage to look and spotted gunman planting C4 and running det cord. They might try and bring down the whole building. The demolition would wipe out a lot of the city block."

Thurston came over the line. "Use caution, as always. Blanca will probably have the detonator; if not, Mahlik for sure."

"Yes, ma'am."

"What's your twenty?" she asked.

Kane glanced at the dashboard GPS screen. The blue dot representing the SUV was getting closer to the graphic representing the Liberty Suites. "About a block away. We're going to pull up at the back wall and insert that way."

"Let us know before you go, and we'll start the video."

"Yes, ma'am."

"It will hopefully distract her long enough."

"I'm counting on it."

"Cops and FBI have the front of the hotel blocked off, and they've set up the usual perimeter with uniformed officers and SWAT teams. You'll see them."

"We have our credentials."

"Good hunting."

"Thank you, ma'am. This ends today."

Kane ended the call.

It ends one way or another.

The red light on the camera blinked off.

Blanca Sanchez let out a breath.

She stood in front of a black screen, which blocked out any identifying marks of the room she was in. The camera operator moved to a table where he'd set up computer equipment and said he was uploading the video so the gathering authorities outside and elsewhere in the government could see the footage.

She said to Mahlik, who stood off to the side of the camera: "They aren't going to listen, are they?"

"Maybe not."

"We're going to die here, aren't we?"

"Probably." From behind his back, Mahlik produced a black tube with a cap on it. Blanca took the tube, lifted the cap, and smiled when she saw the red button beneath.

"Just one push?" she asked.

"Just one."

Blanca pushed the detonator down her top.

She took a deep breath and pressed her lips together. "If they don't listen, then I'll take as many with me as I can."

The man at the computer said, "Video is live."

Blanca wanted to smile. She couldn't.

CHAPTER 24

A uniformed patrolman lifted the caution tape blocking the street and let the Team Reaper SUV through. Cara stopped the vehicle curbside, the back wall of the Liberty Suites standing about ten feet tall just off the sidewalk. Trees behind the wall would provide either decent cover or an obstacle. It meant there might be bushes of hedgerows on the other side, too, and those were tough to navigate.

The team climbed out of the SUV. Kane lifted the tailgate and started handing out packs. Cara. Brick. Arenas. Axe. Traynor. The team scattered on the sidewalk and began donning body armor, coms gear, and weapons. A few of the NYPD officers and SWAT team standing around watched curiously. John Kane, in particular, ignored them. He wasn't here to put on a show for the cops. He was here to bring an end to a fight that never should have started in the first place, that never would have started to begin with if he and his crew had been more thorough.

He was trying not to blame himself for thinking Blanca wouldn't be a threat, but it was hard not to. Maybe it would have been easier if there weren't so many dead civilians now involved.

Kane secured his bulletproof vest, tightening the Velcro straps on either side of his body, and put his Motorola com unit in his ear. The main radio unit attached to his belt. The team tested the coms; they worked, everybody hearing each other as they acknowledged the test. Then Kane switched channels to call Thurston in El Paso.

"We're ready," he reported.

"Blanca released a video making the same demands as before. She wants her old man delivered to the hotel without delay. She'll start executing hostages on the hour if we don't comply."

Kane checked his watch. Thirty minutes till the top of the next hour.

"Once we engage, it won't matter."

"There's a lot of people in there, Reaper," Sam Swift said. "All human shields."

"She'll be too distracted with the video to notice us right away, and then it won't matter."

Thurston again, "The FBI have set up loud-speakers out front, so if she somehow disables the televisions in the restaurant, she'll still hear her father's audio."

"Good," Kane said. "Start the video, we're going over."

Brick Peters placed a stepping stool at the base of the wall. Each team member stepped on that first, grabbing the top of the wall, boosting themselves over. They landed on the other side, quickly spreading out, away from the wall, their Heckler & Koch 416 carbines at eye level, scanning for threats.

Kane rolled over the wall last. He charged his HK and took the lead. The promenade lay ahead. There could be shooters in any of the storefronts, hiding behind trees, any other nook they could find. The water fountain trickled audibly.

A frontal assault wasn't the best strategy, but sometimes there was no other way. Blanca had already taken the lives of too many. They had to stop her now. No time for negotiations.

Kane started forward. "Follow me," he said.

Team Reaper didn't need to hear the order a second time.

Inside the restaurant, Blanca sat at the bar, pistol in front of her, the tube detonator next to the gun. The televisions, all tuned to local news channels, gave her a sweeping view of what was going on out front, the mass of cops and Feds, the SWAT teams, a bunch of puppets making a show of force and thinking it helped. Blanca laughed a little. There was nothing they could do. If they didn't release her father, she did not plan to do any talking. She planned only to bring down the guest tower and send a rain of death upon the city. The fact that she wouldn't survive didn't bother her one bit. She had planned to survive, of course, she had things she wanted to do, but now that extreme measures were necessary, she found herself thinking back to the talks she and Mahlik had shared about sacrificing for the cause. Sometimes, there was no other way.

Then the screens blinked out as if somebody had turned them all off at once.

She snapped upright, reaching for the detonator. Mahlik, across the room, motioned for her to get away from the bar, and she complied, taking cover near a table. Some hostages cowered nearby, trying to move away from her, jammed in by more hostages. A man with a crew-cut, his body trim and well-muscled, wrapped an arm around a woman, holding her close and turning her face away from Blanca. She grinned at him. His eyes bored into her own.

Troops moved to the windows behind the bar, which provided a panoramic view of the promenade.

Blanca flipped open the top of the detonator.

The screens flashed on once again. Blanca gasped. Her father was centered on all screens, sitting in a small room with gray walls. He wore his orange jail jumpsuit and looked mad as if he had just caught her joy-riding in one of his Lamborghinis.

As had happened more than once. She'd had a particular fondness for his old Countach.

"Blanca, my darling," her father began, his voice loud over the television speakers, and echoing from outside. *"All my life I worked to give you a better life. One better than mine. And now I see that I have failed. You are more like me than I wanted. I had hoped you'd take after your mother. What you are doing right now is wrong. I do not want you risking your life or the lives of others, for my release. We all make choices in life, some are good, and some are bad, and I made mine. Whether they were good or bad, I will leave to somebody else to decide, but what you are making right now is a bad choice."*

A hot flush started in Blanca's chest, and slowly moved up to her neck. She clenched her jaw tightly.

Her thumb moved to the red button.

Rested there ever so lightly.

"I want you to surrender," her father continued. His face remained strained, but his eyes were focused on the camera, looking directly at her. *"Do not harm anymore people. I have made my choices, and I am going to pay for them. That's what a leader does. I am taking responsibility*

for my choices. They are mine only. As your father, I do not want to see you make the same mistakes. I want you to have the life I never had and enjoy the freedom that I will not. Blanca, my darling daughter, surrender right now. End this. The people making this video have agreed to let you see me if you surrender. Do so. Right now."

The video froze, her father no longer talking, but still staring at her.

The hot flash crawled to Blanca's head. She felt the heat through her body.

"No," she said.

She let go of the detonator and gripped her pistol tight.

"No!"

She jumped up, raising the gun. She fired once. The TV screen on the wall ahead popped as the bullet ripped through the crystal display. She spun around, found another target, and fired again. "No!" Another TV in her sights. *Pop.* Hostages started screaming. She ran through the room, blasting every television in sight. Mahlik ran to her, grabbing her gun arm.

"Stop this!" he shouted.

Blanca glared at him.

"He betrayed me! He betrayed his own daughter!"

"Blanca! Stop!"

Blanca broke away from Mahlik, turned, and started to reach for the detonator she'd left on the floor.

It was gone.

She turned to Crew Cut, who still glared at her. She raised her pistol and shot him in the face. The woman with him screamed as his blood splashed on her. Other hostages behind him reacted in a similar fashion. As Crew Cut fell flat, the detonator he'd stashed in his shirt pocket rolled out. The woman made a grab. Blanca shot her in the back of the head. The woman's body jerked once and lay still. Blanca casually picked up the tube and moved her thumb to the red switch once again.

A gunshot cracked. Blanca jerked back. A sudden scream burst from her gut. The hand that had held the detonator wasn't there any longer, replaced by a bloody stump. Her screams stopped; she slowly turned to the front of the restaurant, where seven wraiths dressed head-to-toe in black appeared, their automatic weapons spitting death.

Kane and his team entered through the lobby as Jorge Sanchez's voice echoed up and down the street.

They avoided the dead bodies and pools of blood on the floor, the carnage stirring rage in Kane's belly. He gripped his HK tighter, the weapon tucked firmly into his shoulder, finger on the trigger, ready. *It ends now.*

The front of the restaurant yawned before them, and the team approached in a horizontal line. Shots cracked inside. They ran faster, spreading out as much as possible as they entered, shouting in unison, *"Hostages, get down! Hostages, down! Hostages, get down!"*

Kane scanned the scene. Gunmen were raising weapons, shouting back, some diving to the floor to mix with the hostages. Kane zeroed on Blanca, who stood near the bar, about twenty yards away. She held what could only be a detonator in her left hand. Kane didn't think. He pressed the trigger. The HK spit flame. The 5.56mm slug crossed the twenty yards true, and took off her hand, leaving behind the bloody stump of a wrist. She screamed. Her hand dropped to the floor, the detonator with it.

More shooting echoed. Kane ran to a ceiling support post, rounds smacking into the wood. He scanned, fired;

gunman down. Another scan. He fired. The second gunman down. His team cut through the room, their HKs mixing with the automatic rifles of the sleeper cell gunmen, hostages in the crossfire, but most scrambling out of the way.

Cara sidestepped as a gunner who'd dived into a cluster of hostages, fired at her. His head was exposed. She took the shot. His head popped open, and he dropped.

Brick shot one gunman, then lurched as another charged at him, swinging the butt of his empty rifle. Brick lifted a heavy boot into the man's groin, stepped back as the man doubled over, and put a string of rounds into his chest.

Kane left the support post and ran to the bar. Behind him, Cara shouted, "On your six!" Kane pushed through a group of hostages who took the opportunity to run for the exit. They jostled him, forcing Kane to lift the muzzle of his HK, but he kept his eyes on Mahlik. The Saudi Arabian had Blanca on the floor near the bar, clutching her with one arm while lifting a pistol with another.

Kane shoved another hostage aside, forcing the woman to the ground. He fired twice. Mahlik's head snapped back, striking the front of the bar as he fell, Blanca turning to watch him die. Her face, white with shock, registered no reaction, but her body moved on its own. Ignoring her destroyed left arm, she grabbed for the detonator with her right. It had rolled under a bar stool. Her first reached missed. She lunged forward for another grab, grasping the tube this time.

Kane and Cara fired as one. Bloody red roses blossomed across her chest, Blanca falling back against the stools, the detonator rolling away once again.

"Everybody out!" Kane shouted into his com unit. "Get them out of here!"

His team copied, their acknowledgments quiet in his ear as his pulse pounded.

He and Cara ran to the bodies of Mahlik and Blanca. Cara pulled Mahlik away, Kane grabbing the detonator. He closed the cap and jammed the tube in a pocket.

He turned. The rest of the team was in the process of herding the hostages out of the room. There was yelling, crying, chaos, but the people moved, helping loved ones and strangers to their feet, leaving behind dead bodies of both gunmen and civilian.

Then, as suddenly as the fight had begun, it ended. Only silence and death lingered.

Kane turned to Cara. She stared at him. Neither had any words.

Manhattan Correctional Facility
Manhattan

Kane and Cara, another jail guard escorting them down the cell block, arrived at Sanchez's cell. They were still dressed for battle, but their weapons and equipment had long been put away. The cell block had its usual chill. The guard stepped back.

Cara had asked if she could tell Sanchez of the outcome. Kane hadn't argued.

Jorge Sanchez sat on his cot, in prison orange as always. He turned his head and his face blanched. His sad eyes communicated more than any words he could say.

"I already know," he said.

"Who told you?" Cara asked.

"I'm her father. I felt it." He rose and approached the bars. "You'll feel it too. We all do."

"I'm sorry, Sanchez," she said. "I really am."

"There was no other way," Kane added.

Sanchez nodded.

"It won't matter what the jury says now, you realize," he said. "You killed me after all."

"You killed yourself, Sanchez," Kane said. "None of this would have happened had you turned left instead of right when you were young. You made your choices."

"You might be right. After all the lies I told myself over the years, I had to tell Blanca the truth."

Sanchez returned to the cot and sat down. The springs creaked. He put his face in his hands and let out a single choked sob.

Kane nudged Cara's arm, but she brushed him off. She watched Sanchez a little longer. He wasn't the enemy anymore; he was a father in mourning, a father who had tried to steer his daughter in the right direction but had failed. Would she fail with her own son?

She wasn't worried about Sanchez retaliating; there was no more Chologos Cartel to answer to his commands, and anybody else who might listen was now too busy taking over his operations and picking up where he left off, to care what *El Tigre* thought about anything. Team Reaper could shut down one avenue of drug smuggling, take out whichever cartel leader was in their sights, but nothing ever changed.

The war continued. Always. There would be more Blanca Sanchezes in the future.

Cara turned from the jail cell and started walking, Kane and the guard following. They walked into the future, into the next battle, wherever it may be. One thing was certain:

Team Reaper would be there, and nothing was going to stop them from winning.

But victory came with a price. A very high price. One they could only pay for so long.

Outside, as Cara pulled open the door of the SUV, Kane stopped her.

"Are you okay?" he asked.

"No."

She climbed behind the wheel and pulled the door shut.

She had the engine running when Kane joined her inside.

A LOOK AT: KILL COUNT

A TEAM REAPER THRILLER

THE GUNS BLAZE, THE BODIES STACK, AND THE KILL-COUNT SKYROCKETS

When a ruthless Colombian cartel kidnaps the 10-year-old son of a DEA agent for leverage, Team Reaper unleashes a blood-and-bullets blitz that uncovers an unholy alliance dirtier than the devil's own heart.

Hunted by both a rogue black ops assassin and a cartel cutthroat, Team Reaper take the fight from sin-soaked city streets to the jungle hell-zones of Colombia. Meanwhile, a devastating series of terrorist attacks strike New York City as al-Qaeda rises from the ashes and ignites a political firestorm that threatens to topple the President.

With a young boy's life on the line and the fate of a nation at stake, Team Reaper refuses to retreat.

A non-stop action-fest – Kill Count is the fifth book in the thrilling Team Reaper Series.

AVAILABLE NOW.

ABOUT THE AUTHOR

A twenty-five year veteran of radio and television broadcast-ing, **Brian Drake** has spent his career in San Francisco where he's filled writing, producing, and reporting duties with stations such as KPIX-TV, KCBS, KQED, among many others.

Currently carrying out sports and traffic reporting duties for Bloomberg 960, Brian Drake spends time between reports and carefully guarded morning and evening hours cranking out action/adventure tales. A love of reading when he was younger inspired him to create his own stories, and he sold his first short story, "The Desperate Minutes," to an obscure webzine when he was 25 (more years ago than he cares to remember, so don't ask). Many more short story sales followed before he expanded to novels, entering the self-publishing field in 2010, and quickly building enough of a following to attract the atten-tion of several publishers and other writing professionals.

Brian Drake lives in California with his wife and two cats, and when he's not writing he is usually blasting along the back roads in his Corvette with his wife telling him not to drive so fast, but the engine is so loud he usually can't hear her.

Made in the USA
Las Vegas, NV
15 February 2023